Teaching the New English

Series Editor

Ben Knights
Teesside University
Durham City, United Kingdom

T0394187

Teaching The New English is an innovative series primarily concerned with the teaching of the English degree in the context of the modern university. The series is simultaneously concerned with addressing exciting new areas that have developed in the curriculum in recent years and those more traditional areas that have reformed in new contexts. It is grounded in an intellectual or theoretical concept of the curriculum, yet is largely concerned with the practicalities of the curriculum's manifestation in the classroom. Volumes will be invaluable for new and more experienced teachers alike.

More information about this series at
http://www.springer.com/series/14458

Katy Shaw
Editor

Teaching 21st Century Genres

palgrave
macmillan

Editor
Katy Shaw
School of Cultural Studies and Humanities
Leeds Beckett University
Leeds, UK

Teaching the New English
ISBN 978-1-137-55390-4 ISBN 978-1-137-55391-1 (eBook)
DOI 10.1057/978-1-137-55391-1

Library of Congress Control Number: 2016957366

© The Editor(s) (if applicable) and The Author(s) 2016
The author(s) has/have asserted their right(s) to be identified as the author(s) of this work in accordance with the Copyright, Designs and Patents Act 1988.
This work is subject to copyright. All rights are solely and exclusively licensed by the Publisher, whether the whole or part of the material is concerned, specifically the rights of translation, reprinting, reuse of illustrations, recitation, broadcasting, reproduction on microfilms or in any other physical way, and transmission or information storage and retrieval, electronic adaptation, computer software, or by similar or dissimilar methodology now known or hereafter developed.
The use of general descriptive names, registered names, trademarks, service marks, etc. in this publication does not imply, even in the absence of a specific statement, that such names are exempt from the relevant protective laws and regulations and therefore free for general use.
The publisher, the authors and the editors are safe to assume that the advice and information in this book are believed to be true and accurate at the date of publication. Neither the publisher nor the authors or the editors give a warranty, express or implied, with respect to the material contained herein or for any errors or omissions that may have been made.

Printed on acid-free paper

This Palgrave Macmillan imprint is published by Springer Nature
The registered company is Macmillan Publishers Ltd.
The registered company address is: The Campus, 4 Crinan Street, London, N1 9XW, United Kingdom

Acknowledgements

This collection originated in a Higher Education Academy UK (HEA) seminar held at the University of Brighton in 2013. The seminar acknowledged the increasing presence and significance of genre in the first decade of twenty-first century literary studies, and its influence on intertextuality and interdisciplinary approaches across media, film and screen studies. The day-long event invited academics to ask whether the politics of new twenty-first century genres could offer insights into developments in the teaching of our subject disciplines across the Arts and Humanities. Speakers presented on a wide range of topics including social media, technology, popular culture and pedagogy. Thanks go to the HEA for their support of that day and the development of this collection. Special thanks to Prof Ben Knights, *Teaching The New English* series editor, for his enthusiasm for the collection, and his helpful guidance throughout the publication process. Thanks also to Ben Doyle at Palgrave for advice on content and style. Personal thanks as Editor are extended to all contributors at the original seminar and to all authors in this collection. It has been an educational and enjoyable experience, and offers an important contribution to the evolving and ever-changing world of new genres entering our classrooms and lecture theatres today.

Contents

Notes on Contributors

Xavier Aldana Reyes is Senior Lecturer in English Literature and Film at Manchester Metropolitan University and a founding member of the Manchester Centre for Gothic Studies. He specialises in Gothic and Horror film and fiction, and is the author of various books in these areas, including *Body Gothic: Corporeal Transgression in Contemporary Literature and Horror Film* (2014), *Digital Horror: Haunted Technologies, Network Panic and the Found Footage Phenomenon* (co-edited with Linnie Blake; 2015), *Horror Film and Affect: Towards a Corporeal Model of Viewership* (2016) and *Horror: A Literary History* (editor; 2016). Xavier is also the Series Editor of the University of Wales Press's Horror Studies series. Pedagogically, Xavier is a Fellow of the Higher Education Academy and was awarded a Postgraduate Certificate in Academic Practice in 2013. Since then, he has contributed to, and participated in, events connected to the teaching of the Gothic for the HEA and for the English and Media Centre.

Kate Aughterson works on seventeenth-century drama, notably with regard to gender and literature, sexuality and literature, performance culture. She is the author of *Renaissance Woman; The English Renaissance: An Anthology of Documents*; *John Webster: The Tragedies*; and *Aphra Behn: The Comedies*, as well as articles on Bacon, Middleton, Behn and Marston. Thematically both her teaching and research interests cross disciplinary boundaries, linking scientific, textual, philosophical and political discourses.

Mark Eaton is Professor of English at Azusa Pacific University. He is co-editor of *The Gift of Story: Narrating Hope in a Postmodern World*

(2006) and a contributor to *A Companion to the Modern American Novel, 1900–1950* (2009); *A Companion to Film Comedy* (2012); and *The Routledge Companion to Literature & Religion* (2016).

Nicole King is Director of Teaching and Learning for the School of Languages and Literature at the University of Reading. Her specialist areas of teaching include African American literature and Anglophone Caribbean literature, Women's Contemporary Writings, and Postcolonial and American literature. She is the author of *C.L.R. James and Creolization: Circles of Influence*, a study that calls attention to James' internationalism as an articulation of creolisation in multiple registers–spatial, temporal and cultural.

Bianca Leggett is a teacher and researcher of contemporary literature who was awarded her PhD from Birkbeck, University of London, in 2013 where she subsequently co-designed and taught the undergraduate module Reading Twenty-First Century Fiction. She is also the co-editor of *Twenty-First-Century British Fiction* (2015). Her research considers the relationship between the novel and the nation in an increasingly cosmopolitan world with a particular focus on travel in English fiction. She is a Teaching Fellow in British Studies at Harlaxton College, the British study abroad campus of the University of Evansville, Indiana, USA.

Deirdre Osborne is a Reader in English Literature and Drama at Goldsmiths University of London where she co-convenes the MA *Black British Writing*. Her research interests span late-Victorian literature and maternity, to Landmark Poetics, mixedness, adoption aesthetics and Black writing. Publications include: editor *The Cambridge Companion to British Black and Asian Literature (1945–2010)* (2016), guest-editor Special Issue, 'Contemporary Black British Women's Writing' for *Women: a Cultural Review* (2009), a commentary and critical edition of Lorraine Hansberry's *A Raisin in the Sun* (2011), edited volumes of critical introductions and the previously unpublished plays of Kwame Kwei-Armah, Malika Booker, SuAndi, Lennie James, Courttia Newland, Lemn Sissay (*Hidden Gems Vols. I and II*, 2008; 2012) and as contributor and co-editor of *Modern and Contemporary Black British Drama* (Palgrave 2014). She is Associate Editor of the scholarly journal *Women's Writing*.

Katy Shaw is Associate Director of the CCA: Centre for Culture and the Arts, Principal Lecturer in Contemporary Literature and Head of English at Leeds Beckett University, UK. Her research interests include twenty-first century literature, especially working class literature, cultural representations of post-industrial regeneration and the languages of comedy.

Her monographs include *David Peace: Texts and Contexts* (2010), *Mining the Meaning: Cultural Representations of the 1984–5 UK Miners' Strike* (2012) and *Crunch Lit* (2014). She is editor of *C21 Literature: Journal of 21st-Century Writings.*

Kristian Shaw is Lecturer in Contemporary and Postcolonial Literature at the University of Lincoln. Prior to this, he was Lecturer in English at the University of Bolton, and an AHRC funded PhD student at Keele University, UK. He is the author of *Cosmopolitanism in Twenty-First Century British and American Fiction* (Palgrave 2016). His primary research concerns the study of globalisation, transnationalism and digital technology on post-millennial literature and culture. He is also interested in working-class literature, specifically literature and politics.

Oliver Tearle is Lecturer in Nineteenth and Twentieth Century literature at Loughborough University, UK. His research is principally in literature of the period 1870–1950, focusing especially on the ghost story, twentieth-century poetry, and the rise of modernism. He is the other of *Belwilderments of Vision* (2013) and *T.E. Hulme and Modernism* (2013). Primarily interested in Modernist poetry, Tearle is researching creative/critical intersections and the concept of citizenship in the works of T.S. Eliot.

Gina Wisker is Professor of Literature, Principal Fellow of the Higher Education Academy, a National Teaching Fellow and the Chair of the Contemporary Women's Writing Association. She researches both learning and teaching, specialising in the postgraduate student learning and supervisory practices, as well as Gothic and postcolonial writings. She is the author of *Getting Published* (2015), *Teaching African American Women's Writing* (2010) and *Atwood's The Handmaid's Tale: A Readers Guide* (2010).

Introduction

Twenty-first century genre fiction has become part of the zeitgeist of academic criticism and teaching since the year 2000. Despite this growing academic and popular appeal, a critical consideration of genre and the development of new genres in the twenty-first century has only recently begun. This collection emerged as a response to the growing presence of a range of new genres, and the re-emergence of older genres, from the year 2000 onwards across the teaching of contemporary writings, as well as in televisual and filmic interventions, adaptations and representations. As a volume in the *Teaching the New English* series, it offers a contribution to important and ongoing interdisciplinary developments in the field, critically examining the emergence of some of the most innovative and interesting contemporary genres represented in teaching at the time of publication.

The politics of genre fiction is significant because it can offer some insight into twenty-first century developments across teaching and popular culture, as well as to the function of new genres in an ever-changing world. Derrida proposed that 'a text cannot belong to no genre, it cannot be without [...] a genre. Every text participates in one or several genres, there is no genreless text' (1981: 61). Yet genre has always been plagued by the problem of definition. It can mean a way of organising a variety of texts both intellectually, in terms of how we think about them, but also physically, in terms of how they are presented by publishers, promoted by distributors and understood by readers. In the post-millennium period, changes in genre have also been influenced by transmedial developments, wider debates about the future of the novel form and the emergence of new platforms for the consumption of writings. The ongoing evolutions that define the teaching of twenty-first-century genre fiction therefore offer both opportunities and challenges for educational practitioners and students.

A keyword that is often used in the teaching of twenty-first-century genres is 'diversity'. As literary critic Jago Morrison argues, contemporary literatures are 'anything but homogeneous. On the contrary, they are interesting precisely for their ability to locate themselves in the interstices—the spaces between national cultures, genders and histories' (Morrison 2003: 7). Contemporary is an equally slippery term, it can mean 'of the moment', but a text is also necessarily 'of the past' as soon as it is published. As far as this collection is concerned, the twenty-first century marks literature published since the year 2000. The year 2000 marked a crucial turning point for society and for contemporary literature. The end of the Cold War created an impression that the threat of global conflict was, for the first time in a hundred years or so, finally receding, but this concern quickly gave way to new threats.

As the millennium approached, it seemed to be carrying a host of disturbing social indicators that culminated in a wider millennial anxiety. A myriad of related fears—about an anticipated 'Y2K' bug, environmental disaster and apocalyptic biblical prophecies—meant that the year 2000 became a source of fear, as well as a time for hope and optimism about the future. As Bradbury argues, 'industrial pollution surges, environmental terrors reign, and plagues and earthquakes spread. Our pleasures have become our pains: our food and drink, our sex and smoking, all threaten to injure us. We have new visions of choking, collapsed, crime and drug ridden cities, wasted landscapes, fundamentalist conflicts and genocidal wars, shrinking ice-caps the widening of the ozone hole [...] seen from this turning point, our century is most likely to seem uniquely terrible, less the age of visionary hopes and fantastic utopian prospects [...] more a time of terrors, crimes, political disasters and technological horrors' (Bradbury 1993: 87). The new millennium did not offer much in the way of respite from these fears as the hopes and aspirations of many were swiftly greeted with a new international challenge in the shape of terrorism. The events of 9/11 and 7/7 in particular, alongside the Mumbai bombings, 'introduced a degree of narrative uncertainty and apocalyptic pessimism' (Bickley 2008: 35).

Genre fiction effectively connects literary structures and accounts of historical change. As a result, it has become 'the meeting place between general poetics and event-based literary history' (Todorov 1990: 19–20) in the twenty-first century. Carolyn Miller argues that 'the number of genres in any society [...] depends on the complexity and diversity of that society' (Miller quoted in Freedman and Medway 1994: 36). In the twenty-first century, the number of genres has increased and continues to expand, matching the rich and varied social makeup of the age. The new genre fictions profiled by this collection developed in response to the anxious contexts informing their creation. Collectively, they suggest how and why genre fiction can function to cast new light not only on social, political and economic events, but also on changing publishing and reading trends in the twenty-first century.

Significantly, these new genres emerge not only in writings but in wider popular culture. Since the new millennium, genres have developed transmedially across literature and screen. The platform-shifting nature of the genres featured in this collection means that the role of media and adaptation are often important considerations in their teaching. The development of twenty-first-century genre fictions equally occurs in a new digital landscape. The Internet has transformed the way literature is viewed, processed and exchanged. Technology has not only resulted in the digitisation of writings but a widening of the creative field to include supplementary 'texts' such as Twitter feeds, Facebook comments, Tumblr blogs and forum exchanges in which readers are able to extend texts in new ways. E-reader apps for mobile phones and computers enable readers to both view and extend a text simultaneously through fan interaction online, or converse with the author through social networking sites.

Working in the contemporary period of any discipline can present new challenges, and resources, for students and teachers, and literature is no exception. Twenty-first century genre fiction is an ever-expanding field—many of its authors are still alive and continue to write. This can be useful but also challenging because these writers can and do talk back—many of the authors of texts discussed by the following chapters can be emailed, googled or tweeted, they can give opinions, change their minds and comment freely, confronting critics and authors with a new dialogic dimension to understanding texts. One of the greatest contradictions encountered by any individual teaching in the field of twenty-first-century genre fiction is that, despite a plethora of 'content' on new media platforms, there remains a relative poverty of academic criticism or secondary reference materials about new genre texts. The cutting-edge and recent nature of twenty-first-century genre fictions mean that students must be prepared and guided by teachers to turn to alternative sources on the contemporary: reviews, interviews, websites, YouTube, twitter or blogs, as well as the more traditional monographs and journal articles. A 'canon' of twenty-first-century genre fiction remains very much in formation, and one of the most exciting and dynamic aspects of teaching and learning in this field is taking part in the process of creating that canon.

No collection can offer an exhaustive or definitive survey of the teaching of twenty-first-century genre fiction. Instead, this volume in the *Teaching The New English* series explores the development of genre and fiction as contemporary forms, as well as a selected range of themes, concepts and key historical and thematic issues central to teaching this ever-growing field of critical and popular enquiry. The chapters aim to offer critical insights into key intellectual and scholarly issues in contemporary literary theory and studies, promoting independence of thought and intellectual rigour. The pathways and configurations outlined are designed for delivery via a range of teaching and learning methods, reflecting a diversity of textual approaches and mobilising blended learning opportunities as a reflection of the digital evolutions in both genre and fiction in the new millennium to offer a more effective learning experience. These may include:

- Tutor-led lectures that introduce subject specific knowledge, underpinned with a range of in class and electronic materials;
- Seminar and workshop sessions that give students an opportunity to engage with the subject matter in greater depth, analyse aspects of twenty-first-century genre fictions by combining theory and practice and engage in discussions that may be facilitated by the students or the tutor;
- Action learning sets, learning diaries and formative assessments to enable students to develop thoughts in reflection, editing and redrafting;
- Individual tutorials that give further opportunities for students to seek information, clarify issues and discuss in detail any controversial or complicated areas of understanding;
- Virtual learning resources to provide students with additional materials that can be used for further individual study, or during seminar sessions;

- Reading materials, particularly secondary criticism and journalism, that will enable students to engage with the wider literary communities and equip them with ways to present their own ideas, research questions and arguments.

The chapters featured in this collection argue that, in the twenty-first century, genre fiction constitutes an important space in which contemporary writers discuss relationships between the local and the global, gender, class and race. As a site to debate issues as diverse as the role of the state and the individual, convergence culture, socio-political trans-national tensions and the relationship between the fan and the writer in contemporary fiction, the teaching of genre fiction emerges from these chapters as a means by which students can represent and critically consider complex global issues. Twenty-first-century genre fictions are marked by reoccurring preoccupations or concerns that a growing range of writers seek to explore or rationalise through their works. The texts under discussion in this collection utilise a staggering range of generic conventions to examine themes central to the contemporary period. As a result, each chapter considers how, why, and with what effect educational practitioners might employ genre as an effective segue into opening up the twenty-first century for a new generation of readers, and writers.

Celebrating a hybridity of history, twenty-first-century genre fictions take an anti-authoritarian approach to heritage, the past, and unequal access to story-telling. Their refusal to submit to closed narratives or sealed histories leads these texts to sift through the ruins of broken or hidden histories and illuminate the past through the eyes of those previously denied a voice. Suggesting a wider crisis of representation, the texts strain at the limits of their fictional form to contain new images and representations, setting the facticity of history against the fictionality of literary representation. In chapters addressing the development and function of twenty-first-century Gothic fiction, Aldana Reyes and Wisker consider the role of the past in the present. There has been a major growth in new Gothic fiction across the past 30 years. Their chapters consider the ways in which Contemporary Gothic fictions present history as an unfinished process, and seek to disrupt or disturb narratives to reveal the past as an enigma to be interrogated. Carving into old landscapes to offer new representations and historical reverberations that echo across the twenty-first-century world, they examine a range of texts that aim to rewrite a past that continues to assert its role in the present, disrupting narratives and engaging readers in a multiplicity of perspectives on recent events.

Post-colonialism, multiculturalism and national identity—or as Bradford terms it, the 'Question of Elsewhere' (Bradford 2007: 191)—quickly became a central theme of twenty-first-century genre fiction. The contemporary period has been marked by crises of identity and new contemporary ways of living. The interconnected relationship between history and memory is a major theme in contemporary genre fiction because we live in a time where past issues relating to gender, class, colonialism and conflict have placed narrative in a vital position of having the potential to tell other, hitherto unheard stories, or to reframe events we know well. Weaving fact and fiction through unspoken slices of history, twenty-first-century genre fictions offer revisionary accounts that enable contemporary readers to recognise past struggles and how they feed into conflicts of the present. Chapters by King and Osborne examine new people's histories and sub-histories of race and suggest ways in which they effectively illuminate global history, shedding new light on, and widening our appreciation of, the past as authored by numerous competing and contradictory sources. Foregrounding the role played by genre in shared and individual histories of consciousness, the teaching strategies offered by their chapters do not simply reflect historical change, but suggests how literature can inspire the actions that author change, and how change can be understood at an individual level.

Apocalypse has always been a major concern of the science fiction genre, but post-millennium genre fiction is concerned not just with a hypothetical end to the world but the 'end of the end', the prospect of a final act of narrative closure on humanity. As Bickley argues, the turn of the century heralded a host of new fictions that suggest 'the past [...] remains troubling and unresolved' (2008: 7). In chapters considering the emergence of new utopian and dystopian genre fictions, Aughterson, Tearle and Eaton examine the extent to which new genre fictions not only reflect but offer agency for readers coping with the onset of a new uncertain dawn. The utopian and dystopian fictions considered by these chapters use the natural world as a platform on which to stage wider discussions regarding a range of contemporary traumas. They consider ways in which landscape can be mobilised as a critical mirror to society, highlighting underlying tensions created by a constant drive for modernity and progress, socialisation and development. Promoting a more sustainable relationship with the contemporary environment, the genre fictions under analysis call for a reshaping of social practices and offer nature as a paradigm for twenty-first-century cultures of knowledge.

The movement of humans across the globe continues to be the subject of contentious debate in the post-millennial world. Chapters by Shaw and Leggett consider ways in which twenty-first-century genre fictions attempt to represent these changes and their consequences for global societies. As the chapters suggest, these debates are related to issues of power, representation, hybridity, heritage and colonisation. Engaging with international discussions about identity, voice and marginalisation and effectively re-voicing formerly hidden communities through pushing generic boundaries, these chapters promote the new genres of 'Cosmopolitanism' and 'Translit' as alternative models for understanding and teaching the inherent interconnectivity of world literature in the new millennium.

As an area of academic and popular cultural study still in formation, twenty-first-century genre fiction is resistant to definitive boundaries, categories or labels. The new genre fictions discussed by this collection tackle a range of issues central to understanding global affairs in the opening decades of the twenty-first century. Not only representing, but also engaging with, some of the more pressing issues and directions of the twenty-first-century world, as well as the many and varied pasts that produced the present, the teaching of the texts analysed by this collection offers contemporary education practitioners an opportunity to consider the vitality and significance of genre fiction today. This collection asks where and why 'new' twenty-first-century genres of writing have originated, and to which other genres they owe a debt of influence. Offering reflections on innovations and evolutions, as well as wider understandings of multi-platformed genre developments across a range of writings, the various chapters pose as many questions as they answer, engaging in a debate that will continue to develop the teaching of genre fiction into the next decades of the twenty-first century.

Leeds, United Kingdom — Katy Shaw

References

Bickley, Pamela (2008) *Contemporary Fiction: The Novel Since 1990: Cambridge Contexts in Literature* (Cambridge: Cambridge University Press)
Bradbury, Malcolm (1993) *The Modern British Novel* (London: Penguin)
Bradford, Richard (2007) *The Novel Now: Contemporary British Fiction* (Malden, MA: Blackwell)
Derrida, Jacques (1981) 'The Law of Genre' in W J T Mitchell (ed.) *On Narrative* (Chicago: University of Chicago Press)
Freedman, Aviva & Medway, Peter (eds.) (1994) *Genre and the New Rhetoric* (London: Taylor & Francis)
Morrison, Jago (2003) *Contemporary Fiction* (London: Routledge)
Peach, Linden (2004) *The Contemporary Irish Novel: Critical Readings* (London: Palgrave)
Todorov, Tzvetan (1990) *Genres in Discourse* (Cambridge: Cambridge University Press)

PART ONE

Contemporary Gothic

Genre Trouble: The Challenges of Designing Modern and Contemporary Gothic Modules

Xavier Aldana Reyes

Formerly relegated to scheduled weeks on Jane Austen's *Northanger Abbey* (1818) and its accompanying horrid novels, or else, considered only in passing in wider surveys of the Enlightenment in traditional English degrees (Powell and Smith 2006: 2; Hughes 2006: 16–18), the Gothic has, since the 1980s, crept its way into the syllabi of schools and universities and become a crucial literary mode. As the critical reputation and value of the Gothic have gone from strength to strength—especially since the foundation of the International Gothic Association in 1991 and the journal *Gothic Studies* in 1999—the desire to learn about it has also grown at an exponential rate.[1] The study of the Gothic first spread via specialised MA programmes in the UK and Ireland.[2] Andrew Smith identified four programmes that contained a significant amount of Gothic material in 2006: those provided by the Universities of Stirling, Glamorgan and Kingston in the UK, and by Trinity College Dublin in Ireland (Smith 2006: 182). To these, we must now add the MA English Studies: The Gothic, offered by Manchester Metropolitan University (MMU), and the MA in Gothic: Culture, Subculture, Counterculture, offered by St Mary's University, Twickenham, as well as MAs elsewhere that include at least one Gothic module (those offered by, for example,

X. Aldana Reyes (✉)
Manchester Metropolitan University, Manchester, UK

© The Author(s) 2016

K. Shaw (ed.), *Teaching 21st Century Genres*,
DOI 10.1057/978-1-137-55391-1_1

Birkbeck College (University of London), Lancaster University and the University of Hertfordshire).[3] Since 2009, the Gothic has also been part of A-Level English literature options (Priest 2011), which has meant, firstly, that students come to BA degrees having some notional knowledge; secondly, that universities like Manchester Metropolitan now run A-Level Gothic Study days; and, thirdly, that Continuing Professional Development courses on the teaching of the Gothic have also begun to blossom.[4] It is, currently, difficult to find degree programmes in the UK which do not teach the Gothic, however cursorily, as part of broader modules on Romanticism, the Enlightenment, Victorian fiction and the fin-de-siècle.[5] The interest in contemporary permutations of the Gothic, especially since Catherine Spooner's well-received book on the topic (2006), has also meant that universities increasingly have research expertise in this area to offer specific modules covering the Modern (twentieth century) and the Contemporary Gothic (post-millennial, generally, but also turn-of-the-century).

The gradual growth in teaching in Modern and Contemporary Gothic has developed alongside a sustained critical enthusiasm for the field and its texts, and this in turn has led to the publication of a number of introductions to the topic (Groom 2012; Botting 2013; Smith 2013), as well as study guides and companions (Stevens 2000; Hogle 2002; Punter and Byron 2004; Wright 2007; Chaplin 2011).[6] What is interesting is that debates around the limitations connected to the genre/mode debate, most obviously the laxity of the term 'Gothic' and its indiscriminate application to all things dark, can play out, on a micro-level, in the classroom, where generic questioning may be at its most active. This chapter seeks to expand on previous research on the teaching of the Gothic (Hoeveler and Heller 2003; Powell and Smith 2006) and to explore some of the key issues that lie at the heart of Gothic Studies today.

As a researcher in the Gothic, I am familiar with the landscape of the field, but my conclusions are largely grounded on my own experience co-teaching, leading or co-designing the following Gothic modules in the UK: 'Screening the Gothic' (MA level 2015), 'Gothic and Modernity' (MA level 2013), Modern Gothic (final year undergraduate 2014) and Gothic and Gender (second year undergraduate 2011), as well as 'Contemporary Literature in English' (final year undergraduate 2012), which included a Gothic component.[7] However, my thoughts are also influenced by my participation in Catherine Spooner's 'Contemporary Gothic' MA module (Lancaster University 2010–11), which originally made me consider the possible generic constraints of the Gothic, and in two Contemporary Gothic reading groups: the Modern and Contemporary Gothic reading group at MMU, which I have attended from 2013 to 2016, and the Contemporary Gothic reading group in Lancaster, which I attended from 2009 to 2012. These groups have been invaluable in assessing contemporary perceptions of the Gothic, especially as they affect evaluations of recent texts that may, in some cases, have received little or no critical attention.[8] In this chapter, I will focus on how the pedagogic challenges connected to curriculum design of Modern and Contemporary Gothic modules reflect the difficulties of the theorisation of the Gothic in academic research. I propose that, whilst the notion of the Gothic is fuzzy and difficult to define, curriculum design actually benefits from the process of questioning what constitutes this artistic mode in its twenty-first century context. As such, this chapter is also intended as a supportive introduction to practitioners who are considering developing related modules.

Generic Indeterminacy as Pedagogic Challenge

Any process of curriculum design requires decision-making and, where teaching groups are involved, compromises may inevitably have to be reached according to areas of expertise, as certain academics may want to give priority to texts they deem foundational. Periodisation, the identification of key texts or finding the right thematic balance and critical input are challenges which are not exclusive to the study of the Gothic, postmillennial or otherwise, and which all teaching practitioners face. Other practical considerations, such as making sure that texts are available, that they are not too expensive (that the bibliographic cost of different modules is similar) or excessively long, as well as doing everything possible to guarantee that modules will provide a reflection of current areas of debate and that the delivery of the module will be lively and provide students with the right tools to study a specific area (as well as comply with general QAA benchmarks for English in the UK context), affect Module Leaders across English degree programmes. All survey modules have also been thoroughly revised in the light of the impact of feminist, queer and postcolonial areas of enquiry, among others, which have pushed lecturers to rethink literary traditions and go beyond the Leavisite approach to literature so popular in the past. Specific agendas, and the ever-changing focus of research funding bodies, are also having a substantial effect on the shape of certain modules, especially at MA level.

Genre modules, whether they are specifically about one single genre or cover more than one, will typically focus on landmark texts that have been historically or critically significant. As such, if *The Exorcist* (William Friedkin, 1973) were to be selected on a module about Horror film, the logic behind the choice would necessarily rely on the film being a good example of that genre, whatever its specific purpose. Alternatively, a hybrid or generically ambiguous film, such as *Don't Look Now* (Nicolas Roeg, 1973), may offer students the possibility of discussing the limits and limitations of generic ascription, or indeed, the process behind it and the way in which this might, ultimately, escape the hands of the film and its marketers. It would be peculiar to pick an example that very obviously does not belong in a genre or that shows very few of its characteristics. One may, for example, struggle to imagine teaching *Casper* (Brad Silberling and Phil Nibbelink, 1995) as a useful example of the Horror film genre simply because it contains a ghost, a figure that appears in countless Horror films. The inclusion of this film would probably raise a few eyebrows: not only does it present itself as a fantasy comedy for a young adult demographic, it also never affectively resorts to Horror. This generic marker is significant, as the film does take place in settings (a haunted castle) that are readily, and generically, recognisable. In this case, it is easy to explain why the choice feels intuitively wrong: Horror is a genre named after the emotions it aims to generate (see Carroll 1990: 10–41; Aldana Reyes 2016) and, as such, is not only, or substantially, defined by its settings and characters. The obvious comparison, a genre that is delimited by these situational, historical and narrative bounds, is the Western (Prince 2013: 252).

The same cannot be said for the Gothic. Unlike Horror, if it was ever premised on an emotional or affective drive—and debates around terror and horror in Ann Radcliffe's own posthumous 'On the Supernatural in Poetry' (1826), among others, would seem to suggest so (Aldana Reyes 2015a)—this has been lost in recent approaches that have focused much more obviously on aesthetic and thematic identifiers. For Catherine Spooner, one of the most influential academics working on the contemporary Gothic today, the Gothic is a revivalist artistic form that, in twenty-first century fashion or film production, 'can be recognised by a combination of features, including intensive chiaroscuro, crowded space, intricate detailing, distorted proportions, a saturated colour palette and deliberately retro or aged styling' (Spooner 2014: 184). The Gothic looks a specific way; we recognise it when we see it because it shows a very particular dark aesthetic allegiance, one that is borne of numerous layers of referentiality and recycling. In terms of its thematic concerns, the Gothic is also obsessed with

> the legacies of the past and its burdens on the present; the radically provisional or divided nature of the self; the construction of peoples or individuals as monstrous or 'other'; the preoccupation with bodies that are modified, grotesque or diseased. (Spooner 2006: 8)

Derived from the narratives of well-known Gothic classics such as Mary Shelley's *Frankenstein* (1818), Robert Louis Stevenson's *Dr Jekyll and Mr Hyde* (1886) or Bram Stoker's *Dracula* (1897), the mode's motifs create a dense net of referentiality that potentially empties the Gothic from a/effect and from its critical potential (Botting 1999; Aldana Reyes 2015b).[9] Any permutation of the vampire myth, regardless of its purpose, needs to be considered, if we are to follow this approach, as Gothic: from romantic hero Edward Cullen in Stephenie Meyer's *Twilight* series (2005–8) to kiddie cereal character Count Chocula. In these instances, the Gothic works aesthetically. *Twilight* does not aim to affect negatively, nor necessarily to negotiate social or cultural anxieties. Count Chocula is a referential character, recognisably vampiric but, ultimately, part of a brand whose purpose is to sell chocolate cereal. For this reason, and to separate aesthetic Gothic from rawer, trauma-centred Gothic, Spooner has proposed the term 'Happy Gothic', meant to designate 'Gothic that isn't at all anxious, at least not in a straightforward way, but which privileges comedy, romance, pleasure and consumption' (Spooner 2011).[10] In this way, the Gothic has been appropriated, like most subversive discourses, by a late capitalist machine that has rendered it another potentially hollow intertextual and allusive image.

Yet, the Gothic also appropriates. Since the mid-to-late 2000s there has been a huge interest in the Gothic as an acceptable area of academic study, one capable of producing notable scholarly work that matters and has impact, and this has helped legitimise the field and propelled further study. The term's association, in the public imagination, with the past (medieval, initially, but increasingly Victorian), is also significant. The Gothic as an architectonic style that has, since the eighteenth century (Groom 2012: 54–62), but especially through the 'war of styles' in 1834 (Townshend 2015), been associated with a patriotic and nationalistic sense of Englishness and heritage cannot be underestimated. The popular turn to the Gothic in public media and by organisations such as the British Film Institute and the British Library, both of which ran important, well-attended seasons and exhibitions in 2013–14 and 2014–15, respectively, have continued to contribute to the Gothic's visibility and to its connection with all things dark and creepy. For example, while slashers and contemporary trends like torture porn have been harder to locate as Gothic (Aldana Reyes 2014), films such as *The Innocents* (Jack Clayton, 1961) or *The Haunting* (Robert Wise, 1963), which were previously understood as Horror, are now also read as Gothic. In a process of reversal—some Horror would have previously been labelled Gothic if it took place in certain settings, time periods or included certain characters and tropes—it is now 'Gothic' that is invoked as an umbrella term covering other generic subdivisions. In fact, as Peter Hutchings once noted (1996: 89), the privileging of the Gothic may have come hand-in-hand with a pejorative rhetoric that reads Horror (its viscerality and explicit nature) as Gothic's poor cousin. This process whereby the Gothic has subsumed other genres has also included the assimilation of the fantastic and the supernatural, both of which have strong independent critical traditions in Europe, and horror science fiction subgenres such as the weird (now sometimes referred to as Lovecraftian Gothic, after the work of key weird writer H. P. Lovecraft).[11] The Gothic, initially a merging of the chivalric romance and the modern novel of the eighteenth century, has also further hybridised (with the weird and science fiction, with the romance novel) to the point where it is sometimes difficult to establish its strict generic boundaries.

Beyond its use as a literary label that defines a text according to well-known tropes and aesthetics, even a mood, the Gothic has also been studied according to the type of critical work it enables. That is to say, the Gothic has increasingly been recuperated by academia as a mode capable of either addressing issues otherwise ignored by mainstream society, or else actively (but also unconsciously, for some) repressed. This approach, one I have elsewhere termed 'cathartic-traumatic' (Aldana Reyes 2015b: 12–16), is interested in the capacity of the Gothic for either sublimating the traumas of postmodern life (Bruhm 2002; Warwick 2007) or, at its most confrontational, for providing a fictional space through which to critique the status quo and the economic and political models that have blossomed in the modern, neoliberal West (Blake 2015; Blake and Soltysik Monnet 2016). In either case, this type of Gothic is theorised in a very different manner, as the focus here is the Gothic's capacity to negotiate certain anxieties through its investment in the socially or personally repressed. The capacity to transgress, which as previously argued has been somewhat dulled by its capitalist co-option, is recast here and recharged by its ability to challenge the way things are and even to uncover dirty 'truths'. This approach is less concerned with traditional ties, something evident in the embrace of the most abject of horrific figures: the zombie. The zombie is 'a distinctly modern contribution to the Gothic tradition' (Luckhurst 2015: 10) and, for this reason, is sometimes perceived as not really Gothic at all.[12] However, for those who favour the Gothic's value beyond its entertaining qualities, such fine-tuning and generic allegiances are less important than the texts' politics.

Such a position is unthinkable without the concomitant development of cultural and literary theory and, perhaps even more pressingly, of post-structuralist philosophy, all of which have provided the critical tools to read contemporary texts, and the Gothic, according to what they might have to say about the society in which we live. In this sense, the cathartic-traumatic approach to the Gothic is the product of, as Jerrold Hogle has put it,

> a reactivated psychoanalysis, a post 1950s feminism which has expanded into 'gender studies', a resurgent Marxism, a genuinely 'new historicism' combining cultural anthropology with Derridean 'deconstruction,' and several forms of 'cultural studies' that have come to include 'postcolonial' theory and criticism, among other strands. All of these together, challenging the standards set by New Criticism and high/low culture distinctions, have brought the Gothic forward as a major cultural force by the very nature of their assumptions and thereby drawn some Gothic 'classics'. (Hogle 2006: 31)

They have also brought along an even newer application of the Gothic itself as a critical tool, so that it is now possible to provide Gothic readings of texts that are only partially, if at all, Gothic.[13] Various critical constructs, originally developed by other subject disciplines (psychoanalysis, most notably, and especially the uncanny, the return of the repressed, the sublime and the hauntological), have become integral to the discussion of contemporary texts, and thus, palimpsestically, an inherent part of what it means to 'do' Gothic Studies. In other words, 'Gothic' is increasingly employed not just as an adjective or a determinant that qualifies the dark nature of a text, be it aesthetically, thematically or in terms of its wider critical purpose, but also as a theoretical toolkit that sheds light on possible hidden social messages, or allows for an uncovering of ancillary, but nonetheless crucial, meanings.

Given this confusion, or rhizomatic expansion, of the Gothic in academia, it is not difficult to imagine that establishing a set of core texts for Modern and Contemporary Gothic modules is far from straightforward. Since there is not one working definition of the Gothic, the selection of primary sources will largely depend on what approaches are chosen. As a way to surmount this genre trouble, in my own experience working individually or with others on the design of modules, I have always begun by focusing on the learning objectives. The focus must remain to offer students, at any learning level, a good sense of the field—both the theoretical tools deployed in Gothic Studies and how they can be used effectively—and this, in turn, will influence the best pedagogic division of the material.

In our MA module 'Gothic and Modernity' at MMU, my colleague Dr Linnie Blake and I adopted a broadly chronological approach to the teaching of the Gothic, mainly because one of our objectives was for students to finish the programme with a general survey-level knowledge. As such, the module was structured to enable students to become acquainted with trends at the level of genre; favoured critical approaches that have shaped the look of the modern and contemporary canon, as well as significant contemporary debates; and a sense of the development of both throughout a large expanse of time (the module covers more than a century). This is why we began the module by focusing on the 'abhuman' and fin-de-siècle Gothic, before turning to serial killer Gothic fictions later, when we centred on the popularity of the sympathetic murderer.[14] However, the pairings of primary texts for each week of delivery were determined by other factors, such as more general significant concepts or themes, and did not always belong to the same decade. In this instance, we found it very productive to discuss Bram Stoker's *Dracula* alongside Anne Rice's *Interview with the Vampire* (1976) because of their obvious thematic links and because this allowed us to trace a clearer path through vampiric fiction. Later in the module, our primary texts included a higher percentage of films, one way in which we acknowledged the transmedia nature of the Gothic, that is, its appearance in media beyond the literary, predominantly cinema and television.

In the case of our module 'Modern Gothic', which I co-taught and co-designed with Dr Linnie Blake and Dr Sorcha Ní Fhlainn, our approach was much more thematic. Weeks were dedicated to important critical constructs like abjection, significant thematic pockets of writing, such as the Female Gothic, or to the strategies through which the Gothic explores identity politics (especially, gender, race and sexuality). While our teaching included chronological approximations to each and every topic, the selection of sources, its division and order, as well as the nature of the assignments, was more concerned with ensuring that the students developed a solid knowledge of what the Gothic is, and means, in and outside academia. The module was a third-year specialist module, and our students were unlikely to have taken other modules on the Gothic, so we assumed a starter's level. This meant that the texts we chose as primary sources—films such as *Rebecca* (Alfred Hitchcock, 1940), *Alien* (Ridley Scott, 1979) or *The Wicker Man* (Robin Hardy, 1973)—are canonical and fit the specific intellectual and critical outcomes we agreed upon. The module was also a Film Studies module elective, which posed its own challenges. As a result, it was difficult to assess how far to examine the literature that some of the films are based on, or to know how familiar students would be with the Gothic canon. During a session on *Bram Stoker's Dracula* (Francis Ford Coppola, 1992), for example, where we aimed to analyse the role of intertextuality and adaptation in the Gothic, we were quite surprised to find that a number of students had never actually read the novel.[15]

A key strategy that the teaching team found useful in addressing the generic indeterminacy of the Gothic, especially in its contemporary incarnations, was to build the very questioning of the term and its legacy into the learning objectives. In the module 'Gothic and Modernity', a first assignment asked students to read a piece of contemporary criticism that has been particularly influential and to review it critically. We provided a selection of three pieces, but students were encouraged to read widely from the bibliography in order to get a sense of the nature of the debates at hand and their conclusions. Ultimately, we asked students to reflect on the piece by positioning themselves on the nature and value of the Gothic. The second piece of assessment, a longer essay, allowed them to investigate these issues further through a more sustained study of the Gothic via an essay in a Gothic topic and texts of their own choosing. In the case of second or third year modules, where students may be less confident about settling on a subject, we offer them a number of questions, all connected to the critical and cultural ideas explored in the module, and ask them to answer them in relation to one studied text and one of their choice. We found that these open questions were an effective way of assessing engagement beyond the classroom, since particularly productive parings generally show both an interest in exploring specific aspects of questions, or else, a good working knowledge of the texts that constitute the Gothic or that can be read productively through it.

Era-Specific Challenges: Contemporary Periodisation and the Fragmentation of the Gothic

The contemporary period, indeed the 'contemporary' label itself, poses further challenges to the task of working through the ambiguous nature of the Gothic and what it should cover, aesthetically, thematically or critically. This has not been the case for other key eras. There is a general agreement that 'first wave Gothic', as it has been termed, may be neatly periodised (1764–1820), the starting point being Horace Walpole's *The Castle of Otranto* (1764), whose second edition in 1765 was the first self-professed 'Gothic story', and with Charles Robert Maturin's rather late *Melmoth the Wanderer* (1820) understood as a species of swansong. Similarly, the Victorian Gothic normally picks up where *Melmoth* leaves off, experiences an infusion of new 'blood' through penny dreadfuls such as James Malcom Rymer's *Varney the Vampyre* (1845–47) and George W. M. Reynolds's *The Mysteries of London* (1846–50), and is said to end just before the fin-de-siècle string of novels that have been most foundational to the Gothic, those by Bram Stoker, Robert Louis Stevenson, Oscar Wilde, H. G. Wells or Arthur Machen.[16] Even Modernist Gothic, which, until recently (Riquelme 2008, 2014), had not been thoroughly demarcated, can now be roughly located by turning to similar efforts to periodise modernist writing.[17] It has not been so easy to find a working timeline for the Modern and the Contemporary Gothic, no doubt, in part, due to the incredible difficulty in pinning down the differences and overlaps between the terms 'modern' and 'contemporary' more broadly, as well as their own beginnings and ends.[18]

Efforts and attempts have been made, and very important ones too, to provide starting places for academics looking for primary critical material for Modern and Contemporary modules, such as the monographs by Spooner (2006), Armitt (2009) and Botting (2008), the edited collections by Sage and Lloyd Smith (1996) and Hogle (2014), and an anthology by McGrath and Morrow (1993). The closest thing the field has to a working bibliography—and even this only covers the twenty-first century—is an edited collection by Olson (2011). A large part of relevant material is actually dispersed among a number of collections, journal issues and blogs, and indicative chronologies are only available in volumes that span broader periods, such as Smith (2013). To further complicate matters, these sources adopt different approaches in their understanding and cataloguing of the Gothic, so a final, or definitive, list is even harder to write. These tensions collectively indicate that the Gothic is alive and well, that boundaries are still being drawn—that they are, in fact, more flexible and stretchy than they have ever been—and this is exciting. On the other hand, it also means that the process of selecting primary texts for teaching the Gothic is very much at the discretion of the lecturers and their understanding of the field. It is difficult to justify not including *Dracula* on a module on Victorian and/or fin-de-siècle Gothic literature, but whether Mark Z. Danielewski's *House of Leaves* (2000) should be a comparable evident candidate for modules on Modern and Contemporary Gothic is less clear. This situation is more acute for post-millennial modules, as the period under survey is so relatively brief that trends and patterns may be difficult to identify.

Disagreement over key texts are, of course, connected to the lack of hindsight that teaching contemporary literature entails. How contemporary the 'contemporary' is and where the modern ends and the contemporary begins (that is, if they are not seen to coincide) are both points that need to be discussed. Post-millennial Gothic offers the advantage of limiting texts to the twenty-first century, but where precisely the break should be, or whether a neat break can be established in the first instance, is also arguable. Increasingly, 9/11 is used as a dividing line, but modules that follow this organisational principle might be forced to invest some degree of political intent to fictions that may operate outside of that framework or are not interested in it at all. Lack of hindsight can also result in the overlooking of texts that might eventually become canonical, or in the prioritisation of others that may become difficult to obtain, especially as Gothic publishing has never been as vibrant.[19] The postmodern embrace of high and low cultures, alongside the Gothic's wild popularity, translates into a further challenge, namely, to strike a good balance between works that we feel are worthy of study or, in other words, that we think will stand the test of time, and the consideration of popular texts that may be less critically interesting but have, nonetheless, shaped the look of the field. The classic question is whether to include a novel like *Twilight* (2005) in a module on the Contemporary or Post-millennial Gothic, especially since it has been the victim of countless journalistic and academic attacks since its rise to fame.[20] While it can be incredibly profitable in helping students tackle issues connected to reading practices, as well as technical aspects of the Gothic like marketing, or the gendering of readerships by publishers and public media, it also could be argued that the novel is thin on Gothic tropes, beyond the institutionalisation of the sympathetic vampire (Botting 2013: 201–2), and that it is not particularly well written.

At my institution, as well as in others such as the Universities of Stirling, Lancaster and Sheffield, we have found a productive way of beginning to operate with, and through, these generic shortcomings by establishing Modern and Contemporary Gothic reading groups. Meetings which are generally attended by the very same MA students who are likely to be taking our Gothic and Modernity module, serve as a place to discuss the limits and benefits of the Gothic label, its terminology, application and usefulness, as well as to assess the critical value of certain works. The experience is enriching for both staff and students: staff keep abreast of their field, since texts are decided on by the group collectively and this often forces us to read outside of our comfort zone and to encounter texts we may otherwise never have. For students, this is a valuable, voluntary way of engaging with the field beyond the classroom and to test their skills within a context that may feed into the teaching of further cohorts. In short, as with the issue of critical indeterminacy, our experience tells us that the best way of dealing with the complications arising from the Gothic's ambiguity is to study the areas of conflict themselves. Opening up the debate to students who may not have the same academic baggage is also useful in assessing where the Gothic is at, where the new generation of thinkers place it and what it means, or has come to mean, for them.

The fragmentation of the Gothic in the twentieth and twenty-first centuries, its dispersion and eminent transmediality, has also, inevitably, led us to the point where considering novels or short stories in teaching no longer effectively captures the mode's wide appeal. Some argue that interesting work in the Gothic is now being carried out not in literature, after the perceived slump following the flood of paranormal romances, but in television. Although the cult of *Buffy the Vampire Slayer* (1997–2003) is legendary in Gothic Studies, there has been a surge in interest in Gothic television since the influx of popular Gothic and Horror programmes such as *True Blood* (2008–14), *Dexter* (2006–13), *The Walking Dead* (2010–), *American Horror Story* (2011–), *Penny Dreadful* (2014–16) and *The Strain* (2014–). There is, naturally, an argument to be made for the sequentiality of these texts, which resembles the three/four-volume or instalment publication strategies of the Gothic novel and the penny dreadful. The inclusion of television series is a good way of making sure that the genre permutations are captured, but this has its own methodological implications and problems. Students who encounter this audiovisual material in English modules having never previously studied film or television modules may not be equipped with the critical vocabulary necessary to discuss the texts beyond their plots. Additionally, the length of these series makes a holistic discussion difficult, as does having to negotiate 'spoilers' where only one season is being covered.

Issues of availability also reappear. Where television series are available electronically, via institutional services such as *Box of Broadcasts*, ensuring that students can access these materials is less problematic, but these services rely on recordings, which are not always up-to-date or complete, and are not easy to browse. Otherwise, physical copies of DVDs are impractical for large groups, and the expense of entire box sets is prohibitive for English modules which already include more than the average number of primary texts when compared to other disciplines.[21] The same principles apply to even newer media, such as video games, which, apart from posing the further challenge of requiring certain playing skills, exploit narratives in different ways. These texts may be mentioned in passing in lectures, and I have found that some students can be more versed in them than in the literature, but their sustained analysis becomes complex within the context of modules in English Literature or English Studies programmes. Ultimately, such challenges bring us back to the fact that the Gothic is a transhistorical mode that has evolved and morphed, and that, whilst we may do well to continue to explore its significance in literature, it has found a home in other media. These media, in turn, may be the ones that younger generations are more familiar with, and thus, the ones from which they derive an understanding of the Gothic. It is therefore important, where possible, to bring other media into the classroom and discuss these texts as part of an artistic continuum. Thinking about possibilities and limitations is particularly useful where texts have been adapted to more than one medium, since it provides a way of counteracting the possible deficiencies caused by a lack of discipline-specific knowledge or vocabulary. As a result, a due consideration of where the Gothic has manifested in popular culture should have an effect on selection of texts and overall curriculum design.

The Importance of Genre Debate

I started by highlighting how changes in the public and academic perception of the Gothic, as well as what that term designates and represents, are responsible for the gradual pedagogic embrace of the Gothic that has taken place, most visibly, since the mid-2000s. The popular view of the Gothic as a genre with a definite intellectual heritage and strong national roots, diametrically opposite to the critical reception of the Gothic in the eighteenth century, has had a noticeable impact on this. The Gothic is now 'safe' enough to be taught at A-Level, something that signals its potential 'defanging'. Through a sustained process of academic legitimisation, it has even become its own form of discourse. Given that the Gothic is increasingly being used to uncover hidden or repressed meanings in texts, it is now as much an aesthetic and thematic indicator as it is a theoretical and reading toolkit. But with advances in the ways in which the Gothic is analysed have come a number of challenges connected to the ever-changing, assimilating nature of what has shown itself to be an artistic mode, and not a genre with exclusive time, character and setting constraints. These central challenges are connected to the difficulty of pinning down the Gothic in a way that contains its various permutations (and these are ever-growing) without doing it a critical disservice. In the context of the post-millennial, what is now being called twenty-first century genre fiction, the challenges grow exponentially as the Gothic manifests beyond literature into other disciplines and mediums.

Rather than avoid the potential generic problems that arise from the further fragmentation and recycling of what never really was a solid genre, it is more productive to incorporate debates about what the Gothic is into its teaching. Such an inclusive approach, one I already practise, need not be premised on undecidability, but on the principle that genres and modes are in constant flux and that exploring their limitations—where they stop being ascribed to one genre, and become another—as well as areas of overlap, can function to construct a clearer picture of a specific artistic mode. This allows for the problematisation of received definitions (the Gothic as transgressive, as revivalist, as negative affect, as traumatic sublimation) and gets to the heart of what makes Gothic Studies an exciting academic field today. One of the most positive outcomes of the legitimisation of the study of the Gothic is that it is no longer necessary to spend valuable time defending it. That time can now be used instead to explore exactly what type of palimpsestic monster years of academic investment have created. Such a pedagogic endeavour must be carried out with an inquisitive spirit that will not pit one approach to the Gothic against another. Only through the consideration of all the 'Gothics' I have laid down, through a consideration of genre debate that forces us to confront our own generic assumptions and preconceptions, will it be possible to start building a broader picture of what future may lie ahead for the Gothic genre and those teaching it today.

Notes

1. A sure marker of this shift is the number of journals dedicated specifically to the Gothic which have sprung up since the mid-2000s. These include *the Irish Journal of Gothic and Horror Studies* (2006–), *Studies in Gothic Fiction* (2010–), *Aeternum: The Journal of Contemporary Gothic Studies* (2014–) and *The Dark Arts Journal: New and Emerging Voices in Gothic Studies* (2015–). It must be noted that, despite this, *Gothic Studies* continues to be the only Gothic journal published physically as well as digitally.
2. For reasons connected to the nature of MA programmes in America and their student make-up, the Gothic has not proliferated in the same way there (see Smith 2006: 183–4). At the time of writing (2015), I still have not encountered MA programmes with a strong Gothic content outside the UK and Ireland.
3. The MA Gothic Studies offered by Glamorgan University seems to be no longer available.
4. For example, the 'Teaching the Gothic' CPD at MMU.
5. Gothic modules as part of wider BAs are much more common worldwide, as Gothic modules may be offered as optional, research-specific modules.
6. *eGothicist*, a web-based educational resource for Gothic scholars developed at Edge Hill University, also promised to provide lecturers and students help in their learning and teaching of Gothic Studies. However, as far as I can see, the project has been inactive since 2014.
7. Inevitably, my conclusions are also influenced by my experience of obtaining a PGCAP and of gaining HEA Fellowship. The training I undertook, as well as its connected reflective exercises, changed the way I think about teaching and, importantly, curriculum design.
8. I have recorded some of these experiences in a series of four posts for the International Gothic Association's website, which ran from 16 June to 7 July 2014. See Aldana Reyes (2014).
9. Not incidentally, a recent anonymous survey I ran among 12 MA students showed that the most popular Gothic novels, for them, were not the eighteenth-century classics, but *Frankenstein* and *Dracula*.
10. See also Spooner (2017).

11. See, for example, the abstract for the one-day conference 'What Lies Beneath?', Manchester Metropolitan University, 24 October 2015, https://www.hssr.mmu.ac.uk/gothicmmu/gothic-manchester-festival-2015/what-lies-beneath-one-day-conference. Other genres sometimes collapsed into Gothic include steampunk and neo-Victorian literature.
12. See, for example, the reaction of the local press to our inclusion of zombies in the Gothic Manchester Festival: '[q]uite what Zombies have to do with Gothic studies we're unsure, Frankenstein's monster perhaps, but was he even a Zombie? Certainly not *I Am Legend* Zombies, they're about as Gothic as Abba. We're confused' (The Confidentials 2013).
13. See, for example, the Gothic reading of *Skyfall* (Sam Mendes, 2012) at the *Gothic Technologies / Gothic Techniques: Eleventh Biennial Conference of the International Gothic Association* (5–8 August 2013).
14. It is worth noting that our students also take a core module, 'The Rise of the Gothic', prior to 'Gothic and Modernity', which furnishes them with basic Gothic concepts and takes them up to the fin-de-siècle. Our module picks up where the former leaves off.
15. This problem was easily solved by focusing on other adaptations of the original text and providing summaries and key passages of the original novel.
16. Of course, these writers are also often studied in Victorian Literature or Victorian Gothic modules, as the fin-de-siècle is an inherent part of that period (see Mighall 2004; Smith and Hughes 2015). Luckhurst, for example, terms fin-de-siècle stories 'late Victorian Gothic tales' (2009).
17. Modern Gothic can, however, be seen to manifest, thematically, beyond the Second World War (Riquelme 2014).
18. The literature on postmodernism is vast, but see Eagleton (1996) and Hutcheon (2002) for approaches that either see it as contiguous with modernism, a late development, or else, as dead. I have no space here to deal with the rise of 'post-postmodernism' as a movement, but see Nealon (2012).
19. For example, the fiction of Robert Aickman was very difficult and expensive to source until a series of his short stories were published by Faber and Faber in 2014 to commemorate his centenary. Robert Bloch's short stories are similarly hard to obtain.

20. See Crawford (2014: 181–236).
21. I am specifically referring to modules in science or economics, where a handbook may act as the main essential reading.

References

Aldana Reyes, Xavier (2014) '4 Reasons to Run a Contemporary Gothic Reading Group', *International Gothic Association* website, http://www.iga.stir.ac.uk/showblog.php?id=165 <accessed 10 January 2014>

—— (2015a) 'Fear, Divided: Terror and Horror, or the Two Sides of the Gothic Coin', *eMagazine* 68: 49–52.

—— (2015b) 'Gothic Affect: An Alternative Approach to Critical Models of the Contemporary Gothic' in *New Directions in 21st Century Gothic: The Gothic Compass*, (eds.) Lorna Piatti-Farnell and Donna Lee Brien (London and New York: Routledge) 11–23.

—— (2016) *Horror Film and Affect: Towards a Corporeal Model of Viewership* (London and New York: Routledge)

Armitt, Lucie (2009) *Twentieth Century Gothic* (Cardiff: University of Wales Press)

Blake, Linnie (2015) 'Trapped in the Hysterical Sublime: *Twin Peaks*, the Postmodern, and the Neoliberal Now' in *Return to Twin Peaks: New Approaches to Materiality, Theory, and Genre on Television*, (eds.) Jeffrey Weinstock and Catherine Spooner (Basingstoke: Palgrave Macmillan) 229–46.

—— and Soltysik Monnet, Agnieszka (eds.) (2017) *International Gothic in the Neo-Liberal Age* (Manchester: Manchester University Press)

Botting, Fred (1999) 'Future Horror (The Redundancy of Gothic)', *Gothic Studies* 1.2: 139–55.

—— (2008) *Limits of Horror: Technology, Bodies, Gothic* (Manchester: Manchester University Press)

—— (2013) *Gothic* (2nd rev. edn.) (London and New York: Routledge)

Bruhm, Steven (2002) 'The Contemporary Gothic: Why We Need It' in *The Cambridge Companion to the Gothic*, (ed.) Jerrold E. Hogle (Cambridge: Cambridge University Press) 259–76.

Carroll, Noël (1990) *The Philosophy of Horror, or Paradoxes of the Heart* (London and New York: Routledge)

Chaplin, Sue (2011) *Gothic Literature: Texts, Contexts, Connections* (London: York Press)

Confidentials, The (2013) 'Gothic Manchester Festival Preview: Writers, Architecture, Academics, Walking Tours and Zombies... Zombies?' *Manchester Confidential*, 16 October, http://www.manchesterconfidential.co.uk/entertainment-and-sport/events-and-listings/gothic-manchester-festival-preview <accessed 30 October 2013>

Crawford, Joseph (2014) *The Twilight of the Gothic? Vampire Fiction and the Rise of the Paranormal Romance, 1991–2012* (Cardiff: University of Wales Press)

Eagleton, Terry (1996) *Illusions of Postmodernism* (Oxford and Malden, MA: Blackwell Publishing)

Groom, Nick (2012) *The Gothic: A Very Short Introduction* (Oxford: Oxford University Press)

Hogle, Jerrold E. (ed.) (2002) *The Cambridge Companion to Gothic Fiction* (Cambridge: Cambridge University Press)

—— (2006) 'Theorizing the Gothic' in *Teaching the Gothic*, (eds.) Anna Powell and Andrew Smith (Basingstoke: Palgrave Macmillan) 29–47.

—— (ed.) (2014) *The Cambridge Companion to the Modern Gothic* (Cambridge: Cambridge University Press)

Hughes, William (2006) 'Gothic Criticism: A Survey, 1764–2004' in *Teaching the Gothic*, (eds.) Anna Powell and Andrew Smith (Basingstoke: Palgrave Macmillan) 10–28.

Hutcheon, Linda (2002) *The Politics of Postmodernism* (2nd edn.) (London and New York: Routledge)

Hutchings, Peter (1996) 'Tearing Your Soul Apart: Horror's New Monsters' in *Modern Gothic: A Reader*, (eds.) Victor Sage and Allan Lloyd Smith (Manchester: Manchester University Press) 89–103.

Long Hoeveler, Diane, and Heller, Tamar (eds.) (2003) *Gothic Fiction: The British and American Traditions* (New York: The Modern Language Association of America)

Luckhurst, Roger (ed.) (2009) *Late Victorian Gothic Tales* (Oxford: Oxford University Press)

—— (2015) *Zombies: A Cultural History* (London: Reaktion Books)

McGrath, Patrick, and Morrow, Bradford (eds.) (1993) *The Picador Book of the New Gothic* (London: Picador)

Mighall, Robert (2004) *A Geography of Victorian Gothic Fiction: Mapping History's Nightmares* (Oxford: Oxford University Press)

Nealon, Jeffrey T (2012) *Post-Postmodernism: Or, the Cultural Logic of Just-in-Time Capitalism* (Stanford, CA: Stanford University Press)

Olson, Danel (ed.) (2011) *21st-Century Gothic: Great Gothic Novels since 2000* (Plymouth: Scarecrow Press)

Powell, Anna, and Smith, Andrew (2006) 'Introduction: Gothic Pedagogies' in *Teaching the Gothic*, (eds.) Anna Powell and Andrew Smith (Basingstoke: Palgrave Macmillan) 1–9.

Priest, Hannah (2011) 'Teaching A-Level Gothic', *The Gothic Imagination*, http://www.gothic.stir.ac.uk/guestblog/teaching-a-level-gothic <accessed 10 January 2014>

Prince, Stephen (2013) 'The Western' in *An Introduction to Film Genres*, (eds.) Lester Friedman, David Dresser, Sarah Kozloff, Martha P. Nochinsom and Stephen Prince (London and New York: W. W. Norton) 242–77.

Punter, David, and Byron, Glennis (eds.) (2004) *The Gothic* (Oxford and Malden, MA: Blackwell Publishing)

Riquelme, John Paul (ed.) (2008) *Gothic and Modernism: Essaying Dark Literary Modernity* (Baltimore, MD: Johns Hopkins University Press)

—— (2014) 'Modernist Gothic' in *The Cambridge Companion to the Modern Gothic*, (ed.) Jerrold E. Hogle (Cambridge: Cambridge University Press) 20–36.

Sage, Victor, and Lloyd Smith, Alan (eds) (1996) *Modern Gothic: A Reader* (Manchester: Manchester University Press)

Smith, Andrew (2006) 'Postgraduate Developments' in *Teaching the Gothic*, (eds.) Anna Powell and Andrew Smith (Basingstoke: Palgrave Macmillan) 182–96.

—— (2013) *Gothic Literature* (2nd rev. edn) (Edinburgh: Edinburgh University Press)

—— and Hughes, William (eds.) (2015) *The Victorian Gothic: An Edinburgh Companion* (Edinburgh: Edinburgh University Press)

Spooner, Catherine (2006) *Contemporary Gothic* (London: Reaktion)

—— (2011) 'Catherine Spooner Interviewed by Neil McRobert', *The Gothic Imagination*, http://www.gothic.stir.ac.uk/blog/catherine-spooner-interviewed-by-neil-mcrobert <accessed 21 June 2014>

—— (2014) 'Twenty-First Century Gothic' in *Terror and Wonder: The Gothic Imagination*, (ed.) Dale Townshend (London: British Library Publications) 180–207.

—— (2017) *Post-millennial Gothic: Comedy, Romance and the Rise of 'Happy Gothic'* (London: Bloomsbury)

Stevens, David (2000) *The Gothic Tradition* (Cambridge: Cambridge University Press)

Townshend, Dale (2015) '16 October 1834: Architecture, Romance and the Migration of The Gothic Imagination', *Gothic Migrations: Twelfth Biennial Conference of the International Gothic Association*, 28 July–1 August, Simon Fraser University, Vancouver.

Warwick, Alexandra (2007) 'Feeling Gothicky?' *Gothic Studies* 9.1: 5–15.

Wright, Angela (2007) *Gothic Fiction: A Reader's Guide to Essential Criticism* (Basingstoke: Palgrave Macmillan)

Dark Chocolate from the Literary Crypt: Teaching Contemporary Gothic Horror

Gina Wisker

As a genre, Gothic horror has never been more popular on the university syllabus, yet, because it is often seen as low brow, popular culture, distasteful schlock, horror hides behind the 'Gothic', its more respectable half, or behind speculative fiction, or period studies.[1] Gothic horror appears in the work of many classic and contemporary writers. It is ubiquitous, a form of choice to deal with everything from concerns with identity, poverty and violence, to cultural and gendered difference. This chapter will argue that teaching Gothic horror enables academics and students to co-construct culturally inflected understandings through engaging with literary and media representations of those issues that matter in life such as identity, domestic securities, sexuality, race, the family, culture, the body, equality, sustainability, the future. The main examples drawn from my own teaching practice are Bram Stoker's highly influential *Dracula* (1897) and, more extensively, the Gothic horror of twenty-first-century writer Neil Gaiman. While Stoker's nineteenth century canonical text raises issues of cultural and psychological responses to terrors concerning sexuality, race, migration and Otherness, Gaiman's post-millennial works deal with similar issues but do so through referencing another horror master, H. P. Lovecraft, splicing horror with the comic. His twenty-first century work creates teaching and learning opportunities to use the digital

G. Wisker (✉)
University of Brighton, Brighton, UK

© The Author(s) 2016

K. Shaw (ed.), *Teaching 21st Century Genres*,
DOI 10.1057/978-1-137-55391-1_2

to co-construct knowledge through research, popular cultural references, and a seemingly 'live' interaction with the author and his own comic Gothic horror writing processes.

US academic Frances Auld calls Gothic horror 'the dark chocolate, the Guinness stout of Speculative Fiction. It is strong and chewy. It demands an intellectual analysis of what and how we experience' (Auld 2009). She captures its visceral nature and its intellectual, social and personal challenges so in 'the classroom, on a good day, genre fiction begs interactive reading. Gothic horror fiction allows a rupture of emotion, an embrace of the abyss perhaps, but within the hospitable, shared gallery of the classroom. Gothic horror fictions and their analysis allow for real discussions' (Auld 2009). Gothic horror is entertaining, it draws you in, but that is not its only function. At once destabilising and engaging us personally, culturally, aesthetically, it causes us to consider our awareness of how values are culturally and contextually constructed, how they can manipulate us into dangerous blind compliance, and how the nice dose of paradox, irony and critical scrutiny that Gothic horror can offer can enable critical thinking.

Neil Gaiman's Gothic horror is an ideal focus for new interventions, questionings and re-conceptualisations. Discussing the teaching of Gaiman's short stories as Gothic horror, this chapter considers interactive practices, ways of teaching, learning and assessing that make the most of the personal, cultural, imaginative troublesomeness and transformational thinking offered by Gothic horror, channelled through irony, parody, comedy. It uses the theories of threshold concepts (Meyer and Land 2003), arguing that working with Gothic horror can lead students to troublesome, transformational thinking, understanding and knowledge construction. It does this with us and our students through a variety of learning and teaching activities, including personal reflection, critical reading, group work and active involvement with textual sources, responses, the author and the world, enabled by the digital.

US academic and horror writer Mike Arnzen links the destabilisation that horror produces, the uncanny and the uncertainty, with active creative questioning and critical thinking, all good learning outcomes for study in any context, arguing that:

> Horror provides an excellent context for learning. It raises the serious questions that allow critical inquiry to transpire. This is, perhaps, patently true of all literary texts, but the omnipresent mode of 'uncertainty' that underpins most works in the horror genre inherently moulds the reading experience into the shape of a question mark. (Arnzen 2009)

Gothic horror presents the reader with multiple reading pleasures of entertainment, critique of the everyday securities that so easily and dangerously slide into complacencies, and subversion of the orthodoxies of behaviour and belief. This causes us to scrutinise the familiar and the given, from hearth and home to political ideologies. Teaching and learning moments are crucial opportunities for dialogue, since even socially and culturally engaged Gothic horror might just pass us by as no more than schlock if we miss the elements of representation, of signification and argument. Just to take a couple of examples from earlier periods: reading or watching a performance and discussing Webster's *The White Devil* (1612) exposes the historically constructed demonising of women's sexuality and power, seen as spite and vice. Reading and discussing *Dracula* (1897) enables us to see the historically, culturally contextualised influences of gender, race and patriarchal power in the need to punish foreign Others who seek to invade our homelands and the pure bodies of 'our' womenfolk (and so, offspring). Thinking about the processes and effects of Gothic horror, I earlier noted that the:

> dangerous pleasures offered by horror attract us from both sides of the night. It is wild and alternative, its energies, slow, relentless, creeping, exploding, match and encourage the release of our own. It is a catalyst, a catharsis. In horror, events, people, actions move from the unthinkable into a bodied forth version of the unbearable [...] the sudden intrusion or extrusion of the unexpected and the violent; the stupefying feeling of having what you took for granted exposed as quite different, quite the opposite. And in horror we face up to this, and either explain it and close it down, return to order or, in more radical contemporary feminist horror, recognise it as a projection of, a part of ourselves, not Other to us. Then closing it down would be absurd, and futile. Horror figures—vampire, werewolf, femme fatale, a host of monsters, are recuperated, celebrated, or at least tolerated and recognised. (Wisker 2005)

Arnzen, Auld and others were invited for a special edition of the e-journal *Dissections* (2009) to explore how and why they taught Gothic horror, and the ways in which students engaged with it so that disturbance and troublesomeness could lead to transformational learning (Perkins 1999; Meyer and Land 2003). As a teacher I have always loved working with Gothic horror, but only latterly has this become respectable in the Higher Education classroom. Yet Gothic has the ability to undercut complacencies; it is entertaining, 'wild and alternative', destabilising and defamiliarising. As I argued in an earlier work:

> The release of energies it involves exposes pomposity; hypocrisy; power games; the artifice of respectability, hiding deception and violence; the falseness of romantic relationships of family life, of social, political and work hierarchies. This radical, deviant, wild energy assaults and exposes the lies upon which we either base our sense of security or by which others, defended by a status quo which claims to be 'right', ordered, logical, good, healthy, in control, control us. (Wisker 2005)

In teaching horror we expose the ways in which it channels the fears and complacencies of the time, and using our critical reading and research skills we are able to explore their social and cultural origins, and so defuse the power of those controlling beliefs and behaviours. In using comic Gothic horror, Neil Gaiman takes us half way, his comic strategies exposing the overt and covert terrors and panics in the horror texts on which he builds his own work.

The monograph *Horror Fiction: An Introduction* (Wisker 2005), like the special edition of *Dissections* (2009), grew from teaching and working with the Gothic horror genre. I now use excerpts from both in my teaching. These are active texts, which also evidence to students how we interact together with their work, in that we each write from our discussions, and as academics we encourage the students to write with confidence, each creating knowledge to share with others. Together we work with horror and how it enables us to see the world, and to consider serious issues. Context and choice of texts are important, as well as how we teach and learn together. One *Dissections* contributor noted that teaching horror in the Appalachians was a very disturbing experience, since the everyday horror of peoples' lives—brutal, harsh—made it more difficult to dissociate the real from the fictional, and manage the real through the critical stance to enable understanding, the laughter as well as the shudder. Fiction offers an imaginative space in which to deal with what disturbs, but perhaps it is more difficult to gain the critical distance when horror is the lived experience.

In my own practice, I often begin by asking for personal reflections on reading or watching Gothic horror in an attempt to engage students first with their own thoughts, then to share these in small groups or pairs. This surfaces some of the issues about definitions, characteristics, positive and negative reactions, favourite texts and films. It lays the way for making our work with Gothic horror lively and alive, related to their interests, sense of fear and disturbance, identity and power. In my teaching of *Dracula*

(1897) I reference both topical issues and historical roots, marrying the nineteenth-century contexts of the text with our contemporary world. In 2015, this led to discussions on the humanitarian crisis of Syrian refugees, relating the political and media language of 'swarms' and 'hordes' to that used in Gothic horror fiction about vampires, who represent the terrifying, invasive, undead, inhuman Other, and how emotive political language stirs up hidden fears through such resonances. Through teaching *Dracula* simultaneously with the crisis we were able to explore the xenophobia and racism of the 1890s that underpins a postcolonial reading of the text, dramatised in the fear of Dracula's plan to bring his vampire family to Britain. Having bought a house in London and with plans for many more, Dracula himself has his coffin shipped to Whitby. He enters the country both surreptitiously and violently, in advance of the many coffins of his vampire relatives, which are shipped straight into the heart of London. Horror homes in on ongoing fears, such as the instability of identity and of domestic security, and those that are immediate and current.

Doctoral research carried out by Linda Friday (2013) used documentary evidence in the form of newspapers and bills posted on walls to show that there was a blight of anti-Semitic terror of the arrival of Jewish migrants in London's East End in the 1890s. This research, conducted by a PhD student, used digitally presented maps of the period to show the positioning of Dracula's safe houses to which the coffins were being shipped, the Jewish immigration settlements, and the closeness to Jack the Ripper's Whitechapel murders. The elision of the terrors of the East End with Jewish migration in the newspapers set a perfect scene for the transfer of demonisation of the foreign Other into the undead bodies of Dracula's frontrunners for his vampire hordes, his family, thus eliding also a disgust at the spawning of future vampires, which underlies some of the sexual desire and disgust within the novel. The research is meticulous, historical, digitised, accessible; the argument about contemporary terrors embodied in the contemporary Gothic horror novel convincing.

The relationships with contemporary language, fears of the invading Other intent on using up the limited resources of the welfare state to feed their children and houses, is very similar to the fears and language of the 1890s. I also explore the demonisation of women by the representation of them in *Dracula* and other current texts and imagery (Djikstra's *Idols of Perversity* 1986) as femmes fatales guilty of enticing and then emasculating and devouring men. This is the role played by Dracula's three vampire women, one of whom resembles the solicitor, Jonathan Harker's wife Mina, and the role played by the beautiful Lucy, who is desired by three men, her room and her body entered by Dracula himself, his vampire teeth piercing her skin and his disgusting sensual tongue drinking her blood. This demonisation of women's sexuality and their power, even their ability to type (Mina), is coincident with the rise of the New Woman from the 1890s onwards, and with the legal focus on prostitution and sexually transmitted diseases, which resulted in the Contagious Diseases Act (1864).

A contemporary reading of *Dracula* enables the exposure of sexualised terrors and misrepresentation of women as a way of controlling freedoms, particularly sexual, intellectual and economic, which terrors drive much of the novel's trajectory. The 2015 exploration of how *Dracula* vehicles the xenophobia and racism of this period of the late British empire was richer in 2015 because of the humanitarian crisis of those fleeing Syria and other parts of the Middle East from political and physical oppression. The postcolonial reading is brought right up to date, exposing both historical and current terrors and their dramatic exposition in horror fiction. Reading *Dracula* in this way enables twenty-first-century students to unpick how a Gothic horror literary text exposes such terrors, and to critique its psychologically based and propagandist nature and role, to expose the problems expressed in horror through exploring the text, in its times, and in its current topical resonance.

When teaching Gothic horror I always share examples of the historical contexts of the work, and of the sources which influenced it, as well as engaging students with the theoretical perspectives which inform our reading of Gothic horror. Critical dialogues about the texts we are studying often form part of a lecture, which will also have references, quotations, video clips, and overall offer a version of a model of ways of engaging with the texts. I record the lecture when I give it and make it available online along with the PowerPoint, but I refuse to simply read from the script or a PowerPoint. Instead, I update, elaborate, ask the students questions and give them time to think, discuss and answer them, so that even a large lecture is interactive (Jenkins 1991) and followed by a smaller interactive seminar with text extracts, questions and digitally based research and discussion activities. Some of the lecture and seminar work emphasises and engages research skills, indicates the longevity of figures of horror, their replay and reimaging, their consistent relevance. I use and ask students to use media, including YouTube clips, websites, author blogs, social media and web links that engage them with considering some of their own interests in relation to sources, context, influences, and interactions between author, world, text and readers. One of the aims or learning outcomes of all of this is to bring and keep texts alive; to encourage personal engagement and the imagination; valorising the importance of the imagination, storytelling and living with the dimension of the imaginary as well as the real; and to move beyond the shivering fun of entertainment without losing it. Another is to enable us all to see that in our interactions with the history, context, sources, influences, critical dialogues, and the text, through research, reading and discussion, we are co constructing knowledge, making something new.

I have explored some of the issues in teaching *Dracula*—the use of the contemporary to the novel's production, and our own contemporary concerns; the use of archives and digitised artefacts, such as maps and newspapers, to enable students to conduct their own original research, following the engagement with the novel, the historical context and the critical reading. I should like next to make a case for a focus on the fantasy author Neil Gaiman, seeing some of his work as comic Gothic horror. Neil Gaiman's work encompasses graphic novels, blogs, film scripts based on his own novels and short stories. In the tale discussed here we see a form of transatlantic comic horror translation, which moves from H. P. Lovecraft and Poe to Monty Python and Pete and Dud, and in its splicing of the comic with horror also splices American and British references and sensitivities, the great horror masters and the Britishness of sitcoms, comic duos, ironic juxtaposition, referencing a location, intertextuality and naiveté. 'Only the End of the World Again' (1998b) combines all of these with the addition of California detective fiction, since it features an 'adjustor', private investigator, also a werewolf, arriving in a small town, but destined to be sacrificed, off the edge of a cliff, to the elder gods (part of Lovecraft's myths) when the end of the world (much sought by the locals) is on the cusp of arrival.

Neil Gaiman's texts rely on translation and mistranslation. He is an expert in translation between cultures, between comedy and horror. His transatlantic comic horror combines the lurking fears of American horror masters Lovecraft and Poe with international myth, fantasy, fairy tale, and a range of recognisably English humour, from deadpan to farce. When teaching Neil Gaiman's Gothic horror, it is useful to briefly explore segues between and twinning of comedy and horror, each based on defamiliarisation. In considering Neil Gaiman's short stories, I look briefly throughout at H.P Lovecraft's work (nicknamed 'The King of Weird' by Joyce Carol,

Oates 1996). I focus in the main on 'Shoggoth's Old Peculiar' in *Smoke and Mirrors* (1998c), which exemplifies Gaiman's horror/humour/cultural difference splicing. Part of the teaching of Gaiman's work which builds on that of H. P. Lovecraft serves to also reveal the horror of that great influential author. Lovecraft was noted for his disgust at sexuality and miscegenation, rolling together both sexual and racial fears. He was also a master of creating indescribable terrors, a mythos comprising the great Cthulhu, and the elder gods, whose threat is ever present, who are insidiously gradually entering humankind through the bodies of women who spawn half human, half creature offspring. An eventual apocalypse or grand world-changing arrival is imminent. Such arcanely religiously fuelled terrors can also be found in the language of extreme religious cults. The disgust at sex and sexuality, the blame on women, and the terror at invading racially different others is of a piece with that informing *Dracula*, though Lovecraft's migrant hordes were the immigrated population of New York in which he briefly lived, and possibly the Portuguese settlers in Providence where he was born and died, and mainly lived, and his own sexual disgust both as a product of the times, and his own distaste (see Joshi 2001; Lord 2004).

In Neil Gaiman's unique contribution, he revisits then undercuts the terrors of the unnameable, the unspeakable and the unmentionable histories, weird disturbing characters and scenarios frequent in horror, particularly Lovecraft's horror, and brings them into the everyday, with exquisitely amusing results. While an inability to interpret and translate often threatens Lovecraft's characters, among others, in narratives using the characteristics of fantasy (Todorov 1975) and horror (Jancovich 1992; Punter 1996; Wisker 2005), effective translation from culture to culture, and between the nuances of language and interpretation offer Gaiman and his readers opportunities for richly amusing irony, satire or slapstick. The kind of cultural differences that threaten in Lovecraft are manipulated by Gaiman using the same ploys of the uncanny (Freud 1919; Royle 2003), defamiliarisation and misinterpretation, but to comic effect, enriched by horror and mythic (Oktem 2012) intertexts.

The juxtaposition of the homely, the banal and the inept, a tendency to misinterpret, endangers Lovecraft's characters, who are usually tangled up with the source of the often cosmic threat (frequently based in miscegenation) (Lord 2004), at the level of the elemental and otherworldly (Joshi 2001). Much myth and fairy-tale as well as horror emphasises this level, this liminal space. In 'Only the End of the World Again', Gaiman takes the transitory, wolfman, private investigator (adjustor) in Innsmouth to the end of the cliff, where the end of the world and the rising from the deeps will take place once his blood is spilled. In 'Shoggoth's old Peculiar' (1998c), Gaiman gives us the naive American on a walking tour of the worst coastal towns in the North of England, who foolishly decides to stay at the bed and breakfast 'Shub-Niggurath' (named after a Lovecraftian fictional deity intent on procreation, 'The Black Goat of the Woods with a Thousand Young'), instead of 'Mon Repos'. In dipping his own fictional characters into Lovecraft's world, Gaiman transforms it into the everyday, translating the horror into the comic. An encounter with two brown raincoated blokes in a pub, Wilf and Seth (reminders of the Whateley brothers in 'The Dunwich Horror' (1929), spawn of a devilish creature), becomes one with the Pete and Dud characters created by Peter Cook and Dudley Moore. They inform the traveller that the great Cthulhu will soon come and take over the world, but they cannot imagine quite how, so they suggest that once Cthulhu has read the papers he will come out of the ocean depths and consume the world. The old lady purchasing the Holy Grail from a charity shop, visited by Sir Galahad on his white charger in another of Gaiman's tales, 'Chivalry' (1998a), is straight from Monty Python, *Fawlty Towers* (1975–9) and British sitcoms. Gaiman's work offers a comic horror mix of delightful richness based on the splicing and clashing of cultures, the translation between the banal, the everyday, and the language of slapstick, as much as of irony and the unspeakable, the unnameable, the unimaginable.

My first awareness of this liminal space between horror and the comic, the cusp of the boundary between the two, where one slips into the other, was reading and teaching the revenge tragedies. In *The Revenger's Tragedy* (Middleton 1607), as the third round of revengers come on stage, skulls, daggers, blood, cloaks, politics, brutality merge into stylised comic without losing the visceral threat. Some of the humour of the revenge tragedies, including *The Revenger's Tragedy* (1607) and *The White Devil* (Webster 1612), is an acquired taste, since not everyone finds any humour in such dark, violent and psychologically threatening excess. It is black humour, laughing at the unthinkable, at death, funerals, and the movement between response to forms of the comic and their overlap at the most uncomfortable, as well as the most unlikely, verging on the ridiculous. The excess makes us shudder and laugh at the same time. In facing discomfort, recognition, the embodiment of the things that concern, frighten, disturb, worry us—shuddering and laughing are remarkably similar responses, and uneasy, queasy laughing is where they overlap. Disgust, rejection and nervous laughing, laughing at the discrepancies between the expected and the unexpected, is where they dip into farce. Here we have the moments where horror, through becoming excessive, becomes burlesque.

Gaimain's 'Shoggoth's Old Peculiar' (1998c) is a hilarious satire of H. P. Lovecraft, more so if the reader is familiar with the comedy routines of Peter Cook and Dudley Moore. Hapless American Benjamin Lassiter, on a walking tour of the coast of England, discovers that it is not nearly as picturesque as he had been led to believe. He comes to an odd little village and meets two very strange men, Seth and Wilf. Fans of Peter Cook and Dudley Moore's mind-boggling deadpan conversational routines will instantly recognise these two, and Gaiman has acknowledged that historically one night, in a bar with a friend, he decided that the unavoidable (to him) relationship between Lovecraft's two strange Whateley brothers and the comic characters had to be realised and shared.

As a transatlantic writer and traveller from the south coast of England, Gaiman has caught the problems of translation perfectly, the translation of tourist guide descriptions and of English terminology into the 'real'. 'Shoggoth's Old Peculiar' (1998c) is a travel tale, as is Lovecraft's 'The Shadow over Innsmouth' (1936), but one which adds cultural difference to the already complex misinterpretations possible for Lovecraft's warned off lone wanderer figure. The tale has traces of *An American Werewolf in London* (1981), where Jack and his friend stumble wearily into 'The Slaughtered Lamb' on the Yorkshire Moors, are met with covert warnings and hints and threats usually only found in that other familiar travel context, *Dracula* (1897), where Jonathan Harker travels to Transylvania to sell parts of London to the vampire count.

Locals always know secrets, keep them, warn the traveller a little, watch him or her fall straight into the trap, and sometimes, as in 'The Shadow over Innsmouth' (1936) or Kate Mosse's *The Winter Ghosts* (2009), set in Carcassonne, are part of the trap. *Wrong Turn* (2003) and *The Texas Chainsaw Massacre* (1974) operate a similar trajectory, as does Ian McEwan's *The Comfort of Strangers* (1981). Travellers are always a little gauche, confused, liable to fear and misread the unusual, miss hints about the truly dangerous and strange, mistake the strange and excitingly different for the deadly and vice versa. Gothic horror's ability to nudge us out of our comfort zone is set perfectly in the context of the defamiliarisation of people and places, the misreading of signs.

Many travellers in such tales as Gaiman's, Lovecraft's, McEwan's escape completely unaware of what could have happened. Many so utterly misread the situation, inebriated (much of this work has pubs, cafes, meals) by difference, destabilised, that they are cast into being the consumed or consumable, rather than the guest, as in 'The Shadow over Innsmouth' (1936). In the latter, Lovecraft's inquisitive traveller might be in danger but he also faces one of the roots of abjection and Otherising: finding that surprisingly he is a part of what he has newly half discovered. In this case, he realises that it is his family connection with the Lovecraftian Mythos influenced townsfolk, whose ancestors mated with the fishy folk beneath the waves in return for strange golden jewellery and sustained catches of fish.

The naïve American abroad tradition is as old as Henry James and Edith Wharton. Usually it ends in tears. In the British television comic tradition, *An Idiot Abroad* (2010–12), *The League of Gentlemen* (1999–2002), and some of *Little Britain* (2003–5), all capture this—but Gaiman wrote his tale before these, so perhaps was looking at the often culpable naivety of *Carry On* films (1958–92). He takes British sitcoms and Ealing comedy humour and the witty banter of men in the pub, of Peter Cook and Dudley Moore (1960s), and transposes them onto the rather problematic creatures/people in Innsmouth, and in Dunwich (Lovecraft's 'The Dunwich Horror' 1929). In the latter, there are two strange brothers, the Whateleys, sons of Yog-Sothoth, a creature from inner/outer space. One, Wilbur, has tentacles beneath his waist, neatly covered by his long coat, and walks relatively freely among people, while the other, much taller, is shut up in the barn devouring cattle, pledging with the elder gods, intent on bringing about the end of the world as we know it.

Gaiman's tale is set in the North but recognisable and read as any seaside town on the coast of Britain. He combines the language of Lovecraft and insider knowledge, in this case of real ale popular amongst the local working-class drinkers in pubs in the North and Midlands or other edges of the UK. *Shoggoth's Old Peculiar* is modelled surely on *Theakston's Old Peculiar* and other dull, heavy local beers, Real Ale specialities, reliant on exclusive insider knowledge and choice, as much as on the insider language excluding and confusing Ben Lassiter, the American traveller in Gaiman's tale. Ben Lassiter, naïve American tourist on the British coastal north in the off season on a walking tour, has been misinformed that British locals like Americans on walking tours, and can himself read between the lines of the guidebook, whose author, he believes, should be charged under the Trade Descriptions Act. He learns how to translate 'charming' for 'nondescript' and ends up actually North of Bootle, just outside Liverpool. All three local bed and breakfasts are unlikely to be the choice of the discerning traveller. Their names, 'Sea View', or 'Mon Repos', are misleading, and their interiors would be damp and decayed. However, selecting 'Shub Niggurath', another member of Lovecraft's Mythos (the goat with a thousand young), signals for the discerning reader an insider joke referencing Lovecraft's horror. A 'frog faced' woman might merely be an insult to a local, but when we have become familiar with Lovecraft's 'The Shadow over Innsmouth' (1936), we know the sea creatures are just round the corner, about to emerge. The Lovecraftian intertextuality spliced with travel writing and British sitcoms and comic routines is a double delight.

Ben, from dry Texas, is doubtful about pubs, even though recommended in 'A Walking Tour of the British Coastline'. Of course, the British always suggest pubs, thus excluding large chunks of the populace from the only real social hub of a town or village. The pub, 'The Book of Dead Names', run by proprietor 'Al-Hazred', references dubious Eastern foreigners and esoteric texts, the lure and threat of the exotic which underlies much of Lovecraft's fear of Otherness, miscegenation and invading difference. The scenario is a mixture of the threatening, the disturbingly confusing and familiar. The sourcing of references to Lovecraft's work enhances this, as does all good intertextuality, without also excluding those who have no basis to recognise the references. In my lecture I explore and explain the sources, and in the seminar I invite the students to explore whatever they are interested in from the sources for themselves using their shared iPhone, iPad or laptops, so that they follow an aspect which interests them, and make a case for it, and also experience the ways in which sources and intertextual references are used in these texts.

References to Lovecraft's works might supply frissons of horror, but the comedy is very British and also needs exploring. The bottle blonde barmaid is from the *Carry On* films, the two 'gentlemen' wearing 'long grey raincoats and scarves, were playing dominoes and supping dark brown foam-topped beerish drinks from dimpled glass tankards' (46) are Pete and Dud, comic alter egos of Peter Cook and Dudley Moore. The pair are recognisable to those who have seen the politically inspired satirical comedy routines popular in the 1960s and 1970s in the UK beginning with 'Beyond the Fringe' then the 'Dagenham Dialogues', on which Gaiman has built his satirical comic Gothic horror tale. However, these routines are of Gaiman's generation or before, so students also need introducing to their kind of humour, which uses deadpan delivery to mimic and satirise a mixture of the serious made light and the banal made serious. The reversals and defamiliarisations of comedy and of horror are very similar in strategy, but usually used to different ends. In comic Gothic horror, orthodoxies and high seriousness (such as the Cthulhu mythos, the practices of oppressive regimes, culturally based, invented and enforced behaviours) are seen as constructions that can be deconstructed, myths that can be deflated, unreliable investments, however overwhelming they are to those committed to them. This is achieved through that splicing of the banal and the deadly serious. Ben is offered a 'Ploughman's' but that, like 'Saloon Bar', fails to translate. 'The British treated food as some kind of punishment' (148). In cursing the English 'for choosing to dine upon such swill' (148), the archaic language of Britain matches that of Lovecraft, as pointed out by Wilf and Seth, who debate the use of 'eldritch', and 'squamous', each elevated terms in ironic juxtaposition to the meagre reality.

Comedy and horror operate often on such ironic juxtapositions, defamiliarisation, understatement, misunderstanding, that we have to 'mind the gap' between the language and the reality we are offered for deadly or hilarious results. As readers and students we align ourselves as equally unwitting, only slightly more informed than the naïve and unwitting protagonist, and we each also translate the scenarios in which we find ourselves in Gothic comic horror, reliant upon the variety of our own experiences, often getting it all wrong. The references to Westerns place Ben in a Wild West danger zone. He then falls into the linguistic trap of inquiring what they are drinking, which means he has to buy them a round and join them in a pint of *Shoggoth's Old Peculiar*, referred to as 'full-bodied'(148) as a goat, like the Devil, or Shub-Niggurath:

> 'You know what eldritch means?' Ben shook his head. He seemed to be discussing literature with the two strangers in an English pub while drinking beer. He wondered for a moment if he had become someone else, while he wasn't looking? (150)

Ben's estrangement and defamiliarisation as a gauche tourist is matched with the wildly unlikely scenario of being with two old blokes in a pub discussing language and literature, although that very disjunction between the esoteric and the familiar, the relationships between class and belonging, derive from the kind of comic gap that British comedy often pursues, with its use of satire, irony, farce and sometimes threat, its making fun of misunderstanding and painful unexpected conclusions.

Wilf, playing a Pete and Dud role, starts a joke tale about camels, humps and the desert. It's a witty banter based on preposterous pretence and conjecture, as often is the case in the comedy routines in Pete and Dud, where, in one exchange, for instance, they talked about being a judge and doing judging. This comedy routine and boasting, mimicked in Gaiman's story, is based on ignorance and brashness, wisdom fuelled by several pints. Another Lovecraft reference is the 'Tomb of Nyarlathotep', of which one of the men says 'you could have meant someone else with the same name' (151). Colloquialisms are juxtaposed with elevated language, and the sheer unlikeliness of the grafting of the bizarre and comic everyday with the cosmic threat posed in Lovecraft's tales removes any sense of threat. However, Seth and Wilf are 'acolytes' of 'Great Cthulhu' and their routine, based on that of Pete and Dud, of being a judge, emphasises the disjunction between the serious and the funny. They say 'the acolytin' is not really what you might call laborious employment in the middle of its busy season, that is of course because of his 'bein' asleep'(153). Once Cthulhu has read the papers he will 'come out of the ocean depths and consume the world utterly' (153). Ben finds this funny because he sees an ironic juxtaposition between labels such as 'Ploughman's' and 'Great Cthulhu' and what something turns out to be. His inebriated state offers him an angle on the absurd, bizarre and mundane. Lovecraft's terrifying godlike figure Cthulhu is reduced to a dozing heap, his position in the depths transposed to just outside a pub near Bootle. Most readers would probably be 'tourists' in need of translation of terms to appreciate the full set of humorous references, and the effect of Gaiman's language and tale on the reader depends on being an insider of both UK and US cultures, and the scenarios of both Lovecraft and of Pete and Dud. The realm of the mundane is at a ridiculous distance from esoteric elevations, as Gaiman juxtaposes two cultures, history, horror, the comic and popular culture.

It is possible then to teach Gaiman's contemporary Gothic story as comedy, but there is an undertow of potential threat, and that is the danger of the unusual and unknown to the unwary tourist. The tradition from which this comes is that of the horror of travel and tourism. E.M. Forster pointed out some of the problems of relying on guidebooks when his tourists in *Where Angels Fear to Tread* (1905) use Baedeker to find an idyllic Italy and are shaken by blood and a dead body in the fountain in Florence, dentists and laughing gas in Fiesole. The naïvely trusting tourist or self-absorbed traveller seeking adventure and the unusual as well as a resting place is a popular figure for contemporary horror. Using Venice, a labyrinthine city filled with historical secrets, to recuperate from work and revive a relationship, leads to mis-readings, torture and death in Ian McEwan's *The Comfort of Strangers* (1981). Seeking adventure in the less travelled areas (*Deliverance* 1972), turning off road to avoid pile ups or traffic jams and driving through the wrong part of the Appalachians (*Wrong Turn* 2003), hitching and taking a lift, or being towed when your car breaks down in the Australian outback (*Wolf Creek* 2005) are all commonplace scenarios now in popular horror films.

If Gaiman's 'Shoggoth's Old Peculiar' (1998c) isn't directly influenced by the Gothic tourism inherent in these horror films, then contemporary readers will link from the text to them and more recent iterations. We read back into sources direct and indirect, both as pointed out overtly by authors, our own sources, and then we read out into the contemporary use of these works, influences on them, their influences on other work, of film, event and social media. This is a comic tale, and it grows from translating an American Abroad, the naïve traveller, as in *An American Werewolf in London* (1981), into a local northern seaside pub in the winter season when everything is shut and all guidebooks misleading, so that, in an out of the way place, he might meet Lovecraft's Whateley brothers, the kind of strange incestuously or confusingly originated 'locals' who might provide fascinating entertainment for the tourist or who might prey on their insouciance, misinterpretation, lack of intuition in strange circumstance and lack of maturity. This is a story about entering a safe, comfortable space of the Other, and misunderstanding their intent, a common misinterpretation between cultures, often leading to serious consequences. The traveller in 'The Shadow over Innsmouth' (1936) is not really in major danger, because he is led to realise that these are also his ancestors from under the sea, his relatives, the strangely tentacled land and sea folk. The traveller in 'The Dunwich Horror' (1929) also is not in direct danger, but the Whateley brothers are a problem, since their existence is evidence of Lovecraft's major fear, miscegenation. Lavinia Whateley has mated with a beastly creature, sent by the elder gods, and the overarching plan is to take over the world. The two blokes in brown raincoats in the pub are intent on confusing Ben, the American tourist, so that he drinks, misunderstands their jokes and references to the great Cthulhu and is led out into the wintry wet seaside air along the prom, potentially to his doom in the waves below, as a sacrifice.

Lovecraft's tales emphasise a racialised terror of the foreign Other, more terrible, more insidiously, intrusively dangerous when intermixed with our relatives. Gaiman's comic horror keeps the terror at bay without diminishing the Lovecraftian resonances, by using comedy. He also undercuts the racism, the horror at the unspeakable Other. Gaiman's is a 1998 tale, building on Lovecraft's work from 1929 and 1936. However, even for a contemporary student reader, it is possible to engage in discussions about Lovecraft's racism and sexism, his language of Otherising, his terror of immigration (from the sea, the stars, Africa, with Arthur Jermyn [Lovecraft 1921]) and more fully understand the dangerous rhetoric of racism in the terrors over contemporary migration, where refugees are referred to in language used for invasive insects or 'swarms', 'hordes', language which also reminds now of zombie apocalypse in popular film and text. Gaiman is comic, he uses British sitcom and stand up, but he also engages with Lovecraft's racism and terror of the foreign Other, offering an awareness of its subtext of terror, disgust and misreadings of the Other, seen in Gothic tourist horror, and in the contemporary press. The contemporary resonances of Lovecraft's terror at mixed race intrusion, repeated in comic horrors in Gaiman, make Gaiman's work a layered, rich read of comedy and Gothic horror, with pertinent connections not only to travel and tourism, and cultural confusion, but to political propaganda, and racism. The work is important and it connects with and causes discussion about serious issues.

In a contemporary classroom, with the many digital opportunities offered by iPhones and iPads, students are invited to explore back, round or forward: back to the references to Lovecraft and find out about a great horror master, to the theorised references which horror uses, related to abjection, for example, Julia Kristeva's work (1982). Then they can explore out to other horror Gothic tourist work (such as the writing sof Kate Mosse and Ian McEwan), to British sit-com and stand up, Peter Cook and Dudley Moore, to Gaiman's own, very accessible comments about his inspiration and sources, and to contemporary comments about the Syrian refugee crisis, for example, which uses the language of apocalypse and horror to dehumanise refugees, a strategy familiar from Nazi representation of Jews in the Second World War.

I often ask students to look where they are interested and set out the questions that they can explore individually, then in small groups. They look at what interests them in their brief research and they also talk about why and how they accessed the information they sought, how they determined which sources were helpful, what was poorly researched and ephemeral, what were total side-lines, and then, when comparing what they had each found, and bringing some theory to bear on it, how their work cast new light on that of Gaiman and Lovecraft through considering abjection and horror, Gothic tourism, comic horror, British comedy, contemporary news reporting, and so on. Students carry out their research in the class using their devices, which begins to interlock the world of Gothic horror with the digital, since each takes place in a liminal space; each troubles the familiar yet offers critical insights. The digital world is already uncanny—*unheimlich*—as is the Gothic. This defamiliarisation of familiar forms of engagement and expression naturally fit together our work with Gothic horror, and Neil Gaiman's writing links these into a layered uncanny world (Mills 2010).

Digital connections inspire a new form of interaction with authors, their sources, influences and work. Interacting with Neil Gaiman's own website, with his blog, and with the various references with which he is working or which connect us as readers to the work enables students to take their own research paths and then contribute their own critically informed work to the group, and in their written assignments. On this course they are expected to produce three short pieces, two of which can be research-based blogs, each uploaded online, which enables illustrations, sounds and web links, like Gaiman's own blog, and more informative posts. Skains suggests readers turn to online outlets to prolong the experience of reading novels, and digital communities introduce 'the print-oriented reader to digital storytelling elements, such as online games, multimedia, and hypertext', referencing the *NeilGaiman.com* community as of 'the expanded author-reader dynamic', with interactions introducing digital storytelling conventions. Hillesund (2007) also comments on the relationship between authors who have an online presence, as does Gaiman, to act as a bridge between digital and print storytelling conventions, and between author and reader.

When we undertake research with literary texts we probably usually focus on critical reading, bringing in the work of theorists and critics to bear on themes and issues which we find in the work we are reading. But with the advent of writers who use the postmodernist tendency to intermix their new work with referencing and reuse, who reunderstand and reinterpret the arguments and contributions of those earlier texts, it is vital to have access to some of the influences and sources of the intertextual references to begin to see this dialogue and their contribution, reinterpretation, contradiction. The seminar sessions working with Neil Gaiman deliberately engage students with the practice of twenty-first-century research. When we read and explore literary texts today we follow the trail set by the writers and set our own trails. We engage with and explore their sources, intertext references and the hints and traces we see in the texts ourselves, which link for us out into other films, blogs, images, novels and the news. We make our own lines and spin our own interpretations, constructing new knowledge from literary texts, using the digital resources, links, dialogues and then, in the case of work on a course, expression in assessed work. Students explore their own trails through this work and that of influences, then share responses. The assessments, the three pieces, are part of our module but other assessment forms could be used as co-constructions of knowledge—in individual and group work assessments, including creative products such as individual and group blogs as discussions; diary type capture of developing ideas and reflections; researched, evidence-based explorations of the ways sources lead into new works, or works are constantly reconstructed and rewritten, re-represented in different times through wikis, podcasts and video productions.

Neil Gaiman's comic Gothic horror can be a rich source of learning and teaching to engage students with some of the serious issues about identity, body, gender, power, culture, and with the role played by the imagination, the fantastic, in engaging with such serious issues. Both Gaiman's engagement with the digital and social media, and Linda Friday's research into the context and history behind *Dracula*, for example, offer ways in which students can step into the uncanny world of the digital, engaging with serious issues dealt with through Gothic horror. In his controversial speech at the London Book Fair, Gaiman suggests:

> the whole point of a digital frontier right now is that it's a frontier, all the old rules are falling apart. Anyone who tells you they know what's coming, what things will be like in 10 years' time, is simply lying to you. None of the experts know—nobody knows, which is great [...] When the rules are gone you can make up your own rules. You can fail, you can fail more interestingly, you can try things, and you can succeed in ways nobody would have thought of, because you're pushing through a door marked no entrance, you're walking in through it. (Gaiman 2013)

Neil Gaiman's comic Gothic horror engages us as students and readers with the darkness of horror, and its comic side, its history, and its legacy in popular culture and the contemporary representation of events, which we can discover and research. It enacts for us how learning and teaching horror provides a vital engagement with psychological and social issues, in real time, and for the classroom, real or virtual. It offers the opportunity to make those immediate connections, building new knowledge and understanding to enable dialogue between the digital, the world, self and the text. Gaiman's own 'Dream Lord' comments on the importance of the imagination, the fantastic, and I would argue, Gothic horror, for opening up new versions and visions, which in the teaching and learning context can engage students in co-constructing new responses, new knowledge.

Note

1. Gothic literature has been seen to start with three key texts, first Horace Walpole's *Castle of Otranto* (1764), featuring objects coming alive, inheritance, sexual danger and romance, then Anne Radcliffe's *Mysteries of Udolpho* (1794), both of which are set in Italy. Matthew Lewis's *The Monk* (1796) develops the sexual predation and prurience theme in a religious context, while much Gothic work that followed these focuses on romance. Gothic horror is a specialist subset of both Gothic and horror springing from early Gothic writing's interest in gender and power, violence, property ownership. It is likely to avoid the romance element (except to expose and undercut it) and explore issues to do with the body, identity, family, inheritance, spaces, knowledge and fundamental and everyday concerns, as does the Gothic, in order to disturb these, make the reader uncomfortable, threatened about them, even endangered. It is likely to use shock and dis-ease alongside the disturbance of complacency and the questioning of forms and beliefs found in Gothic. Horror which is not Gothic is more likely to be violent, visceral, 'shlock', which shocks for the entertainment of it. It could be more gratuitous, without always having a specific social, cultural, political engagement and questioning at its core. *Texas Chainsaw Massacre* (1974) is more likely to be considered as horror, as there is much gratuitous violence and little if any questioning of social and cultural norms and givens, in order to lead to change; however, *Dr Jekyll and Mr Hyde* (1886), while also containing violence, provides questioning about social issues such as the wholeness of identity, the security and trustworthiness of middle-class professional rules, roles and behaviours, so it is Gothic and horror, that is, Gothic horror.

References

Arnzen, Michael (2009) 'Horror and the Responsibilities of the Liberal Educator', *Dissections,* http://www.simegen.com/writers/dissections/May%202009/dissections_page_03.html <accessed 18 February 2016>

Auld, Frances (2009) 'Teaching Horror: Subversion, Sublimity, and SO MUCH BLOOD!' *Dissections,* http://www.simegen.com/writers/dissections/May%20 2009/dissections_page_07.html <accessed 18th February 2016>

Boorman, John (1972) *Deliverance.*

Cleese, John and Booth, Connie (1975–9) *Fawlty Towers.*

Dijkstra, Bram (1986) *Idols of Perversity: Fantasies of Feminine Evil in Fin-de-siècle Culture* (Oxford: Oxford University Press)

Dissections, May 2009, http://www.simegen.com/writers/dissections/May%20 2009/dissections_contents_page.html <accessed 18th February 2016>

Friday, Linda (2013) 'Exhuming Dracula's Coffin via e-Learning', paper delivered to the *International Gothic Conference*, Surrey (unpublished PhD).

Forster, Edward Morgan (1905) *Where Angels Fear to Tread* (Edinburgh: William Blackwood and Sons)

Freud, Sigmund [1919] (1953) 'The Uncanny', in *The Standard Edition of the Complete Psychological Works of Sigmund Freud,* Vol. XVII, James Strachey (ed. and trans.) (London: Hogarth) 217–256.

Gaiman, Neil (1989–1996) *The Sandman* (New York: DC Comics)

——— (1998a) 'Chivalry' in *Smoke and Mirrors* (New York: Avon) 33–47.

——— (1998b) 'Only the End of the World Again', in *Smoke and Mirrors* (New York: Avon) 171–189.

——— (1998c) 'Shoggoth's Old Peculiar', in *Smoke and Mirrors* (New York: Avon) 144–155.

——— (2013) Keynote at the *Digital Minds Conference* 2013, QEII Conference Centre, Westminster, London, http://www38.theguardian.com/books/neil-gaimanurges publishers-make-mistakes <accessed 18th February 2016>

Gervais, Ricky and Merchant, Stephen (2010–12) *An Idiot Abroad.*

Hillesund, Terje (2007) 'Reading Books in the Digital Age Subsequent to Amazon, Google and the Long Tail," *First Monday*, 12:9, http://firstmonday.org/htbin/cgiwrap/bin/ojs/index.php/fm/article/view/2012/1887 <accessed 26 October 2009>

Hooper, Tobe (1974) *The Texas Chainsaw Massacre.*

Jancovich, Mark (1992) *Horror* (London: Batsford)

Jenkins, James J. (1991) 'Teaching Psychology in Large Classes: Research and Personal Experience', *Teaching of Psychology* 18(2):74–80.

Joshi, Sunand Tryambak (2001) *A Dreamer and a Visionary: H.P. Lovecraft in his Time.* (Liverpool: Liverpool University Press)

Joshi, Sunand Tryambak (2001) *H. P. Lovecraft: A Life* (West Warwick, RI: Necronomicon Press)

Kristeva, Julia (1982) *The Powers of Horror: An Essay on Abjection*, Leon Roudiez (trans.) (New York: Columbia University Press)

Landis, John (1981) *An American Werewolf in London.*

Lord, Bruce (2004) *The Genetics of Horror: Sex and Racism in H.P. Lovecraft's Fiction,* http://www.contrasoma.com/writing/lovecraft.html <accessed 18 February 2016>

Lovecraft, Howard Phillips (1921) 'Facts Concerning the Late Arthur Jermyn and His Family', in *The Wolverine,* No. 9, 3–11.

Lovecraft, Howard Phillips (1929) 'The Dunwich Horror', *Weird Tales,* 13, No. 4 (April 1929), 481–508.

McLean, Greg (2005) *Wolf Creek.*

McEwan, Ian (1981) *The Comfort of Strangers* (London: Jonathan Cape)

Meyer, Jan H.F. and Land, Ray (eds.) (2003) *Overcoming Barriers to Student Understanding: Threshold Concepts and Troublesome Knowledge* (London and New York: Routledge)

Middleton, Thomas [1607] (1996) *The Revenger's Tragedy* (London: Nick Hern Books)

Mills, Kathy Ann (2010) 'A Review of the "Digital Turn" in the New Literacy Studies', *Review of Educational Research,* June, 80: 2, 246–271.

Mosse, Kate (2009) *The Winter Ghosts* (London: Orion)

Oktem, Zuleyha Cetiner (2012) 'The Sandman as a Neomedieval Text', in *Image to Text,* 4:1, http://www.english.ufl.edu/imagetext/archives/v4_1/introduction.shtml, <accessed 10 November 2012>

Perkins, David (1999) 'The Many Faces of Constructivism', *Educational Leadership,* 57:3, 6–11.

Punter, David (1996) *The Literature of Terror: A History of Gothic Fictions from 1765 to the Present Day, Vol. 2, The Modern Gothic* (Abingdon: Routledge).

Royle, Nicholas (2003) *The Uncanny: An Introduction* (Manchester: Manchester University Press, 2003)

Schmidt, Rob (2003) *Wrong Turn*

Shearsmith, Reece, Gatiss, Mark, Pemberton, Steve and Dyson, Jeremy (1999–2002) *The League of Gentlemen.*

Stevenson, Robert Louis [1886] (2004) *Dr Jekyll and Mr Hyde* (Harmondsworth: Penguin Books)

Stoker, Bram [1897] (1979) *Dracula* (London: Penguin Books)

Thomas, Gerald (1958–92) *Carry On.*

Todorov, Tzvetan [1973] (1975) *The Fantastic: A Structural Approach to a Literary Genre* (New York: Cornell UP)

Walliams, David and Lucas, Matt, (2003–5) *Little Britain.*

Webster, John [1612] (1971) *The White Devil* (Otterup: Scholar Press)

Wisker, Gina (2005) *Horror Fiction: An Introduction* (New York and London Continuum)

PART TWO

Writing Race

Teaching Crime Fiction and the African American Literary Canon

Nicole King

Teaching African American literature, whether it is designated as 'literary' or 'popular,' is political and carries with it a political resonance. According to some calculations, detective stories are the most widely read literary genre in the United States, but the fact that African American writers have been writing in this genre since the early twentieth century is less well known (Dietzel 2006: 159). Rudolph Fisher's novel *The Conjure Man Dies: A Mystery of Dark Harlem* (1932) is understood as an important precursor to the mid and late twentieth-century crime fiction of Chester Himes and Walter Mosley. Earlier still, Pauline E. Hopkins used the *Colored American* magazine to serialize her novel *Hagar's Daughter* (March 1901–March 1902) which features the first black female detective in fiction (Dietzel 2006: 158).

Both Fisher and Hopkins are regularly anthologised and recognised by scholars as important contributors to the canon of African American literature, but neither *Hagar's Daughter* nor *The Conjure Man Dies* are chosen by editors of anthologies of African American writing.[1] Similarly, despite the common practice in English literature departments to teach popular and genre fiction such as romance, science or crime, an informal survey of UK university courses reveals that the appearance of crime fiction modules which focus exclusively on African American writers are uncommon. It is

N. King (✉)
University of Reading, Reading, UK

© The Author(s) 2016

K. Shaw (ed.), *Teaching 21st Century Genres*,
DOI 10.1057/978-1-137-55391-1_3

far more likely to encounter African American crime fiction on broadly defined modules in which 'genre' or 'crime' is the main focus.[2] Perhaps this is due to an implicit respect for the different attributes and histories of crime fiction (and other popular genres) and African American literary fiction, but beyond such impressions is there a robust pedagogical reason not to devise an African American crime fiction module? Or to incorporate crime fiction into African American literature modules focused on novels or short stories? As a specialist in African American literature, would I hesitate to teach such a module in my own university?[3] In short, yes, in the past I would hesitate and I have hesitated. Moreover, the absence of such modules on English literature programmes at under- and postgraduate levels at universities across the world suggests that others have hesitated too.

To understand why African American literature modules tend not to teach crime and literary fiction in equal measure requires an examination of how African American literature is defined in addition to a focus on the pedagogical possibilities offered by forthrightly addressing concepts of the popular and the literary within an African American cultural context. This chapter makes a tripartite argument: firstly, it examines how attitudes towards teaching, as well as the contexts in which we teach, have a profound effect on what we choose to teach; secondly, it argues that if a general pedagogical aim in teaching African American literature can be summarised as a project that acknowledges and interrogates the literature's distinctive, shared themes and tropes (Gates 1992: 39), then African American crime fiction can be understood as an under-utilised component of such a pedagogical project; thirdly it uses a close reading of crime fiction novel, *The Cutting Season* (2013) by Attica Locke, as a case study to illustrate how particular texts blur the boundaries between literary and popular and how such texts might be successfully used to structure and populate a module devoted to African American literature.[4] *The Cutting Season* is a text where an ethos of teaching and learning also functions to inform the plot, setting and characterisations. I therefore employ the novel to suggest that a combination of popular and literary, or canonical, texts can provide new ways of teaching African American literature to university students. Importantly, it is a method that includes students in a conversation about the continued, if sometimes implicit, judgements about literary value which in turn inform which texts are placed on reading lists and how they are taught.

Contexts and Consequences

Although some literary critics argue that distinctions between high-brow and low-brow, serious and pulp, popular and literary fiction are spurious, such distinctions have a long a history, and they do persist (Swirksi 2005: 5). New Criticism teaches a particular valuation of literature and keeps in place 'a rigid division between high and low, or elite and mass culture, an emphasis on invention over convention, and a distinction between literary and commercial forms of literature' (Dietzel 2006: 156). Within the classroom (as opposed to a more capacious anthology) a tendency to exclude so-called 'low-brow' literature is sometimes as true for African American literature as for any other kind of writing. On a personal level, although my research and teaching has been predominantly shaped by feminist, postcolonial and poststructuralist discourses, I have not automatically escaped some of the influences of New Criticism when tasked with curriculum design. Equally, what I observed in my own teaching practice is often mirrored on the larger stages of US and UK academia.

One of the implicit reasons for maintaining boundaries between literary and popular African American fiction in my own teaching is linked to the situation of African American literary instruction in the academy. Often there does not seem to be the space to accommodate both the popular and the literary within the curriculum of a single module. In higher education contexts such as that of the UK, the opportunity to study African American literature as an undergraduate are also limited by programmatic specifications such as the typical three-year degree length.[5] At my current institution, the University of Reading, first- and second-year English literature students encounter African American literature in the form of one or two major texts—such as *Invisible Man* (1952), *Their Eyes Were Watching God* (1937) or *Erasure* (2002)—studied on deliberately broad modules including 'Twentieth Century American Literature', and 'Contemporary Fiction'. Students have the chance to take a selection of African American Literature option modules in their final year, but without any previous foundational study in African American canonical works. Their American counterparts, however, have access to these foundations in their first, second or third year.[6] An example common in many US universities is a survey course open to majors and non-majors called something like 'Introduction to African American Literature'. Previously, I reasoned that given the very limited opportunities to teach African American literature in a three-year degree, there was a pedagogical imperative to concentrate only on canonical texts and to sacrifice popular or genre fiction when teaching an African American module. I saw the two categories of literature as distinct and with different pedigrees, but there were additional layers of reasoning that I was less inclined to acknowledge, and which actually exposed an often obscured vulnerability that comes with teaching, one that speaks to more personal aspects of teaching practice than academics are commonly asked to articulate.

Most prominent among these perceived vulnerabilities is the notion of how literary value is linked to intellectual standing. If colleagues are teaching canonical texts in a jointly taught module, as is common in the UK, then I have felt compelled to do the same. My default position would always be to choose an author like Nobel prize-winning Toni Morrison over the hugely popular Terry McMillan for either an American literature or an African American literature survey module. In contrast, when teaching at three quite different universities in the United States (the University of Pennsylvania, the University of Maryland and the University of California, San Diego) colleagues and I had opportunities to teach modules devoted solely to African American Satire, Women's Literature, Neo-slave Narratives, Poetry, and to historical periods such as the Harlem Renaissance, the Cold War and the Black Arts Movement. Within the latter three examples in particular, it was not uncommon for us to incorporate the study of popular and visual culture, as well as popular fiction. Therefore, in addition to perceptions of academic standing, there are structural differences and limitations to how we might teach African American literature in the UK, or elsewhere, where curricular flexibility might be, or simply feel, restricted. As these examples illustrate, the spaces and contexts in which we teach are intimately bound to what we teach, and the approaches to teaching we choose to adopt.

How specialists conceive and teach the African American literary canon is further implicated in how African American literature is positioned within the broader American literary canon, and how academics of all ethnicities and subject positions who teach non-white and/or non-canonical literatures are situated within the institutions in which they work. In the UK, perhaps understandably, African American literature is a minoritized literature, subordinated to American literature in which 'American' stands in for literature penned by ethnically white men and women which in turn stands in for canonical, in the 'New Criticism' sense of the canon. To teach the breadth and diversity of African American literature—to accurately signal its cultural reach and significance beyond higher education, the literary establishment and the milieu of Anglo-American culture—then requires the installation of a different pedagogical framework. Such a framework could use African American literature to delegitimise boundaries between high and low culture, between canonical and popular literature, and thereby destabilise foundations that might be sexist, racist, and elitist (Beavers 2009: 264–5). Crime fiction is one component of African American literature that could achieve this aim.

The student-led 'Why is my Curriculum White' campaign attests to how the feeling amongst some UK students that a monocultural curriculum fails to deliver a high-quality education is made more visible than ever through social media (UCL TV 2015). This popular movement highlights the political impact of the curriculum choices lecturers make. African American crime fiction, although it is not always about social justice, does frequently use realism, plot and genre conventions to expose and comment upon a history of subjugation and unequal treatment of black people (and other minority communities) in the US, the legacy of slavery and state-sanctioned violence against African American citizens. As Lee Horsley notes, '[c]rime fiction has qualities that make it well-suited to the task of critique and protest [...] its protagonists are marginalised, outsiders forced into awareness of the failings of established power structures' (Horsley 2005: 5–6). It is an added pedagogical bonus that African American literary fiction and crime fiction share overlapping imperatives. The familiarity of a popular genre such as crime fiction can prove to be a useful pairing with African American literary fiction for students with little knowledge of the latter. While this chapter will turn to a full discussion of *The Cutting Season* in the final section, it is worth noting that Locke's characters Donovan Isaacs and Caran Gray, as well as the ancestral figure of Jason, are each marginalised and become aware, in very different ways, of the failings of established power structures and each offer 'oppositional critiques' of these structures (Horsley 2005: 6). The fact that some crime fiction draws upon the shared themes and tropes of the African American literary tradition effectively contravenes my previous assumptions and makes it both a logical and a canny choice for a module that aims to provide a broad view of African American fiction.

It must be noted that other popular literary genres, such as science fiction, could be used in a similar way to teach African American literature. This is especially true of texts which foreground how American society is and has been organised as a racial state and of texts that call attention to figures and tropes of African American literature. The focus on crime, criminality and injustice in crime fiction has an added advantage when this genre is used to teach African American literature. What Omi and Winant call the 'racial dictatorship' that has structured American politics and social life from the colonial period to the Civil Rights Movement of the 1960s also facilitated the theft and exploitation of Africans and then African Americans and provided the wealth on which the nation was founded (1994: 65–6). Omi and Winant point out that racial dictatorship also 'consolidated [...] oppositional racial consciousness and organisation' (1994: 66). I argue that by using its distinct conventions and tropes, African American crime fiction is perfectly situated to thematise and represent both the crime of the transatlantic slave trade and its aftermath. Conjoining African American literature and crime fiction in the classroom creates the opportunity to explore the structures of genre alongside the structures of the nation and dominant cultural traditions.

Despite such parallels and affinities between crime fiction and African American literary fiction, the argument against bringing any popular or genre fiction in the literary classroom is familiar, if not necessarily robust. Helen Carr reports the twinned attitude that crime fiction lacks intellectual currency and depth and is conservative rather than subversive, indeed genre fiction is often perceived as a 'low-level, formulaic production' (Carr 1989: 6). Yet, speaking broadly of both popular culture and specifically of popular fiction, Herman Beavers reminds us, 'the narrative variety of popular culture produces a set of sophisticated reading strategies that belie the charge that popular fiction is characterized by a mindless adherence to plot and fantasy' (Beavers 2009: 264). Further, given the relatively small number of African American texts that have been canonized 'it is a mistake to uncouple popular fiction from literary fiction or *belles-lettres*' (Beavers 2009: 265). I would add to this that the notion of crime fiction being conservative rather than subversive varies considerably when we are discussing specific examples of African American crime fiction. Some fictions might be conservative in terms of following crime fiction conventions and reproducing familiar narrative arcs, but all genres do this in some form. One way in which African American crime fiction in particular can be understood as unconventional is in terms of its giving voice to protagonists who are themselves marginalised people of colour, and therefore more likely to be silenced in other works of crime fiction, or altogether absent from literary fiction written by Anglo-American authors. Another way is in terms of its narrative innovation. Citing Ishmael Reed and Clarence Major, Stephen F. Soitos writes that 'both authors revise the traditional classical and hardboiled formulas' and transform the formulas previously adhered to by other African American authors of crime fiction through 'experimentation with the double-conscious detective trope (Soitos 1996: 180). Their detectives, in other words, make use of the Du Bosian concept of double consciousness to aid their perceptions as detectives.

My argument that African American popular and literary fiction function differently is not anomalous, but is indicative of what Dietzel calls a web of 'exclusionary' reading practices derived from New Criticism. Since the ethos of black crime fiction has been said to have some of the same critical intentions as black literary fiction—to critique racism, to focus on racial uplift, to 'affirm' (Dietzel 2006: 160) blackness while it also demonstrates a double-voiced, signifying text—a perceived division between high and low culture, or literary and commercial fiction, among African Americanists is only part of the issue. In practice, it points to a wider cultural phenomenon, one that infiltrates the spaces in which we teach, and in which students learn. An important intervention then is to call attention to these permeable boundaries even if we choose to teach texts that skilfully transgress them.[7] Conversely, as Wells asserts, where crime fiction has been understood as 'a notoriously conservative genre', crime writers who critically engage with racialization and introduce complex racialized characters to their narratives, work 'to disturb the genre' and break down its boundaries (Wells 1999: 206). Crime fiction by African American authors (and Black British authors as Wells demonstrates) works in conversation with literary fiction as it goes about the work of contestation and the questioning of racial and cultural monoliths.

Although there is a dearth of university modules focused exclusively on African American crime fiction, it is important to note that no specific statistics are available on how or where African American crime fiction is taught in UK universities. In my research for this chapter, I have learned that Dr Sam Thomas at the University of Durham offers an MA module in US Crime Fiction, which includes texts by Attica Locke.[8] Also, Dr Will Norman at the University of Kent has been teaching an American Crime Fiction module to undergraduate students in their final year for six years, and it includes texts by both Chester Himes and Attica Locke (Dietzel 2006: 158). Dr Lee Horsley pioneered undergraduate and postgraduate crime fiction modules at the University of Lancaster in the first part of this century and, like Helen Oakley at the Open University, is particularly attentive to the position of, and narratives by, non-white writers in the context of research and teaching about crime fiction. There is a notably growing expertise in the UK regarding African American crime fiction but, on a module-by-module basis, significant interventions are being made in terms of how American literature and crime fiction are conceptualised and taught.

The 'Literariness' of African American Crime Fiction

There is a wealth of African American crime fiction to choose from that troubles the boundaries between literary and popular fiction. Prominent examples include texts such as Walter Mosley's Easy Rawlings series, Barbara Neely's Blanche on the Lam series, and Chester Himes's Coffin Ed Johnson and Gravedigger Jones series. Within this milieu, *The Cutting Season* functions as an exemplar text because although it is written in the crime fiction genre, and is sold and marketed as crime fiction, like its predecessors listed above it actively dissolves the boundary between literary and crime fiction by negotiating both the conventions of crime fiction and African American literary tropes, the so-called 'high' and 'low'. As such, it highlights the paradox of an African American literary canon which has always included fiction that began life as popular, only later 'became' literary such as *Native Son* (1941), as well as texts that are firmly within the canon but which have never been bestsellers, such as Ralph Ellison's *Invisible Man* (1952) and Toni Morrison's *Beloved* (1987) (Dietzel 2006: 158). Such texts suggest that aspects of literary and popular African American fiction are both concerned with history, racial identity, double-voiced texts and signifying.

Dietzel also calls attention to the breadth and depth of African American literature that, by virtue of being popular and produced for a mass market, is highly significant to the African American reading public and yet all too easily ignored by literary scholars. Thus there exist cultural, political and historical arguments for reading popular African American literature alongside texts that have entered into the canon. In their discussions of popular African American fiction and crime fiction, Dietzel, like Carr, Beavers and others, argues forcefully against the separation of the popular and the literary that continues in the twenty-first century. She calls attention not only to the rigid divisions of literary categories, but also highlights the gap which exists between how literature is experienced and evaluated by the general public, and how it is experienced and evaluated by some university lecturers:

> In the fields of literary criticism and the teaching of African American literature, for example, scholars and critics alike have restricted their efforts to reviewing, promoting, and canonizing only those texts that fit the prevailing aesthetic and literary standards [...] Applying these standards to African American literary texts (and indeed all literary traditions) has pushed much of its literary production out of the classroom, off the bookshelves, and into the dustbin of literary history. (Dietzel 2006: 156)

Dietzel makes a strong case for thinking carefully about what we choose not to teach. By excluding the popular by design or by default we impoverish the literary diet of the very people keen to expand and diversify their intake. I would add that when we consider that there is more to lose than to gain by keeping the popular and literary separate, the inclusion of the popular automatically becomes part of the familiar enterprise of recovery and restitution from which much of the literary fiction of African American literature has benefited. By using authors who have established themselves as popular by virtue of book sales, such as Terry McMillan (*Waiting to Exhale* 1992) or by virtue of writing within a popular genre such as crime fiction, such as Mat Johnson (*Hunting in Harlem* 2003), as a core part of teaching the multi-faceted world of fiction by and about black Americans, practitioners are engaging in vital work that expands the breadth and depth of African American fiction. It is work in a similar mode to that of the Schomburg Library of Nineteenth-Century Black Women Writers series which brought 30 works to scholarly prominence in 1988.[9] It is work that is also similar to the scholarship of Jean Fagin Yellin, which rescued *Incidents in the Life of a Slave Girl* (1861) from being considered a 'fabrication' and confirmed it for many as 'the most important book in the antebellum era by an Afro-American woman'.[10] The aim of including the likes of Locke, McMillan, and Johnson on an African American literature syllabus is often to initiate a discussion regarding what questions their inclusion raise about the usefulness of qualitative divisions between categories of literature when texts can be found in all categories which deploy standard tropes of African American literary and cultural expression. I have become convinced that the university classroom is a place where it is problematic to make a pedagogical justification for separating out the study of different forms of African American literary expression based on oppositional notions of popularity and literary value. When opportunities to study African American literature are restricted to one module, a broad spectrum can ultimately be as useful to and informing for the student as a single author study.

Crossing the Threshold

By situating the contingent nature of identity in both the present and the past, Locke's contemporary, popular text of genre fiction enables readers to acquire a threshold concept of African American literature: the fallacy of race as a natural, biological marker of difference between human beings (Meyer and Land 2003). *The Cutting Season*'s presentation of markers of racialisation and identity as neither stable nor inherent are two key messages of canonical African American literature such as *The Narrative of The Life of Frederick Douglass* (1845), *Their Eyes Were Watching God* (1937), *Passing* (1929), *Invisible Man* (1952), *A Raisin in the Sun* (1959) and others. These are texts that teach the reader to examine the complex interplay between representations of gender, history, location, class and sexuality in the portraits of black Americans and American culture(s). *The Cutting Season* uses a wide variety of plot and character devices to present itself as a text that teaches, and as a text that values the types of questions (and questioners) found on the margins of established norms and ways of knowing.

As Meyer and Land elaborate, threshold concepts that allow students to make transformative leaps in their understanding of a subject or discipline can be, and often are, simultaneously troublesome (Meyer and Land 2003: 10). The fallacy of race can be a counter-intuitive concept for students to grasp and requires an undoing of understanding 'race' as biology and moving towards the notion of racialisation as cultural, social, and political. I argue that popular, commercial, genre fiction is no more or less able than literary fiction to present such pedagogical projects, though it may have the advantage of accessibility. No matter what type of fiction students are reading, I have found it impossible to rely on their tacit knowledge of African American literary expression or tacit understandings of race as a construct. Rather, in guiding them over this threshold of their understanding, how words are used and in what context are the key to helping students access new angles from which to think about the idea of 'race'. As Meyer and Land state, with well-chosen examples for our students 'the inert, superficial mimetic use of language of a threshold concept becomes enlivened' (Meyer and Land 2003: 6). Such examples are frequent in *The Cutting Season*, and the troublesome concepts are potentially less so as they are delivered within the familiar contexts of the crime fiction genre, that borrows knowingly from conventions of African American literary fiction. *The Cutting Season* generously provides a layered presentation of the malleability of racial thinking and racial identities. For the student of either African American fiction or crime fiction the setting of *The Cutting Season* will likely be immediately evocative and disconcerting. While the images of slavery and slave plantations will no doubt be familiar, the fact that in the twenty-first century there are restored, operational plantations, albeit with migrant rather than slave labour, which serve both a business and cultural heritage function, may feel jarring to the reader who presumed that the social and cultural relations occasioned by chattel slavery were safely confined to a two-dimensional past.

The Cutting Season is set on the restored grounds of a Louisiana sugar cane plantation home, Belle Vie. The protagonist, Caran Gray, grew up there and returns, at age 37, as its general manager when she relocates with her 9-year-old daughter from New Orleans in the aftermath of 2005's Hurricane Katrina; we meet her in 2009. Belle Vie can be rented out for weddings, offers tours to school groups and other members of the public curious about 'the old South'. A feature of Belle Vie (like many actual tourist attractions in the American South) is its live re-enactments centred on a romanticised theatrical production called 'The Olden Days of Belle Vie' that portrays life on the plantation before, during and just after the Civil War. The murder that drives the narrative of *The Cutting Season* is that of a migrant worker from the adjacent, active, 500-acre sugar cane plantation. This active plantation is one of the text's many complex representations of the 'new' South.[11] The body of the murdered woman, Inés Avalo, is found by Caran Gray on Belle Vie's grounds, and Gray goes on to assist, confound and ultimately solve the police investigation of the murder plus another one that happened a century and a half earlier and which involved her great, great, great grandfather, Jason, a former Belle Vie slave. How history is understood and which histories are known is a central theme of the text and one which links it to the work of archival literary scholarship mentioned in the previous section. In an interview Locke states that in *The Cutting Season* she was particularly concerned with the position occupied by history in the contemporary moment, how 'the narrative of American history gets—who gets to own it, how does it get presented, how do we consume that history?' She mentions in the same interview that she sees fiction's 'power as an instrument of social justice almost unparalleled' (Locke quoted in Marshall 2015). Significantly she does not make a distinction between the power of popular and literary fiction, which affirms the idea that crime fiction need not be segregated within the African American literary canon.

The Cutting Season overtly challenges the boundaries between so-called popular and literary fiction by braiding together key attributes of crime fiction and African American literature. Deborah Madsen writes that African American literature is centrally concerned with issues of 'memory and memorialisation, of history and historical reconstruction, of literature and social justice, of language and identity' (Madsen in Wisker 2010: 60). *The Cutting Season* reflects this emphasis with its juxtaposition of the contemporary and the historical, the forward driving narrative of solving the crime with the backwards movement through history and family relations. In these ways *The Cutting Season* sits alongside texts like *Native Son* (1940), *The Street* (1946), *and If He Hollers Let Him Go* (1945), which are now part of the African American literary canon and which, for example, feature murderous or wrongly accused protagonists and deliver commentaries on racialized social injustice.

The Cutting Season also announces its affinity with the African American canon and its concerns through intertextuality. It names *Gone with the Wind* and *Uncle Tom's Cabin* (1852), and at other times signifies upon Toni Morrison's *Song of Solomon* (1987) and Ralph Ellison's *Invisible Man. The Cutting Season* is crime fiction and yet participates in the same conversation as African American literary fiction, using similar tropes of invisibility, ancestor texts, and the talking book in concert with a narrative that uses history to help make sense of the present. Significantly, the text blurs the boundaries between popular and literary fiction in its simultaneous adherence to certain conventions of crime fiction such as the alienated outsider figure (Caran Gray and Donovan Isaacs both fulfil this role) and to the formal and stylistic moves of canonical African American authors, known as double-voiced or signifying. As such, *The Cutting Season* invites both students and lecturers to foreground questions about the categorical and qualitative divisions of literature. In doing so, it suggests the need to account for the popular in literary fiction and the literary in popular fiction, while also providing a context in which students can learn the value of critically engaged reading no matter what the context or genre of text they encounter.

In addition to the 'whodunit' narrative of *The Cutting Season*, part of the tension of the novel revolves around how and why the theatre piece, 'The Olden Days of Belle Vie', topples from its pedestal as the canonical narrative of the plantation's history. 'The Olden Days of Belle Vie' is a key paratext for this later novel and functions as the literary convention that Locke uses to highlight the performativity of racial identities as contingent upon, and produced within, a very particular historical narrative of the nation. As a 'doubled' text the play script is highlighted by Locke as unstable and variable. Donovan Isaacs, a member of the 'Olden Days' cast who plays FIELD SLAVE #1, eventually gets fed up with the banality of his role, and of the whole play. As one of Caran Gray's most unreliable workers and the prime suspect for the murder, he also rewrites the racist, stereotype-laden play script to tell a different story, unearth a buried history and in doing so rewrite the way in which history is consumed on the plantation by its owners, workers and the visiting public. The contemporary setting of the text in the year 2009 is particularly relevant in this respect: it is one year into the first term of Barack Obama's presidency, and the scripting of a different American narrative, one which rejects static concepts of race and identity, is still quite possible.

Although Caren Gray is the main protagonist and helps solve the present-day murder of Avalo, Isaacs' social position in the text is of inverse importance to the teacherly role he occupies and the significance of his work in revealing the hidden history of Jason. He is initially presented as a disaffected youth, just getting by at the local community college. He is 'off-stage' and occupies the margins of the text, while his work itself is hidden in the shadows. This marginality is not only symbolic of the rebellious enslaved men and women who plotted in secret to overturn slavery, but of the many authors who write against the odds of their condition to counter dominant social, cultural and economic structures.

The reader eventually learns that Isaacs not only persuades the other cast members to learn new lines, but convinces them to create something new: a film that leaves behind the hackneyed southern belles and white patriarchs, the stereotypes of mammies and field slaves contained within the characterisations of 'Olden Days'. Isaacs's film, 'Raising Cane: A New Sheriff in Town', focuses on a brief period during the Reconstruction Era when ex-slaves held some political power and during which the Parish of Belle Vie, where Isaacs and Gray and the others still live and work, had a black sheriff. The film subverts and rewrites the publically consumed view of the Old South presented by 'The Olden Days of Belle Vie' in a similar fashion to the way African American literature subverts and rewrites the canon of American fiction and crime fiction written from a multicultural perspective subverts the hard-boiled formula.[12]

Drawing on Maureen Reddy's work on detective fiction featuring black women, it is evident that there are both reverse and counter discourses at work in *The Cutting Season*. Writing about black women detective series, Reddy notes that they all 'question the conventional crime plot's movement from disorder to order and injustice to justice, and collectively redraw the borders of the crime fiction genre' (Reddy 2002: 52). The film script nested within the narrative of the crime which structures *The Cutting Season* conforms to such a model where untidy narratives, disorder and injustice are deployed to expose and teach a different version, and ultimately a different understanding of both nineteenth-century history, and the 2009 world of the protagonists. In the context of *The Cutting Season* as a text that teaches, it is incredibly significant that Isaacs uses the plantation archives, housed in the plantation library, to write, stage and create 'Raising Cane' and that the film begins life as a project for one of his classes. His labour is the key to solving the mystery of Jason's disappearance, the theft of his property and his murder but this historical recovery is perhaps less significant than the feat that Locke pulls off in forcing her reader, through the perspective of Caran Gray, to see Donovan Isaacs as someone to learn from. Locke asserts, 'we need to balance stories about the past with stories that deal deeply with racial issues in the present' and for the characters in *The Cutting Season* one way this is realised is through the acknowledgement of black identities as shifting, diverse and subject to intra-racial conflict in addition to the persistence of racism and racial terror.

The traditional neatness of the crime novel is treated with scepticism by Locke, who instead offers space for an ironic commentary on the crimes of American and Europe against black people. She weaves her subversive narratives together with finesse—the murders of ancestor Jason and migrant worker Inés Avalo are solved, but order is not restored—in part because the complex history of Belle Vie plantation as well as American slavery were founded on violence, disorder and mayhem, and as a result there is no foundational order or stability to recover or return to. Yet she equally moulds the crime fiction genre to her own purpose, which Soitos asserts is common to African American writers of crime fiction (Soitos 1996: 11). By the conclusion of *The Cutting Season* the plantation of Belle Vie, its history and present twenty-first-century meanings are neither recuperated as a nostalgic haven of white superiority or for a putatively liberating sense of black empowerment. Rather, Locke emphatically questions idealised and essentialising modes of cultural identity. This questioning is emblematic of *The Cutting Season*'s teacherly tropes. It repeatedly represents formal and informal education and examines how certain versions of history (such as 'The Olden Days of Belle Vie') are reiterated and reproduced, while others lay buried or on the margins. The reader is invited to view the significance of Inés Avalo's body being found literally on the margins, on the border between the active and the inactive plantations, and relate this to contemporary labour relations as well as to cultural conflicts and allegiances. Locke's text is crowded with everything we expect from the crime genre: false leads, twists and turns, a protagonist with her own share of flaws. The text makes it difficult to read American history as a narrative of forward progress in which racial, ethnic, and social divisions or political power was ever absolute for any particular group. It is a crime fiction novel that patiently prompts the reader to cross various thresholds of understanding and to revise any notion they may have brought to the text about singular identities or singular truths.

If Donovan Isaacs can be understood as a teacher forged in the clamour of Obama gaining the White House, then Morgan, Caran Gray's daughter, must also be examined as the text's prototypical student of the contemporary moment. She is central to the plot of the novel—she discovers key clues—as well as to the play within the novel. She literally bears witness to key events as well as bearing witness more symbolically to the changing script of Americanness as it unfolds around her. The rehearsals for the play take place in an old plantation building that functioned as a school house during the Reconstruction era, and she learns from the play script as well as from the adults around her about the suddenness of violence and the slipperiness of truth. Like Lutie Johnson in *The Street*, like Ellison's protagonist in *Invisible Man*, like Bigger Thomas in *Native Son*, Morgan is taught about and influenced by a different way of reading racial identity and that there are always multiple ways to tell a particular story. These are overlapping themes in African American literary texts as well as in African American crime fiction.

Locke opens a space for unknowability, open questions, and diverse perspectives on truth and history. As such, she subverts the conventions of the genre in much the same way as Douglass subverted the adventure narrative in *Narrative of the Life of Frederick Douglass* (1845) and Jacobs subverted the romance genre in *Incidents in the Life of a Slave Girl* (1861). Indeed Locke reminds us of how much commonality there is between what is categorised as popular versus literary African American texts. Her readers know there will be a resolution—not just to a problem, but to a crime—since this is a generic agreement that the author commits to. But

Locke, like other authors of crime fiction who are not only concerned with adhering to reader expectations of generic conventions, complicates this expected readerly pleasure by presenting competing narratives that cumulatively reveal truth to be a relative and contingent concept in the contemporary period.

Crime Pays (or Why We Should Teach African American Crime Fiction)

Locke's use of the crime genre opens up multiple epistemological frameworks for both contemporary teachers and students. By critiquing how knowledge has been framed in the past, it offers new frameworks of understanding and provides provocative representations of how learning occurs. Thus, employing *The Cutting Season* to frame a module that attends to the teaching of literary and popular African American fiction is doubly profitable, since it allows students access to questions about how their own teaching and learning is framed and how canons frame our knowledge of particular literary traditions, and enables teachers to show how the text simultaneously works in conversation with a variety of other texts, popular and literary, to impart some of the key features of African American writing, including social protest, signifying, memorialisation and the troubling of genre conventions. Furthermore, as a crime fiction novel, *The Cutting Season* suggests how a more creative and questioning pedagogical practice is possible within the teaching of African American fiction and, in my own practice, forced questions about the categorical and qualitative division of literature to the surface.

In this chapter I have argued for a renewed interrogation of canonicity in the teaching of African American literature because talking about the canon offers an opportunity for students to understand and question not only how they are taught, but also what they are taught. In this way, the development of critical awareness is achieved through close reading, the theorisation of identity, as well as reflective learning practices. A popular literary genre like crime fiction, with its attention to form and freedom to 'play' can therefore function as an entertaining and effective means through which readers come to understand and map the contingencies and contradictions of the prose, poetry and drama that is taught and presented as African American literature in the twenty-first-century academy.

Notes

1. See, for example, Henry Louis Gates Jr and Nellie Y. McKay, editors, *The Norton Anthology of African American Literature* Second Edition (W.W. Norton & Co, 1997, 2004) xiii.
2. This is true of the University of Kent, Lancaster and Durham, for instance, where their popular crime fiction modules focus on the genre and include contributions by African American authors.
3. I have taught and written about Walter Mosley's *Devil in A Blue Dress*, see Nicole King (2002) '"You think like you white": Questioning Race and Racial Community through the Lens of Middle Class Desire(s).' *Novel: A Forum on Fiction*, Spring/Summer, 211–30. I have also taught *Hunting in Harlem* by Mat Johnson and *The Cutting Season*.
4. Locke is also the author of two other crime fiction novels, *Black Water Rising* (2009) and *Pleasantville* (2015).
5. It is important to note that the typical four-year degree structure and specific cultural activism within higher education institutions in the US mean that the concentrated study of types of American literatures, such as Native American, Asian American, Latino/a, and African American literature is far more common in the US than it is in the UK.
6. The University of Pennsylvania demonstrates a typical pattern in US universities where broad modules such as 'Introduction to Black American Writing' are open to non-majors and honours modules such as 'African American Autobiography' are restricted to advanced students who have 'declared' themselves as English majors. Each group could potentially encounter African American literature on broadly defined modules such as 'Great Traditions in American Literature' or 'The Poet in America'. Similar structures and offerings can be found at a wide variety of universities from Princeton to Wake Forest, to the University of Michigan, Yale and UC San Diego. Once my UK students reach their final third year they do have several modules other than mine to choose from that feature African American content, including 'Literature of the Civil Rights Movement' and 'Fiction and Ethnicity.' A key difference between the US and UK systems is volume and choice, with the US, to generalise, providing more of both.

7. My argument for the inclusion of crime fiction recalls previous interrogations of how canonicity shapes teaching and learning practices for African American literature, as vigorously debated in 'culture wars' of the 1990s, to the contemporary, student-led interrogation of similar issues in UK universities' classrooms, epitomised by the Why is My Curriculum White campaign.
8. Interview with the author 19 October 2015.
9. The 30-volume collection was published in 1988 by Oxford University Press in collaboration with the Schomburg Center for Research in Black Culture, a research unit of the New York Public Library.
10. William Andrews, review of *Incidents in the Life of a Slave Girl. Written by Herself* by Harriet A. Jacobs, Jean Fagan Yellin *Black American Literature Forum* Vol. 21, No. 4 (Winter, 1987), pp. 463–5. Andrews' review gives a concise account of the significance of Yellin's research for the status of Jacobs' narrative within African American and women's literature.
11. The 'New South' refers to the period after the American Civil War when the southern states both had to rebuild themselves and shift away from an entirely agrarian economy. A later meaning, and the one I am invoking, emerges at the end of the twentieth century, led by a resurgent and growing black middle class, one which was both home grown and which migrated in reverse, from the North. In the late twentieth century, the 'New' South becomes a destination whereas the Old South had for generations been a place black people had been desperate to leave. Atlanta, after hosting the 1996 Olympics, is seen as a city which epitomises this New South.
12. See for instance, *Traces, Codes, and Clues Reading Race in Crime Fiction* by Maureen T. Reddy, *Diversity and Detective Fiction*, edited by Kathleen Gregory Klein and *The Blues Detective: A Study of African American Detective Fiction* by Stephen F. Soitos. In addition, several edited collections on crime fiction published in the last 15–20 years include chapters on feminist, 'ethnic', postcolonial or African American crime fiction.

References

Beavers, Herman (2009) 'African American Woman Writers and Popular Fiction: Theorizing Black Womanhood' in Angelyn Mitchell and Danille K. Taylor (eds) *The Cambridge Companion to African American Women's Literature* (Cambridge and New York: Cambridge University Press) 262–277.

Carr, Helen (1989) 'Introduction: genre and women's writing in the postmodern world' in Helen Carr (ed) *From My Guy to Sci-Fi: Genre and Women's Writing in the Postmodern World* (London: Pandora) 3–14.

Dietzel, Suzanne B (2006) 'The African American Novel and Popular Culture' in Maryemma Graham (ed.) *The Cambridge Companion to the African American Novel* (Cambridge University Press).

Gates Jr, Henry Louis (1992) 'The Master's Pieces: On Canon Formation and the African American Tradition' in *Loose Canons: Notes on the Culture Wars* (New York: Oxford University Press) 17–42.

Horsley, Lee (2005) *Twentieth-Century Crime Fiction* (Oxford: Oxford University Press)

Locke, Attica (2009) *Black Water Rising* (London: Serpent's Tail)

___ (2015) *Pleasantville* (London: Serpent's Tail)

___ (2012) *The Cutting Season* (London: Serpent's Tail)

Madsen, Deborah L (2010) 'Teaching Trauma: (Neo-) Slave Narratives and Cultural (Re-) Memory' in (ed.) Gina Wisker *Teaching African American Women's Writing* (Basingstoke Palgrave McMillan) 60–74.

Marshall, Colin (2015) 'Colin Marshall interviews Attica Locke', *Los Angles Review of Books Podcast*, 5 March 2014, https://lareviewofbooks.org/interview/podcast-54-attica-locke/ <accessed 18 October>

Meyer, Jan and Land, Ray (2003) 'Threshold Concepts and Troublesome Knowledge: Linkages to ways of Thinking and Practicing within the Disciplines', *Occasional Report 4* (ETL Project: Universities of Edinburgh, Coventry and Durham).

Omi, Michael and Winant, Howard (1994) *Racial Formation in the United States: from the 1960s to the 1990s* (2nd edn.) (London and New York: Routledge).

Reddy, Maureen (2002) *Traces, Codes, and Clues: Reading Race in Crime Fiction.* (Rutgers University Press)

Soitos, Stephen F (1996) *The Blues Detective: A Study of African American Detective Fiction* (Amherst: University of Massachusetts Press)

Swirksi, Peter (2005) *From Lobrow to Nobrow* (Montreal: McGill-Queen's University Press)

UCL TV, 'Why is my Curriculum White?' https://www.youtube.com/watch?v=Dscx4h2l-Pk <accessed 7 August 2015>

Wells, Claire (1999) 'Writing Black: Crime Fiction's Other' in Klein, Kathleen Gregory (ed.) *Diversity and Detective Fiction* (Bowling Green: BGSU Popular Press) 205–223.

Genre and its 'Diss-contents': Twenty-First-Century Black British Writing on Page and Stage

Deirdre Osborne

Writing on genre and its delineations, Daniel Chandler observes that in 'literature the broadest division is between poetry, prose and drama'. Although a consensus is identifiable in the loose groupings of texts according to their generic characteristics, Chandler notes that 'one theorist's genre may be another's sub-genre or even super-genre (and indeed what is technique, style, mode, formula or thematic grouping to one may be treated as a genre by another)' (1997: 1). The designation of genre blending or crossing—as framed by the perception of how certain genres are 'meant' to operate for certain creative modes—can signal a writer's position in relation to mainstream culture and its processes of critical reception, canon-making and ultimately, cultural longevity. While the protean capacities of language as sounded and heard, or written and read, offers two distinctive conduits for creative expression—that are not mutually exclusive but mutually implicated—certain frameworks of cultural reception and critique have accorded differential status to the spoken and

The dual meaning evoked in 'diss' is from the 1980s US-derived hip-hop slang meaning to disrespect, show disdain for, and homophonically in the prefix 'dis', to convey dissatisfaction with something. Linguistic and cultural polysemy is a key factor in this chapter's discussion of genre and aesthetics.

D. Osborne (✉)
Goldsmiths, University of London, London, UK

© The Author(s) 2016

K. Shaw (ed.), *Teaching 21st Century Genres*,
DOI 10.1057/978-1-137-55391-1_4

the printed word. This is especially identifiable when accounting for the intermediality of dramatic-poetics and the poetics of performance in contemporary black British literature, where the possibilities of trans-generic and poly-generic writing disrupt the straightforward application of critical generic verities. Intermediality is understood here as offering separate material conduits for a text (printed in a book, performed live in a theatre), its communication by more than one modality, and the relationship of the chosen medium to social and cultural institutions. As Nirmal Puwar (2004) argues, it should be remembered that projections of neutrality onto social and cultural spaces is highly questionable. These are as racialised and gendered by power relations as the bodies who enter into them—or who are perennially absent.

In considering the intermixing of the genres of both poetry and drama, this chapter explores the dual indebtedness of two (self-termed) contemporary black British writers—debbie tucker green and Lemn Sissay—to both spoken-word and stage-performance contexts, to show how their use of combinational generic categories elicits inter-compositional framings of poetry and plays that acknowledge a text's performance on and off the page. (Although it is beyond the scope of this chapter to indicate the fullest history of the print–page, performance dichotomy, the work of Kwame Dawes, Lauri Ramey, R. Victoria Arana, Samera Owusu Tutu, Romana Huk, Beth-Sarah Wright, Keir Elam, Deirdre Osborne and Corinne Fowler offers counter-active critique to ethno-cultural compartmentalization.)

British-born, and of African-diasporic heritage (tucker green is of Caribbean descent, Sissay of Ethiopian parentage), their work is contoured by the legacies of migratory-arrivaliste-settler sensibilities that were articulated by post-1945 generations of writers whose work subverted and revitalised Anglophone literature and the English language, refashioning its very sound and producing most significantly, a vibrant politicised-aesthetic of multi-accented, spoken-word poetry in performance. Furthermore, black dramatists introduced new voices and uncharacteristic presences (both in casting and socio-cultural experiences) to the post-war English stage and its white-dominant audience demographic. Both tucker green's and Sissay's works magnify this legacy, with black-centring, British indigene perspectives via their represented subject matter, and also in their experiments with form, language, performativity and anticipated auditors and audiences.

Michael Eldridge argues through employing Frantz Fanon's claim that nations have 'a fundamentally recitative or performative quality to them', that the cultural category of black Britain was 'performed into being, deliberately conjured by artists and intellectuals' (1997: 34). In particular Eldridge identifies the influence of the Caribbean Artists Movement (1966–72) in establishing 'an aesthetic rooted in the vernacular' (1997: 35) wherein poets performing their work made it 'acceptable for young blacks to publicly adopt certain tones of voice, certain registers of speaking, certain ways of inhabiting space; to remove blackness from what Arjun Appadurai calls "the pathological spaces reserved for it" in British culture' (1997: 36). Writers such as tucker green and Sissay are not faced with the nation of the CAM generation where racialised identity categories positioned black people as the antithesis to white Britain, and although British passport holders, could never be truly British. Far from existing as alternatives to the mainstream, contemporary black dramatists and poets in Britain create an aesthetic that while contoured by multifaceted diasporic heritages, is derived from indigeneity. Their work forms a vital constituent of Britain's national culture in foregrounding black British citizens' experiences—even as these are still disproportionately under-represented in mainstream creative and critical circles, and the canon-making which consolidates cultural prominence and longevity. This was recently further ratified by the absence of *any* black British or Asian writers on the 2016 World Book Night giveaway list, in the lack of ethnic diversity in publishing compiled by Keane and Larsen for Spread the Word (2015); while the most recent Forward Poetry Prize winners are the Jamaican-born British resident Kei Miller (2014) and Claudia Rankine, a Jamaican-born American resident (2015).

The dramatic-poetic idiom of tucker green demonstrated in the plays *dirty butterfly* (2003), and *trade* (2005) and in poems from Sissay's third poetry collection *Morning Breaks in the Elevator* (1999) (notably 'Mourning Breaks in the Elevator', which reappears in his play *Storm* 2002) follows W. B. Worthen's thinking that two instabilities lurk 'in the assimilation of drama to print [...] the place of dramatic writing in the canons of print authorship, and the bearing of performance on the print identity of drama' (2005: 105). Moreover, the inter-relation between drama and poetry is evident in the work of tucker green (primarily a playwright) and Sissay (primarily a poet). tucker green has also written screenplays: *spoil* (2007), a feature film, *second coming* (2014) and adapted *random* (2011) for television, while Sissay's other plays include: *No Details* (1988), monodramas *Something Dark* (2008), *Why I Don't Hate White People* (2009), and his dramatisation of Benjamin Zephaniah's novel *Refugee Boy* (2013).

This porousness of genre boundaries is also locatable in trans and poly-generic work by contemporaries including Jackie Kay, Zephaniah, Maud Sulter, SuAndi, Dorothea Smartt, Bernardine Evaristo, Patience Agbabi, Mojisola Adebayo, Malika Booker, Alex Wheatle, Valerie Mason-John and Inua Ellams. In particular the multiple heritages of the dramatic monologue and griot suffuse the performed work of SuAndi's, *The Story of M* (2002), *In My Father's House* (2007), Adebayo's *Moj of the Antarctic* (2008), Booker's *Absolution* (2012), and Ellams's *The 14th Tale* (2009), *Untitled* (2010), and *Black T-Shirt Collection* (2012).

As a codicil, my own coinage of 'Landmark Poetics' as a conceptual framework within which to view poetry on material surfaces (pavements, headstones, lift counter-balances, statues, commemorative discs, sculptures, projections onto buildings, fabric, clothing, carved into the natural environment) recognises not only the extent of these genre-crossings and intermediality, but also emphasises how contemporary black British writers refuse the silence or invisibility of a history beset by cultural erasure and disregard. Through their creative coterie, these writer-performers herald a developmental direction in changing the spatial borders that have conventionally determined what gets staged in custom-built theatre, those spaces that are associated with oral presentations (readings, recitations, poetry-slam), live-art contexts, and the place and space for inscribing the creatively rendered 'word'.

Walter J. Ong has referred to the written word's superior capacity in terms of providing 'a grapholect, a power far exceeding that of any purely oral dialect' (2002: 8). Einar Haugen's 1964 neologism, 'grapholect' that Ong employs here characterizes written language as an ever-increasing lexical storehouse wherein writing's archival capaciousness offers 'a recorded vocabulary of at least a million and a half words, of which not only the present meanings but also hundreds of thousands of past meanings are known' (2002: 8).

However, in any culture, speaking generally precedes writing in human primary language acquisition and its expression and, as Peter Elbow explains:

> Spoken language has more semiotic channels than writing. That is, speech contains more channels for carrying meaning, more room for the play of difference. [...] there is volume (loud and soft), pitch (high and low), speed (fast and slow), accent (present or absent), intensity (relaxed and tense). And [...] there is a range of subtle degrees all the way between extremes. In addition there are many patterned sequences: for example tune is a pattern

> of pitches; rhythm is a pattern of slow and fast and accent. Furthermore there is a wide spectrum of timbres (breathy, shrill, nasal, &c); there are glides and jumps; there are pauses of varying lengths. And all these factors carry meaning. (1994: xxi)

In the light of Ong's and Elbow's observations, the chapter proposes that fresh critical languages are needed to account for trans-generic performativity, to consider the sonic properties in the multi-sensory reach of genre-crossing texts (as read, seen, heard) and the methods of textual delivery.

tucker green's and Sissay's texts' use-and-value secures a dual history through their dramatic-poetics that encapsulates Worthen's model where, 'reading poetry and plays reciprocally provides a final sense of the modern drama's encounter with the page: how the mise-en-page of dramatic language defines modern drama's poetics of agency' (2005: 101). J. L. Austin's scepticism regarding theatrical performatives in his speech-act model excluded plays, as he felt utterances in theatre (plays) were conveyed through hollow, insincere speech by virtue of having an agent, the actor. While his speech-act theory offers ways for literary criticism to negotiate drama and performance, at the same time it congeals speech as the focus of theatrical performance indices, as a perlocutionary vehicle. This suggests, as Worthen argues, that 'the performance onstage is a direct consequence of performatives inscribed in the text [...] performances are scripted by their texts' (1998: 1098). While the field of Performance Studies—often referenced by literary scholars to engage with poetry in performance (Novak 2011; Gräbner 2007)—challenges the staging of drama as performance norm or endpoint (the so-called labouring under a pre-text), this assumes a textual stability that denies the multiple strategies of Worthen's 'mise-en-page'. Many artistic attributes and interpretative possibilities are only accessible through reading tucker green's and Sissay's work, which supports Worthen's point that play texts are not always 'stable vehicles for the production of authorial intent, but complex sites where a variety of interpretive and representational activities take place' (1995: 42). The distinct page and stage performativities are also determined 'within an elaborate, historically contingent, dynamic network of citational possibilities' (Worthen 1998: 1099) as both writers produce a consequentialist dramatic-poetics that speaks broadly to the after-effects of colonial dispossession embedded within contemporary British social institutions and cultural practices. The flexing and mixing of generic categories is therefore fundamental to their innovative work.

If, as Michael Sinding considers, 'literary genres create more powerful roles for "tradition" or "antecedent genre"; and for the sense of a "system" of genres, since literary genres are defined by what they contrast with' (2010: 115), he also notes that 'generic mixture interests critics of every stripe because it opens a window on the processes that define literary history' (2005: 589). Jacques Derrida's classic treatise identifies genre as operating along the lines of taxonomic purity in an authoritarian manner for 'as soon as genre announces itself, one must respect a norm, one must not cross a line of demarcation, one must not risk impurity, anomaly, or monstrosity' (1980: 57). Whereas Tzvetan Todorov argues that in crossing the lines of demarcation, or 'laws' of genre, the norm is revealed through its transgression to create a new genre—a 'transformation' of its antecedents 'by inversion, by displacement, by combination' (1990: 14)—to undo the sense of fixed rules that designate a text 'belonging' to a particular genre. As a result, the categories are never airtight but modulated and moderated constantly by acts of creativity and experimentation through the writer's design.

However, as Glynnis Byron (2003) points out, if generic categories are only viewed through formal characteristics where the literary text functions as autonomous aesthetic object, this also leads to a potential dehistoricisation of the text from its specific material circumstances of production and the political and cultural conditions that have contoured the development of the work. In the case of tucker green and Sissay, the dramatic-poetics of both writer-performers can be both aesthetically inventive, and constitute testimony to the ongoing consequences of Britain's colonizing legacy. A number of aspects in tucker green's writing attest to this distinctive duality as perceivable in her stage language (articulated text), and her page language (reading text). The authority of Standard English occupies secondary status, as patois-associative, choreo-poetical, and non-grammatical syntax are her articulatory textual signature. Through her spare and exacting stage language, she resists and escapes the restrictions posed by a number of frameworks that might standardise her use of English. Notwithstanding the auto-correction feature on MS Word® that imposes capitalisation on tucker green's name, so too have many publishers and theatre critics sought to 'correct' or point out tucker green's deviations from their Standard—be that grammar, punctuation or generic purity—confirming the (dis)comfort zone she creates for establishment circles together with her uncompromising subject-matter. Disdain is evident in

Fiona Mountford's review of *dirty butterfly*, criticising lower-case letters (*Evening Standard*, 3 March 2003) and in Quentin Letts's reprimanding review of *hang* where his non-problematised use of 'us' and 'our' is telling in signalling the conventional insider–outsider (or even outcast) dynamic of culturally elite gatekeeping against post-war cultural claimants that haunts contemporary British society and is preserved in its cultural institutions:

> You will notice from the top of this theatre review that playwright debbie tucker green abjures capitals and spells the titles of her plays in lower case letters. I feel almost guilty using that full stop—punctuation tut tut. You perhaps see how irritating it is when someone declares rules of form to be redundant. Miss Green may think that she is above capital letters but inconveniently for her, most of the rest of us need convention to aid our comprehension. (Letts 2015)

trade centralises women's sex tourism to countries once colonised by Europe and still oppressed by a service role in the hospitality industry. It also unequivocally presents historicised citations to past and present meanings of trade: in human bodies, or exported produce from enforced colonial agriculture that nourished imperial Britain's insatiable industrial economy. The play creates dialogism between inheritors of the imperial legacy in Britain with those who reside in the contemporary tourist resort regions such as the Caribbean. The unequal weighting of the power transaction—personally, culturally and socio-economically—is expressly reinforced by the angle of sex-gender in the female characters Novice, Regular and Local through which tucker green filters her plot. The cross-race, cross-sex, cross-generational playing of all roles (women, men, black, white) by her specified 'three black actresses' (2005: 4) who are the sole vocalisers, subtly implicates black British women in the play's subject-matter and problematizes any clear-cut economic power differentiations according to imperial race politics since post-war migration. Significantly, tucker green prevents affinities developing between the three women characters, to challenge the tenets of automatic female solidarity. The complex shifting allegiances are reinforced through verbal alliances that then become antagonistic, although tucker green's lyrical technique makes the sound of the textual delivery harmonious and continuous:

LOCAL Mi do what mi do.
NOVICE You do that.
LOCAL Mi do what mi do –
mi do what mi do well.
Mi noh mi do hair well.
Even theirs.
Even them.
Even that (11).

The anaphorae of this extract lulls the listener/reader into the rhythm of 'mi do'. While Novice thinks she is chatting about Local's hair plaiting business, the use of 'that' becomes a traded put down between them. Local generalisingly objectifies her clients, as possessive pronouns become object and relative pronouns—heightened by the anaphoric 'Even' as a scornful concession to having to earn money through contact with tourists. In his commentary on Clifford Geertz's 'Deep Play: Notes on a Balinese Cockfight', George E. Marcus describes an 'ironic entanglement of complicity with rapport' (1997: 86) which characterises the transaction between Local and tourist women (Novice and Regular) and gestures meta-theatrically to the spectre of the imperial-colonial relationship—in which the majority of British theatre-going audiences, irrespective of ethnic origins, are implicated.

This extract demonstrates how tucker green's linguistic strategies alert readers to the materiality of the printed text while demanding its embodiment through performance. The process is captured in Pulitzer Prize-winning African American playwright Suzan-Lori Parks's account of printed texts as undifferentiated, 'something that involves yr whole bod./ Write with yr whole bod./Read with yr whole bod' (1995: 18) and in Worthen's description of the ground-breaking compositional forms of Anna Deveare Smith's and Sarah Kane's play texts as displaying 'an absorbing fascination with the materiality of the word and its potential to be objectified—even spectacularized on the page— …' (2005: 121). tucker green's long-time director Sacha Wares (before tucker green's self-directing of all of her subsequent work) actually describes rehearsals of *random* (2008) akin to a literary close reading: 'the rhythm of the dialogue is really, really, communicated to you through the page layout and punctuation. So a huge amount of the rehearsal time was spent literally on analysing that punctuation and on accuracy' (Sierz 2008). This consolidates the sense of tucker green's work as print-text-oriented, wherein meanings for the stage are to be discerned from the precincts of the antecedent (but not precedent), dramatic text. Divertingly, George Bernard Shaw (who, unlike tucker green employed extensive prose directions) describes a similar sense of transposition: 'the notation at my disposal cannot convey the play as it should really exist: that is, its oral delivery. I have to write melodies without bars, without indications of pitch, pace or timbre, and without modulation, leaving the actor or producer to divine the proper treatment of what is essentially word-music' (1921: 178). tucker green's text's enunciation demands a verbal baton-passing for actors, as characters' voices interweave, overlap, complete each other's thoughts, echo lines and re-cycle phrases with shifts in emphasis:

LOCAL Old...
NOVICE you look
REGULAR I am
LOCAL she is
NOVICE she's not that –
REGULAR old.
I am (59).

The primacy of ensemble playing heightens the awareness of actors as physical and literal 'bearers' of the text's typographical orchestrations—its Shavian 'word-music'. In *trade* she tests how far audiences are conversant with vernacular, its resonances with Jamaican patois, estuary English, dub poetry and the sound scatter of jazz lyrical traditions:

REGULAR 'Nice' / I / uh / haven't been called for...
years.
Beat.
I haven't been called anything for years.
I haven't called myself / even / well you
(don't) / for / uh / for / for...for...
years.
NOVICE 'Nice'?
'Nice' came with another drink?
'Nice' came with the drink did it?'
LOCAL 'Nice'...ice and a slice –
NOVICE 'Nice' was what did it was it?
[...]
NOVICE Nice and easy.

LOCAL She is.
Emotional.
Emotionally easy.
You are.
(14)

The repetition of 'nice' evokes a myriad of interpretative possibilities, an undertow of desperation and vulnerability, cynicism and exploitation in sex tourism's rituals, while its sibilant quality elicits Noam Chomsky's grammatical category of 'word as word' before being clarified in meaning by the actor's performance of it. What might seem at times a freewheeling wordplay that has been disparaged by various critics as mannered and overwritten, or out of place in a theatre, poetic rather than dramatic—eminent theatre critic Michael Billington considers *stoning mary* 'feels more like an acted poem than a play' (2006)—is in fact a tightly constructed poetic patterning that best serves her play's embodiment.

In Lorine Niedecker's 'condensery' poetics, Peter Quartermain observes how 'complex play forces us to let go of the manic compulsion so deeply ingrained in most readers, to zoom in on the meaning' (1996: 220). Extending Niedecker's aesthetic to claim for tucker green a condensery dramatic-poetics recognises the same forestalling of an audience's default tendency to impose meaning. Her playwriting language takes conceptualisation challengingly to the cliff edge of discerning comprehension, yet reprieves it from linguistic nihilism through the semantic relationships she constructs, that signal language's distinct aesthetic functions. The poet Fanny Howe (1999) refers to the state of 'bewilderment' as a way of entering into a work ethically and poetically, a state also pertinent to encounters with reading (and hearing) tucker green's drama, where other features move into prominence, and audiences must release themselves to these fresh sensations and processes of receptivity. Wayne Blair who directed *dirty butterfly* at the Belvoir Theatre, Sydney, Australia (2010), registers this when he notes, 'you read it, and you know it's good, but you just don't know why it's good, and then you start wanting more' (2010). This statement indicates that the visceral appeal of this work resists an imposition of orthodoxy and foregrounds a different logic to the textual and linguistic standard. Worthen's citing of adversarial couplings—'Stage vs. page, literature vs. theatre, text vs. performance' (1995: 15)—are inapplicable to her drama's print and stage performativity. tucker green's writing is not simply drama accessorised with poetic conventions, these are integral to all of its manifestations as rendered on the page, as heard upon the stage in its performance, in the verbal as both spoken and unspoken.

Integral to encounters with tucker green's work is receptivity to its soundings. Charles Bernstein's advocacy of 'close listening' (1998) restores the live encounter with contemporary poetry as constituted by sound as a material feature that operates in collusion with the performance style of the poet—an immediacy of receptive involvement that is part and parcel of being in a spoken-word poetry audience. In such settings 'sound is involvement with the present, with here-and-now existence and activity' (Ong 1994: 19), and tucker green elicits this kind of listening in the theatre. Although no comprehensive research into audiences has yet been undertaken in relation to her plays in performance, the theatre critic as audience member presents one recorded source, albeit housed within the specific framework of theatre journalism. Critic Kirsty Brown's 2006 review of *trade* describes an actor sounding as though they had Tourette's syndrome, perceiving that the syntax was lashed together by units that had little to do with coherent speech and more with disconcerting random language sounds. In contrast, tucker green's long-standing advocate Lyn Gardner offers a different perspective in reviewing the same play:

> No playwright makes you sit up and listen like Debbie Tucker Green. While others struggle to find a distinctive voice, Tucker Green has developed her own unique way of saying things. There is something both beautiful and jagged about her theatrical collages: they are poetry laced with shards of broken glass. She makes you hang on every word. (2006)

While one critic describes seemingly arbitrary language sounds or attributes incoherence to what she hears, another identifies the involved listening redolent of that required to fully experience spoken-word poetry. Gardner describes a process of attuning her ears to what she hears and, implicitly, her expectations are altered. This confirms the difference between listening to and listening for. Furthermore, for both black and white 'audience' cultural demographics, the process of reading or hearing black writers' texts can activate an auto-errata towards creolised, vernacular or phonetically rendered language. The work of black poets and dramatists in the UK during the post-war period has displayed and deconstructed an internalised auto-corrective that is set to Standard English and sustained via the formal education system. In live performance, culturally diverse experiences of listening and hearing can contrast white audience members—whose ears might refuse, reject, or interrupt receptivity—with black audience members who may hear with effortless joy, the sounds of experiences so intimately familiar in daily life, but not unilaterally acknowledged in publicly sanctioned discourse.

tucker green's staged plays further privilege an oral-aural culture as the performance visuals are stripped down to minimalism and actors are generally static. The sets are austere or hollow spaces, scenographically non-realist, with functionary sets of a table, chairs, boxes, pens and paper, and few props such as cigarettes, cups, and bags. Ong observes that 'in oral-aural cultures it is thus eminently credible that words can be used to achieve an effect such as weapons or tools can achieve' (1994: 21). Augusta Supple's review of *dirty butterfly* supports this claim, arguing that 'all language is loaded. All words are ready to be used—actors point their words at each other—language is artillery—and is used as such' (2010).

Yet within an apparently syntactical straitjacket, indeterminacy and ambiguity can also function. Like Parks, tucker green employs dynamic silences that extend the capacities of Harold Pinter's legendary 'dramatic pause'. Where characters are stated (in the playwriting typographical convention) in the left side margin to signpost their speech, in dynamic silences, this is indicated without any accompanying dialogue. In *dirty butterfly*, names can appear in succession or as alternating:

AMELIA. I wouldn't wait on you for nothing, Jo.
JO.
AMELIA.
JO.
JASON.
JO. What are you waiting for then?
Beat
...No.
I won't apologise for it.
Thank-you (37).

This space demands that an actor fills it with a continuity of subjectivity that does not involve vocalised words or sounds. Dramatic silence mirrors—what Nick Piombino (1998) terms for poetry—'aural ellipsis' where 'rather than only being asked to observe and comprehend a pattern of thinking, here listeners and readers, by means of a process of close, but freely imaginative, listening are encouraged to actively participate in it' (1998: 62). The eloquence of Piombino's 'holding environment' (derived from D. W. Winnicott's concept) in tucker green's plays also means 'holding up' readerly expectations of seeing words 'ready' for reading. The printed layout oxymoronically, creates a textual space of nothing—which is either to be filled in by the reader's imagination or even skipped over. In staged live performance, the specified dynamic silence might be physicalised or notated by some means (gestures, facial expression)—in an embodied interpretation by the (non) articulator (as the actor vocally becomes). Nonetheless, playing the aural ellipsis or dynamic silence live does not show how the writer has applied the breaks—or the brakes—to the written text, unless an audience member has read it beforehand.

In poetry the holding environment enables an intensified collaborative and organisational sharing between poets and listeners. In reading a play that employs this technique, the reader-writer relationship creates the indeterminateness and ambiguity—for an audience of one. The reader becomes only partially dependent upon the text, to wonder at, or wander around the lacunae. The author's omnipotence is thereby reduced through orchestrating this simultaneous holding and letting go—in confronting an audience/reader with the gaps—as neither strictly subjective nor objective, but transitional. An aural ellipsis leaves a space for invention on the part of the listener and reader to develop an intuition and facility with what are sometimes unfamiliar, or even inaccessible language features, or beyond articulable language. As Piombino notes, the 'result is nothing less than a radical transformation in the architectonic topology of the text/sound relationship' (1998: 70).

The live experience in the theatre and at poetry readings produces different requirements of an audience. Plays in theatre are bound by the necessarily reductive processes of selection and interpretation, through rehearsal, dramaturgy, and ensemble playing that are required for staging. The concurrent multiple meanings that a reader can appreciate, an actor cannot generate simultaneously during a performance as the actor negotiates the space in the rehearsed way—while the poet generally turns up and reads. Unlike theatre performance, in poetry readings or performances, as Peter Middleton observes, 'the speaker is making no attempt to conceal the text' (2005: 31). Effort is needed to stay attentive in poetry readings where the space is often makeshift, intersects with other demands of its venue—whether pub, gallery, bar, bookshop—that can heighten possible distractions. Middleton names these interferences as 'grating, nonsemiotic aural intrusions, and other seemingly irrelevant signs of unwanted occupancies' (31). In this context, the 'auditory effort' (25) of the audience is requisite. Through performing their poetry and evoking associations with staging and drama, poets can debunk the expectations of poetry as a remote, complex and highly stylised medium. In a communal setting of the reading or spoken word event, the liveness and guise of interaction renders it personally communicable. The importance of the stage for black British artists' expression is crucial for, unlike the introspective process of reading novels or poetry, spoken-word or performance poetry modes and plays generally require live people as recipients and participants which, although bounded by physical spatial separation (off-stage and stage areas, audiences in separate seating), there is potentially created, a shared area of racial proximities. Kamau Brathwaite identifies the reciprocity underlying oral traditions and their liveness in order to produce total expression requiring 'not only the griot but the audience to complete the community: the noise and sounds that the maker makes are responded to by the audience and are returned to him. Hence we have the creation of a continuum where meaning truly resides' (1984: 19).

In most cases, the poet's ability to perform or recite or read their work is secondary to the poem they are performing, reciting or reading and the poetry audience more readily overlooks any shortcomings in the skills of performance, than would a theatre audience towards an actor. Sissay's dramatic monologue, 'A Reading in Stanstead', of a poetry reading in a pub, vividly reverses such an expectation. Its conceit articulates the politics of poetry and the politics of performance as intertwined with the backdrop of post-war Britain's racial politics where demography and cultural spaces accord domains of belonging and unbelonging along race lines, through the poet-persona's realization at being the only black person in a white clientele—thus doubly 'on show' as performance poet and black person. 'They ogled./ The mirror behind the bar became a cluster of fascinated faces.' (the 's' and alliterative 'f' onomatopoeically evoking a hiss). The persona is unwitting prey to this greater narrative against which art is insignificant and defenseless: 'As contracted I began reading my poetry/But the air thickened around my words/As if I'd bruised it. [...] Dying wilting words fighting for air, clutching their necks on the carpet/ Clawing themselves up walls, staggering to the bar' (Sissay 2006: 56). A first-person filtering is activated by the dramatic monologue form as the poet removes himself from the frame of comprehension through the creation of a speaker. This stratagem relies upon the (reading) listener's powers of detecting inference, awareness of the ways in which shaping layers surround how information is communicated via a sole conduit who is undeniably a black speaker. Sissay's persona plays ingenuously with the situation, 'Something had disturbed this olde English pub' where, later, 'Everyone was a little too undisturbed for comfort'. A process of involvement with a monologue's speaker co-exists with alertness to the implications of the material, to produce what Alan Sinfield describes as, 'an ironic discrepancy between the speaker's view of himself and a larger judgement which the poet implies and the reader must develop' (1977: 7). Although Stanstead Airport, a gateway for low-cost tourism to and from Britain presents a trans-national environment, it devolves little of this to Stanstead itself, reflecting the demographic realities of Britain where black citizens are geographically and ideologically located in ways that are culturally contested by writers such as Sissay, whose persona has 'travelled two hundred and fifty miles to get here' (1977: 7). The poet creates a trans-historic lineage of racist hostility that links back to the experiences of post-war migrant generations, while claiming his literary lineage from those writers who spoke back to and refashioned British culture from within its borders.

Sissay is part of a generation of writers whose trans-raised backgrounds as black or mixed children raised in white care homes or placed with white families in the 1960s and 70s have provided the catalyst for textual and experiential innovation. The non-fiction, non-literary starting point of their narratives is imaginatively reworked in genres of poetry, prose, and drama. According to Sinding, 'the institutional contexts of nonliterary genres pressure participants to conform to assigned roles and values—and discourage and punish distancing and resistance—literary genres, on the other hand, often positively invite such play with conventions' (2010: 123). The dissonant and daring aspects of textual and experiential unconventionality means that the generic boundaries fluctuate as Sissay interpolates whole or partial poems in his plays that he has had published or performed elsewhere, in his poetic corpus about the care system. Alfred Hickling's review of his second play *Storm* observes, 'Sissay has claimed that he survived the system with only poetry to cling on to [...] he writes as if words were one of the world's last precious resources. Every sentence is composed urgently, as though it could be his last' (2002). Like Brown's response to tucker green's *trade* above, Hickling attributes a creative deficiency to what he attempts to impose meaning upon—rather than responding to the text's soundings: 'It makes for muscular self-expression, but just as poetry needs blank space on the page, a play-text needs a little room to breathe and expand. Sometimes Sissay's language becomes so tightly knotted that it is hard to unpick his meaning' (2002).

The poem which opens *Storm* functions as a prologue, and is read in unison by Mrs Jones and Mrs Spot, the foster home's matrons, whose names immediately conjure the one-dimensionality of children's primary school readers with which they are to be viewed: 'This storm carefully creeps, hidden in its own silence,/Twisting the scowling face, the breathless body,/The weakening pulse of the sky…/Hold onto your children (!!!) Or they'll be swept away.' The final line constitutes a refrain interspersed with 'The storm is here' (2). Like the characters of children's stories, these two characters operate in a straightforward world of cause and effect that Sissay aligns with a lack of imagination, flexibility, and sensitivity: 'rules is rules is. I don't make em and you don't break em' (14). Sissay draws upon the tantalising nightmarishness of fairytales where children have to stay inside for safety, in a world characterised by sudden and inexplicable evil-doing and life-threatening dangers. The children's torment is underpinned by the set and in performance by the actors' physicalisations that, as Hickling observes, create a 'sense of the whole world having gone into spasm […] the furniture is folded at right angles […] the characters suddenly jerk and convulse mid-speech as if a live current has been tripped through the stage' (2002). In this way intense traumatisation is conveyed in a non-realist performing technique in tandem with a non-realist uttered text, heightened by its poetic-dramatic aesthetic.

The first child character, Elaine, does jigsaws, and plays 'paper, scissors, stone', but by herself, ratifying the isolation and loneliness of the home's inhabitants. Her games are based upon fragments that try to create a whole from jigsaw pieces, or the shock of the unknown outcome of the paper, scissors, stone game where one's victory is arbitrary. These symbolically and poignantly ratify the powerlessness of the looked-after child. The stage directions state that Elaine, 'can or cannot be played as never speaking' to the on-stage adults or other children. Leaving the decision to others, rather than stipulating it in his stage directions, Sissay hands her over to a system of performance as though matching Elaine's powerlessness within the textual world of the fostering system. Mrs Jones reels off Elaine's trajectory through it as though she is a commodity or an appliance:

> They take her. They have her. They leave her. They take her they have her they leave here. They take her they have here they deceive her, they break her they bereave her, they deceive leave and they grieve her (6).

The aural anaphora (also a favoured tucker green device) of 'they' underscores Elaine's pawn-like disposableness in the hands of the anonymous adults, mirroring her almost irrelevance rather than centrality in the fostering transactions. The diminishing punctuation between each sentence and the subtle change between 'her' and 'here', where the addition of one letter alters entirely the grammatical syntax and meaning, signals the haphazard misnomer of 'care' and as tucker green's similar syntactical technique enacts, the multiple performances and power of even single letters in words.

Sissay reprises his dramatic monologue 'Mourning Breaks' (from *Morning Breaks in the Elevator* 1999) in an act of self-sampling so that it is delivered by three children, but predominantly by Elaine. Divided between three speakers in *Storm* the same wilful spirit is evident as infuses the persona in his poem 'Mourning Breaks'. Both works equate the mantra ('I am hanging on') with the super-human survival instinct needed. Sissay's inter-referential use of the same material across poem and play illustrates the textual and personal dominance of the experience of survival in care as transcending generic partitions. 'Mourning Breaks' captures the torment, rebirth, and ecstasy of this retrieval and renaissance in an uncompromising evocation of the persona's self-awareness and faith in himself as an artist and human being. The mantra protects him against all enticements towards his defeat and obliteration, 'I am hanging on. I am hanging on. I am hanging on'. Voices of authority woo him to give in, give up, let go, as both poetic auditors, and readers witness the spectacle of the speaker's suffering.

However, a counterpoint of reassurance vibrates throughout—that the fingers will grasp, that faith in the gripping will be sustained against the odds, that the outside voices will be disregarded and the inner voice heeded, that these words will not prove his last. As such, the poem is a testimony to a life survived so far, represented as the self-gestation of identity, from within 'Because I was growing. I was growing wings all the time. And I can fly.' As embodied in this poem, the outside world did not nurture Sissay's creative persona (Osborne 2009: 267). The source of liberation against oppressive odds was a chrysalis within himself. Given that Sissay's own genealogical odyssey has consumed the majority of his adult life, the replaying or gestating of one work inside another is unsurprising.

If a poem invites a reader to posit an audience, a play assumes one. In contemplation of just who this audience might be—as suggested by the play; as suggested by the venue; as suggested by the commissioning and programming trajectory that sees it produced in the first place—might elicit a fuller productive encounter with the cultural stratification that arises from the social categories which position writers and their audiences in mainstream or peripheral, elite or popular contexts. This also influences the genres of drama with which certain playwrights have become associated, and what modes of delivery (printed or performed) are expected of certain poets due to a perceived socio-cultural profile. In relation to black British writers, theatre and literary histories problematise just how 'close' experientially any audiences or readers really are to the playwright or poet. Suzanne Scafe has referred to Paul Gilroy's 'need for the black artist to address a "plurality of publics"' which, in relation to the black arts movement, Gilroy argued, 'requires both artist and critic to consider the difficulties that surround the *heretical suggestion* [my italics] that white audiences may be becoming more significant in the development of black art than any black ones' (quoted in Scafe 2007: 81). While Sissay has filtered much of his dramatic writing through autobiographical material, this has become increasingly 'everyman' and as much a musing upon the intricacy of identity-creation processes as it is about his survival of the care system and a white-dominant social ordering. His monodrama *Why I Don't Hate White People* (2009) is an exploration or explanation of the title through a rhetorical and evidential quest. In performance, his inversion of the title in the penultimate line to, 'Why don't I hate white people?' is answered by Sissay to close the play: 'White people made me.' He affirms himself as a British artist who must acknowledge the influences of his birth land's heritages and all that that entails as shaping his own life and his creativity. Yet his aesthetics also steps away from his work only being read through an inevitably autobiographical filter. As an internationally prominent British poet, recipient of an MBE, and latterly elected as ceremonial Chancellor to the University of Manchester, Sissay's own life is a positive transcendence of the brutalities of the care system and its child casualties even though his poetry and plays on the topic do not always offer this narrative outcome.

The focus upon tucker green and Sissay illustrates the trans-generic porousness between poetry and drama that has reconfigured contemporary British writing and is in particular, associated with spoken-word poetry and performance traditions to which black writers have been innovative and prominent contributors. tucker green's dramatic-poetic stage idiom blitzes conceptions of textual stability in the multiple possibilities of her plays' transmissions and receptions via their inter-medial properties:

audiotextually, linguistically, typographically, and grapholectically. Her plays indicate explicitly how poetry pulses in the arteries of theatre and vice versa, in the work of Sissay live performance strategies most associated with theatre are at the forefront of his poetry readings, while spoken-word techniques pervade his dramas.

As their work frequently slips between and reworks literary genres and performance traditions, this raises questions about the need for critical languages that can serve the demands of the forms and experiential aesthetics they forge. How do we 'develop a genre-blending analysis' towards how we teach, to 'understand something of how genres overlap and contrast'? (Sinding 2010). Clearly it requires the probing of (perhaps irreconcilable) differences, as well as interfaces, and incompatibilities and in placing distinct genres such as poetry and drama, media, books and live performance into an appreciative dialogue. Trans-generic writing reveals how working with the constraints of pre-existing categories can engender new forms and experimentation with the sense—meaning both the logic and feeling—of the permeability of the 'rules' that have evolved. To employ a cognitive approach to genres through focusing upon how we use them—rather than thinking about them (which already constrains us within their definitional compass), can lead to a rethinking of genre's categories. Foregrounding tucker green's and Sissay's genre-crossings in their respective aesthetics intervenes in their work being viewed as evidence for white critical traditions that 'focus and judge work on the basis of ethnic or racial markers' (Fisher 2010: 63). As Jean Fisher points out, the oft-replayed assumption that a black writer's text provides insights for white critics who might be marginalised by its reference points has seen a forensic critique that endeavours 'on the one hand, to look for confirmation of expectation, even prejudice—the artist as anthropological "native informer"—and on the other, to ignore the unique artistic dimension and experience of the work' which can actually 'deterritoralise' these assumptions (63).

This chapter's method has been to respond to the deterritorialising of generic borders through examining the artistic dimensions, while remembering that the positioning of black writers in English literary and dramatic histories has been an experience of exclusion, selective admission and frequently determined by the degree to which the work approximates, approaches or displays credentials of white-dominated cultural traditions. The sampling, blending, rewriting, and referencing detectable in writers' works do not detract from the ingenuity and inventiveness of their creativities as techniques for literary 'devising' and signify the ease and entitlement that contemporary generations feel towards a number of traditions and methods.

However, there are also problematic over-steppings that can position academic-creative, derivative-imitation categories antagonistically. Although I coined Landmark Poetics to critically recognise Sissay's and others poetry on surfaces, in his 2015 BBC Radio 4 programme, titled 'Landmark Poetics' he did not attribute its origin, thus exacting a degree of creative plagiarism of an academic text, not tolerated in a poetic one. Recent controversy surrounded Sheree Mack's anthology *Laventille* (2015)—pulped after Mack was revealed as having stolen whole lines, or substituted changes in personal pronouns, name or location of at least 12 poems by other poets across the world. Wole Soyinka writes, 'neither history nor culture is static' (38–9). He urges 'the conversion of the enslaving medium into an insurgent weapon' (139) which would be one result of letting loose the capabilities of trans-generic writing. But one must remain mindful of the fact that the differentiation between literary influences or inter-textuality in imitation and homage reveals the fine line that exists ethically, between sampling and plagiarism. Where derivative and generative techniques are the springboards for new work and their genres, James Baldwin's heritage declaration of 'know whence you came' (1985: xix), remains sage counsel.

References

Baldwin, J. (1985) *The Price of the Ticket: Collected Non-Fiction (1948–1985)* (London: Michael Joseph)

Bernstein, C. (ed.) (1998) *Close Listening: Poetry and the Performed Word* (New York; Oxford: Oxford University Press)

Billington, M. (2006) 'Review of *stoning mary*', *The Guardian*, 21 March, 28.

Brathwaite, K. (1984) *History of the Voice: the Development of Nation Language in Anglophone Caribbean Poetry* (London: New Beacon Books)

Brown, K. (2006) 'Review of *trade*', *London Theatre Review*, 25 March', 27.

Byron. G. (2003) *Dramatic Monologue* (London and New York: Routledge)

Chandler, D. (1997) 'An Introduction to Genre Theory', *Genre Theory*, http://www.aber.ac.uk/media/Documents/intgenre/chandler_genre_theory.pdf <accessed 13 January 2016>

Derrida, J. (1980) 'The Law of Genre', (trans.) A. Ronell. *Critical Inquiry*, 7:1, 55–81.

Elbow, P. (ed.) (1994) *Landmark Essays on Voice and Writing* (Hermagoras Press: Davis, California)

Eldridge, M. (1997) 'The Rise and Fall of Black Britain', *Transition*, 74, 32–43.

Fisher, J. (2010) 'Cultural Diversity and Institutional Policy', in *Beyond Cultural Diversity, The Case for Creativity* (ed.) R. Appignanesi (London: Third Text Publications) 61–8.

Gardner, L. (2006) 'Review of *trade*', *The Guardian*, http://www.theguardian.com/stage/2006/mar/21/theatre <accessed 24 January 2016>

Gräbner, C. (2007) 'Is Performance Poetry Dead?', *Poetry Review*, 97:2, 78–82.

green, d. tucker. (2003) *dirty butterfly* (London: Nick Hern Books)

——— (2008) *random* (London: Nick Hern Books)

Hickling, A. (2002) 'Review of *Storm*, 18 April', *The Guardian*, http://www.theguardian.com/stage/2002/apr/18/theatre.artsfeatures2 <accessed 24 January 2016>

Howe, F. (1999) 'Bewilderment' *HOW2* 1:1, http://www.asu.edu/pipercwcenter/how2journal/archive/online_archive/v1_1_1999/index.html <accessed 24 January 2016>

Keane, D. and Larsen, M. (2015) (eds.) *Writing the Future: Black and Asian Writers and Publishers in the UK Market Place* (London: Spread the Word; ACE)

Letts, Q. (2015) 'Review of *hang*', *Daily Mail*, http://www.dailymail.co.uk/news/article-3127369/QUENTIN-LETTS-night-review-hang.html#ixzz3yveaq9Kb <Accessed 24/01/2016>

Marcus, George E. (1998) 'The Use of Complicity in the Changing Mise-en-Scene of Anthropological Fieldwork', In George E. Marcus, *Ethnography Through Thick & Thin* (Princeton: Princeton University Press) 105–131.

Middleton, P. (2005) *Distant Reading: Performance, Readership, and Consumption in Contemporary Poetry* (Tuscaloosa: The University of Alabama Press)

Novak, J. (2011) *Live Poetry: An Integrated Approach to Poetry in Performance* (Amsterdam; New York: Rodopi)

Ong, W.J. (1994) 'Word as Sound' in Elbow, P. (ed.) *Landmark Essays on Voice and Writing* (Hermagoras Press: Davis, California) 19–34.

——— [1982] (2002) *Orality and Literacy: The Technologizing of the Word* (London and New York: Routledge)

Osborne, D. (2009) 'Lemn Sissay' in *Dictionary of Literary Biography: Twenty-First-Century "Black" British Writers* (ed.) R.V. Arana (Sumter, South Carolina: Bruccoli, Clark, and Layman; & Detroit, Michigan: Gale Research Company) 261–272.

Parks, S-L. (1995) 'An Equation for Black People Onstage' in *The America Play* (New York: Theatre Communications Group) 19–22.

Puwar, N. (2004) *Space Invaders: Race, Gender and Bodies Out of Place* (Oxford: Berg)

Piombino, Nick (1998) 'The Aural Ellipsis and the Nature of Listening in Contemporary Poetry' in Charles Bernstein (ed.) *Close Listening: Poetry and the Performed Word* (Oxford: Oxford University Press)

Quatermain, P. (1996) 'Reading Niedecker' in *Lorine Niedecker: Woman and Poet* (ed.) J. Penberthy (Orono, Maine: National Poetry Foundation, University of Maine) 219–228.

Scafe, S. (2007) 'Displacing the Centre: Home and Belonging in the Drama of Roy Williams' in *I Am Black/White/Yellow: An Introduction to the Black Body in Europe* (eds.) J. Anim-Addo and S. Scafe (London: Mango Publishing) 71–87.

Shaw, G.B. (1921) 'Shakespeare: A Standard Text', *Times Literary Supplement*, 17 March, 178.

Sierz, A. (2008) 'Interview with Sacha Wares', *Theatre Voice*, http://www.theatrevoice.com/2243/director-sacha-wares-on-random/ <accessed 24 January 2016>

Sinding, M. (2005) 'Genera Mixta: Conceptual Blending and Mixed Genres in *Ulysses*, *New Literary History*, 36:4, 589–619.

——— (2010) 'From Fact to Fiction: The Question of Genre in Autobiography and Early First-Person Novels', *SubStance*, 39: 2,107–130.

Sinfield, A. (1977) *Dramatic Monologues* (London: Methuen)

Sissay, L. [1999]; (2006) 'A Reading in Stansted', 55–6.,'Mourning Breaks', 62–5 in *Morning Breaks in the Elevator* (Edinburgh: Canongate)

——— (2002) *Storm* MS. 9950 (London: British Library)

——— (2009) *Why I Don't Hate White People* MS.11945 (London: British Library)

Supple, A. (2010) 'Review of *dirty butterfly*', *Augusta Supple*, http://augustasupple.com/2010/08/dirty-butterfly-flour-sugar-tea-arts-radar-b-sharp/ <accessed 24 January 2016>

Tzvetan, T. (1990) *Genres in Discourse* (Cambridge: Cambridge University Press)

Tucker green, Debbie (2005) *Trade and generations* (London: Nick Hern Books)

Worthen, W.B. (1995) 'Worthen Replies', *TDR: The Drama Review: The Journal of Performance Studies*, 39:1, 41–4.

——— (1998) 'Drama, Performativity, and Performance', *PMLA*, 113:5, 1093–1107.

——— (2005) *Print and the Poetics of Modern Drama* (Cambridge: Cambridge University Press)

PART THREE

Utopias and Dystopias

Teaching Utopia Matters from More, to Piercy and Atwood

Kate Aughterson

In 2016, Thomas More's *Utopia* is 500 years old, a quin-centenary celebrated by innumerable articles, conferences and exhibitions.[1] However, the genre and mode which he invented continue to be repeatedly misprisioned as both static and finished (Eagleton 2015; Kumar 2010), and are substituted instead by apocalyptic and dystopian visions of the contemporary and near-future world(s).[2] The term 'utopian' is used often by contemporary cultural critics as a broad term of insult to apply to a pie-in-the-sky naive political blueprint, as opposed to the term 'reality', or to 'the end of times in Slavoj Zizek's terms (Zizek 2011). However, this mis-prisioning and death-knell of both the original and the genre depends on an over-literalised reading, one that blinds readers to the nuances of the narratorial process and places utopia as a discursive debate, not as a place: to 'utopia' as genre, not content.

This chapter will contend (*contra* Kumar and Zizek) that by attending to the fluid generic characteristics of utopia we can be equipped to read contemporary utopias/dystopias less literally as end-of-the-world prophecies and more as interventionist debates in global and personal politics. More's 'invention' of the utopian genre—at a point in history when exploration and communication first became global—makes it a perfect prism through which to debate contemporary cultural and literary texts during

---

K. Aughterson (✉)
University of Brighton, Brighton, UK

© The Author(s) 2016

K. Shaw (ed.), *Teaching 21st Century Genres*,
DOI 10.1057/978-1-137-55391-1_5

a time in which the global consequences of that historical moment are coalescing in economic, political and environmental crises. The reading effect/affect of utopian misreading is to disenfranchise our students from an understanding of genre as dynamic and diachronic, and to depoliticise their sense of this particular genre. Additionally, this chapter draws implicitly on recent feminist and queer theory which argues that future ideas and possibilities can best be figured through renewed cyclical engagements with the past, rather than teleological or apocalyptic ones,[3] through a circling back and forwards in time: a movement which itself echoes the discursive practices of the utopian mode. It ultimately argues that by proposing 'utopia' as both mode and genre, we can see how contemporary writers have moulded, adapted and developed the original genre.

Jameson acknowledges this: 'The text thus reconstituted is [...] Thomas More's *Utopia*, one of those rare works which, whatever its precursors, inaugurates a whole genre, which it names at the same time that it exhausts its whole range of formal possibilities' (1977: 4) Modern theoretical and critical discussions of both genre and the intersection of Literature and globalization continue to ignore the radical dialogics and potential of utopian writing: critics and publishers relegate Utopian writing to fan (s/f) fiction. Even Jameson allows his political biases to dominate how he defines contemporary utopia, more recently in his 'The Politics of Utopia' when he states that 'in utopia politics is supposed to be over' (2004: 42).

Critical interpretations and appropriations of More's 'Utopia' erase *Utopia's* playful fictionality and typically debate More's 'utopian' vision as though the content of one part of the book can be extracted and interpreted literally. 'Utopia' has two originary meanings: More's book, and the island place. It is this dialogic framework where the hypothetical place is imagined as 'utopia'. The legacy of nineteenth-century Marxist readings of More's work harnessed the second book containing the blue-print for utopia as though it existed autonomously of the dialogic work. The adjective 'utopian' thus became a term of approbation for the Left, and critique for the Right. The cumulative consequences of twentieth-century developments including the fall of the Berlin wall, the rise of Moslem fundamentalism, and the spread of globalisation have fuelled a Western intellectual scepticism about grand narratives and idealised political projects and, as a result, the post-nineteenth century meaning of 'utopia' has become widely discredited by both Left and Right. Similarly, the label 'dystopian' can effectively shut down the formal dialectic between text, world and reader, focusing primarily on content. Yet the silent erosion of both the semantics and revolutionary representational and political possibilities of 'utopics' by a neo-liberal consensus can be exposed if we return to More's original text, and read its structural complexities and its generic self-consciousness. By acknowledging its radical formal practices, we can revivify the radical rhetoric of both word and genre, and rediscover its vibrancy in contemporary writing.

Utopia consists of two books and a number of paratexts, including the title page and several appended 'letters'. The first book is a narration by the character 'More' of a series of leisurely meetings and conversations with ambassadors and businessmen in Antwerp whilst on a diplomatic mission, focusing in particular on his meeting with the stranger Raphael Hytholodeus, and their long lunch and conversation in a pleasant secluded garden. The topics of conversation are about pressing political and philosophical conundrums of the day in France, England and Holland: the huge gap between rich and poor; how enclosures are changing land use and rights; the role of an educated man (sic) in political life; the corruption of the church; political authoritarianism; how to find worthwhile labour. Throughout these debates, Hytholodeus uses examples of political and social alternatives experienced during his travels in the West and South of the globe, all of which are given names, albeit fictional ones. He teasingly mentions the island of Utopia a few times, and at the end of Book One More begs him to reveal more about the island and its customs. Hytholodeus promises to do so after dinner, and thus the second book opens. Book Two is narrated in Hytholodeus's voice, describing the practices, beliefs and politics of the Utopians. The character More's only direct words are a final concluding paragraph:

> Meanwhile, though he is a man of unquestioned learning and highly experienced in the ways of the world, yet I cannot agree with everything he said. Yet I confess there are many things in the Commonwealth of Utopia which I wish our own country would imitate, though I don't really expect it will (More quoted in Adams 1973: 91).

There are a number of things an astute reader should notice immediately from this summary. Firstly, that Thomas More's *Utopia* is not the blueprint of the second book, but the whole volume of two books and paratexts. The two books of *Utopia* exist in a dialectical relationship to each other: early modern social and political problems are anatomised in one, and an alternate social order is narrated in the other, and then displaced by More's final commentary. More's point of view dominates Book 1, and Hytholodeus's Book 2. Secondly, More's invention of the name 'utopia', a compound formed from Greek roots meaning simultaneously 'no-place' and 'happy-place', playfully codes the imagined alternative as an impossibility, a playfulness conjoined with the semantic origins of Raphael Hytholodeus's name (angel/speaker of nonsense). More's final sentence foregrounds both the formal and fictional qualities of his narrative and its (serious) playfulness. These qualities are central to all utopian writings which collectively offer their formal structure as a dialectical debate between the present and alternate futures. By acknowledging these roots in a playful literariness (albeit with serious political intent) we see utopia as a genre that does not represent an impossible and foolish dream, but one that offers a continuous and dialectical discourse between an analysis of the present and imagined alternatives and solutions. It is in this space between the present and the future that utopian discourse exists, and continually renews itself. Thirdly, the staged encounter occurs between a comfortable set of characters in whom we recognise some of our own habits, thoughts and characteristics and one who is a stranger, a traveller, with views from a place unknown: so structurally the axis between present and otherness (here and there) is grounded in character. Fourthly, the imagined place is a space elsewhere, but one which precisely realised is an inverse mirrored relationship to the expressed present of both characters and readers (and thus future 'dystopian' literature still utilises this same dialectical utopian discourse). Finally, any authorial point of view is oblique or denied, emphasising utopia as discursive debate between present and future, ideas and readers. We can visually represent the structural relationship in Fig. 1.

The reader, context and the world sit outside the rectangular field, and interpret the relationships between all three as intersectional. Utopia is therefore not simply a genre in the sense of a set of formal structures, but a mode, a way of representing and arguing about political ideas that involves fictionality and possibilities, and a readerly and referential perspective in the present. As such, the conventional and contemporary sense of a dystopia is incorporated into this broad sense of the utopian mode. More's original text defines the generic modalities of utopia as an open-ended dialectical form, but in debating modern and contemporary utopias, we must not fall into the trap of those early readers whom More joked about who believed there really was an island called Utopus, and failed to read the playful formal layers of the genre which draw attention to the subtleties

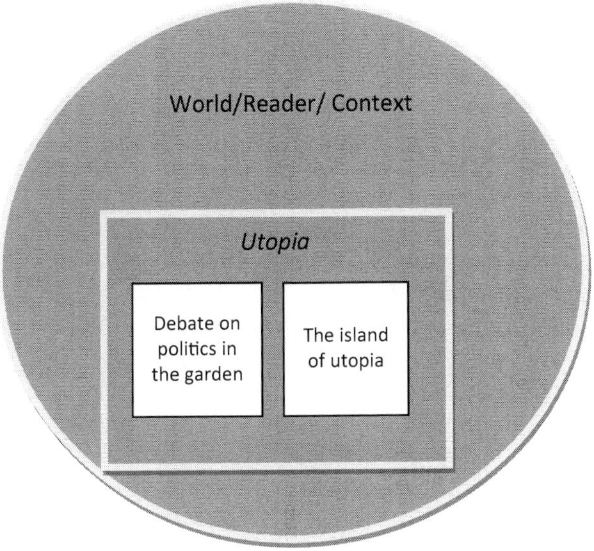

Fig. 1

of the reading and interpretative process as themselves both radical and political 'Utopia' necessitates and includes its opposites, others and contradictions. Naturally polylogical, it is self-consciously open-ended and paradoxically celebrates the possibility of the impossible. In offering an open invitation for readers to join in, the Utopian genre is the perfect embodiment of how generic hybridity can encompass cultural hybridity in a non-authoritarian and open way.

The seminal feminist utopia, Marge Piercy's *Woman on the Edge of Time* (1979), features on many contemporary undergraduate reading lists, and it is possible to recalibrate some of the interpretative difficulties students encounter by reading it through the prism of More's utopics and genre. For many initial readers Connie is judged as both a child abuser and schizophrenic, whose daydreams about a future world are proof of both her shame and illness. Even for highly skilled critical readers, the alternate world that is Mattapoisset 2137 is read literally as Piercy's ideal place and space.[4] However, by reading structure and mode rather than content, Piercy's project becomes clearer.

The title alerts us simultaneously to Connie's psychological status ('woman on the edge') and to the time-/conception-travel motif ('on the edge of time'). The dual facing grammatical function of the phrase 'on the edge' self-consciously names the novel's character and narrative as janus-like and liminal, discursively poised between one thing and another. This liminality is a motif which threads its way through the story: Connie is between one (real) world and another (fictional one): New York 1976 and Mattapoisset 2137; the present and the future; the outside world and the inside world of an asylum; the world of white privileged America and the world of the underclasses. Her edginess defines her as a stranger/outsider in each environment: and it is here that Piercy subtly shifts More's binary opposition in *Utopia* where the More/Hytholodeus axis always posits the stranger's ideas as estranging/outsider. In Piercy's work the focalising character time/space travels as much as the stranger-visitor (Luciente), so that the two worlds which are often alternates in utopias (as in More's), are continually bridged. This formal adaptation enables us to see how Piercy makes clear the dialectical nature of the utopian project: it is literally about making bridges.

Although all action and perspective is filtered through Connie's eyes and voice: the nurses' and doctors' words and those in Mattapoisset are reported to us as direct speech, enhance the appearance of reliable narration, strengthening our empathy for Connie's experiences. However, the final chapter of the book consists only of medical case notes (titled 'excerpts from the Official history of Consuelo Comacho Ramos', 377), a series of perspectives on the actions and viewpoints on the previous 19 chapters from the viewpoints of social workers and medical practitioners who have encountered Connie, including such summaries as:

> SENSORIUM, MENTAL GRASP AND CAPACITY: Sensorium clear. Oriented times three. Recent and remote memory appear weak. The patient has somewhat slow intelligence and answers questions poorly.
>
> DIAGNOSIS: Schizophrenia, undiff. Type 295.90 (378).

The novel appends one authorially voiced sentence to these diagnostic extracts: 'there were one hundred thirteen more pages. They all followed Connie back to Rockover' (Piercy: 381). This chapter appears to query Connie's version of events and experiences. However, by placing this as the final chapter (as opposed to the opening one, for example) Piercy posits another interpretative 'edge'. Do we read this as an authoritative (authorial) intervention on the action of the book, a commentary on the apparent time-travel and alternate worlds described, a conventional formal closure to a novel which 'explains' inconsistencies? There is no final answer: but the very turning back into the narrative makes this text utopic: it posits a dialectical relationship between our logical present and the fictional narrative spaces. Narrative structure echoes and creates a dialogic relationship between different ideas and different spaces.

Furthermore, the final chapter contributes to that narrative movement through our readerly positioning both in relation to the previous time travel and in relation to medical and scientific discourse. The novel's tripartite places and timeframes (the asylum Rockoverin 1976; Mattapoissett in 2137; and Gildina's alternate future New York, which Connie mistakenly visits in a blundered time-travel in 2137) create juxtapositional dialogue between the actions and ideas in each, all focalised through Connie. The doctors' language in the final chapter remains outside and beyond Connie's viewpoint, albeit located in 1976, and within the frame of the book as a whole. Our position as outsiders is re-emphasised by the formal shifts between time-frames and perspectives. Figure 2 represents this.

This structure is especially significant in relation to the language of the final chapter. The plot in each timeframe both debates and represents the discourse of medical and scientific practitioners. In Rockover, the treatment of patients and the language of the medical profession are scrutinised indirectly

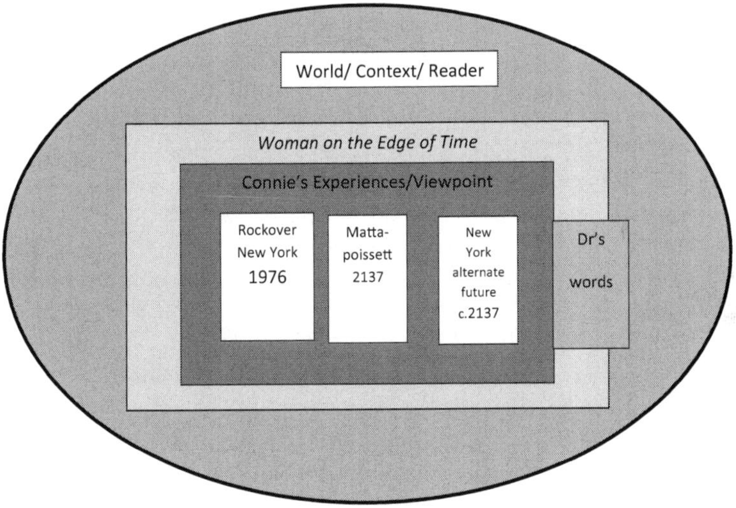

Fig. 2

through the focalisation of Connie's experience, but also through the future characters disbelief about medical practices in 1976. Equally, the series of planned brain operations on the patients at Rockover, narrated through their words, their escape plans, and the loss of core identities, represent medical practitioners, their diagnostic tools and discourses as conditional upon personality, class and individual ambition. In Mattapoissett, characters debate a different medico-physical culture, and when Erzulia is dying, Connie says 'I haven't met any doctors. How come there's no doctor?' (159). In Mattapoissett doctors are "healers" in a world where everyone is technologically cognisant, where medicine and medical knowledge are integral to community, and in which "madness" is celebrated as a prophetic and nurtured state. In Gildina's New York, by contrast, medical and scientific language and practice dominates identities: all humans are modified in some way to meet social and sexual demands; surveillance is maintained by both internal implants and external cameras; the objectification of the human as workable flesh seems complete. When Connie visits Mattapoisset after the first brain operations, and asks why she has been chosen to travel, Bee answers:

> Nobody's supposed to discuss advances in science with you. It might be dangerous – for you, for us. Your scientists were so [...] childish? Carefully brought up through a course of study entered on early never to ask consequences, never to consider a broad range of effects, never to consider on whose behalf. (196)

Connie says to Luciente 'Its so hard for me to think of you as a scientist' (274) because her personal negative experiences have demonized the medico-scientific. The twisting narrative thread of these three time frames—which share plot-lines on medical and scientific practice and discourses—generates a discursive debate about both the role of medical and technical science in human lives, and about the supposedly 'objective' language of science and diagnostics. These narratorial juxtapositions are distinct, but also function to create contrasts, and only together do they create the complete novel. The medico-technological language and perspective of the final chapter, which appears to be 'objective' and final, has been subjected throughout the novel's action and debate to alternate interpretations. It exists, therefore only in that context, and not outside or above the novel. The effect of this juxtapositional threading is to enable and display a series of debates about alternatives and possibilities so that even the ending of a novel is not really an ending (as Barbarossa says 'alternate futures are equally or almost equally probable', 197), simultaneously throwing us back into the narrative and moving us forward into the world. Consequently, Piercy models utopia not as a particular place, but a way of thinking and an enablement to political action, although place remains key to locating sensibilities about what is wrong with our current world. Piercy's seminal work is self-consciously situated in (and at the beginning of) a postmodern feminist tradition, which both looks back to More's open-ended dialogism and forward to contemporary writers such as Atwood, Winterson and Hall. It is this open-endedness, an acute sense of political crisis, and the articulation of alternate (im)possibilities, which define utopianism, often voiced by the dispossessed and the marginalised, who are often also women.[5]

Margaret Atwood's trilogy (*Oryx and Crake*, 2003; *The Year of the Flood*, 2009; *MaddAddam*, 2013), has been consistently labelled by reviewers and critics as 'dystopian' and apocalyptic: a critical labelling which denies her writing's dialogic nuances (intrinsic to the utopian dialectic) and ignores the conceptual issue that the label 'dystopian' necessarily entails broader utopian modalities.[6] Critical analyses focus on content: both the pre- and post-apocalyptic world discussed in all three novels is one in which technology, science, authoritarian political power and big business dominate and control both planet and individuals. It is a world recognisable from other literary and filmic dystopias, from *Brave New World* onwards, and one in which such technical and political authoritarianism has caused the near obliteration of humans.

Yet in conducting a close reading of the structure, focalisation and comedy in Atwood's novels it is possible to illustrate how they should be debated within the utopian frame and how such generic and modal reading displaces and reconfigures the 'dystopian' label. The publishing and marketing of the novels draw attention to their identity as a trilogy, and thus to both structural readings and rereadings, a process of reimagining, returning, and rethinking fundamental to the utopian mode. *Oryx and Crake* narrates events from the perspective of Snowman, who has survived a pandemic engineered and marketed through 'blysspills' by his friend Crake. The novel moves between his present, encountering and helping the Crakers (bio-engineered humanoids genetically spliced by Crake to survive the post-pandemic world to lack human competitive and aggressive characteristics) and Snowman's past, including reflection on how technological and ecological crises formed Crake's decision to end the human race, from his scientific base 'paradice'. The novel ends on a cliff-hanger with Snowman's discovery of three other unknown humans who have escaped the plague.

The Year of the Flood parallels the timeline of the first novel, but is set outside Snowman's Compound world, and is focalised through Toby (despite her name, a woman), Ren and Amanda. The narrative moves between the present (post-plague) in which a few survivors battle with genetically engineered species freed to roam now humans are wiped out, and the past which describes an alternative community called Gods' Gardeners, who 'teach the convergence of Nature and Scripture' (Atwood 2013: xv), a green religion founded by 'Adam One'. The three surviving women encounter and capture the 'Painballers', criminals manipulated by the Compound into killing machines, the story ending in the same cliff-hanger moment as *Oryx and Crake* as all key characters meet at the sea edge. The final novel, *MaddAddam* is narrated alternately from the perspectives of Toby and Zeb, and tells the story of the days and months after the endings of the first two novels, with a final postscript chapter ('Book: The Story of Toby') which is narrated by one of the Crakers, Blackbeard. The present of the story focuses on how the surviving humans protect and live with the Crakers, whose innocence about their environment and human motivations make them easy potential victims of the painballers; the history focuses on Toby and Zed's personal pasts; whilst the future of the story lies in the final chapter.

As Fig. 3 shows, the three books echo the narrative of human, animal and planetary evolution structurally, at first by the first two books' intertwined parallel stories, and latterly in the forward narrative trajectory of the third. Content and structure have circular and teleological movement across the trilogy, both in the readers' experience of events and in terms of plot, and this double movement itself replicates utopian modal discourse. The places (of Paradice, or God's Gardeners' roofs, of the Compound) contain elements of the 'blueprint' model of the utopian mode: however, these places in the trilogy have significance only in relation to each other within the narrative, not to an external referent or stable utopian place. This juxtapositioning of alternative places, possibilities and universes makes the texts utopic, as we shall see.

The first two novels explicitly utilise intertextual biblical frames of reference. Crake's master plan conceived in 'Paradice' (in *Oryx and Crake*) to root out evil from the world through the simultaneous eradication of humans and the invention of a new species (the Crakers) parallels Adam

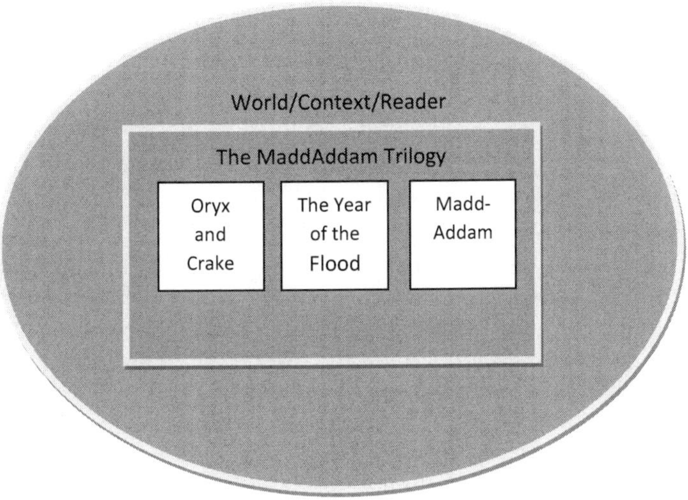

Fig. 3

One's reinvention of religion as an alliance between Christianity and green politics and himself as a founding father in *The Year of the Flood*, both invoking the story of creation in Genesis. The plague (which God's Gardeners call 'the flood') echoes other biblical 'falls': that of the angels from heaven; that of humans from Eden; and that of the world and humans before the flood. It reminds us of the history of human power, desire and our relationship to the natural world through our cultural narratives about those relationships and divergent interpretations of these (disaster for many/ salvation for a few). This locates the trilogy within that historical and narratorial trajectory. It also suggests that narratives of megalomaniacal power (whether theological, political or ecological) consistently 'fall' and fail. However, the dual parallel structure of the first two books posits the third book as a resolution or answer, one of potential salvation, but a salvation beyond that dictated by God-like figures. In both novels the god-substitute or/and sinning figure (Crake/Adam) do not survive and their legacies (the Crakers/Toby) develop and evolve in ways not programmed by either deliberate genetic engineering (Crake of the Crakers) or eco/ political ideology (Adam One). Blue-prints don't work. Whilst both the intertextual and structural trajectories appear to model a present emerging necessarily out of the past (annihilation of the human), the actual events and encounters which happen in the present of the third novel (for example, the mating between humans and Crakers, and the resulting new kinds of humans born at the end of the book) demonstrate instead how serendipity and chance produce alternate futures. Parallel narratives and intertextual referents ask readers to ponder alternatives, the relationships between political situations and possible solutions, and about how stories help us do this: this is the utopian mode.

MaddAddam's structural placing and internal form privilege Toby's voice and stories: those of a woman, as opposed to the previous two focusing on male voices. Her voicing of the narrative begins as a reluctant origin-story narrator for the Crakers, standing in for Snowman whose infection keeps him delirious and out of action until the last third of the novel. Her gradual variations on the origin-story as first told by Snowman in *Oryx and Crake* (Oryx and Crake as foremother/father who birthed the Crakers in an Egg in Paradice) show us both how stories evolve and how humans and Crakers (through their questions) tell stories to resolve questions and make sense of their world(s). The story of Toby's stories and inventions (the novel as a whole) is a metanarrative about how the invention of alternatives works: it functions therefore as commentary on the utopian mode, as well as on the political dreams and analyses of both Crake and Adam One. By enabling us to see these in parallel as Toby looks back at the history of how they all got to the present, as well as watching the process of myth-making at work through her, Atwood simultaneously critiques the idea of utopia-as-blueprint (neither Adam One nor Crake are validated), and utilises the dialectical model invented by More through Toby's present perceptions. The relationship between here and there is not one of place, but one of history and causation. Nevertheless, the axis between here and there retains the dialectical modelling: albeit there is a narrative inversion, a key development of More's sense of the genre. Within the plot, here is the result of mistakes made there, blue-prints that went wrong. Here is post-there, post-blueprint and so Atwood discovers a new twist to the utopian genre, explicitly acknowledging that third potentiality: there/here/somewhere (else).

In *MaddAddam*, Atwood's narrative style and focalisation and their intersection with structure equally alert us to alternatives. The author uses a third person narrative, focalised through Toby's perceptions and experiences. After the first three sections ('Egg', 'Rope' and 'Cobb House') focused on Toby, the subsequent nine sections alternate between Zeb's backstory and Toby's present, represented as part of their courtship in an ongoing dialogue, but culminating in a section in which focalisation shifts between the two ('Bearlift', 'Scars', 'Zeb in the Dark', 'Snowman's Progress', 'Blacklight Headlamp', 'Bone Cave', 'Vector', 'Piglet', and the dually focalised 'The Train to Cryojeenyus'). The three remaining sections function as narrative conclusions, and radically shift the narrative focus and trajectory: the first ('Eggshell') finalises the return to ANooYoo by the MaddAddamites and their successful alliance with the hybridised Pigoons and the Crakers, which results in the defeat of the violent Painballers. The second section ('Moontime') alternates Toby's focalisation, with that of the Craker child/man Blackbeard, whose intelligence and skills Toby has fostered, in which the last two chapters ('Rites' and 'Moontime') are respectively in Toby's and Blackbeard's words, and both self-consciously explain they are writing for future readers. The final section ('Book') is wholly narrated and written down by Blackbeard, one of the Crakers about whose intelligence the humans had been so dismissive. The finale and future are displaced from the recognisably human as we currently know it: but the Crakers' voices (both written down and sung) carry on the story of Toby and Oryx and Crake and articulate a present in which human, animal and the post-Flood earth co-exist in an acceptable harmony. The focalisation and structural shift in this final novel onto an invented and evolved humanoid species can be read as parallel to the different kinds of engineered humans in Mattapoissett's future, an imagined outcome to our contemporary self-destructive global political, economic and geo-humans actions. Yet although critics might label this ending as either 'dystopian' or 'post-human', both such labels negate the complex dialogic debates in which Atwood's work participates, and focus again on content at the expense of form. Her jokey invocation of pre-texts such as *The Bible 1984* (1949), *Brave New World* (1932) and *Animal Farm* (1945) sites this work as one in open dialogue with those about future possibilities and their emergence from contemporary socio-economic and political conflicts: and it is this mode which marks it as utopian.

Atwood's writing in this trilogy crackles with wit, in ways which return us to Thomas More. At the smallest semantic level, there are numerous punning names for institutions and hybridised animals that satirise our contemporary obsessions with body (the spa called ANOoYoo), and competition (the game 'EXTINCTATHON', the production of cheap food through hybridising animals, including the 'Pigoons', and the dominant corporate conglomerate which names its own death throws, 'CorpSeCorps'). The Crakers' semantics vocatively address whomever they address ('O Toby';

'O Jimmy-the Snowman'). When Snowman wakes up his first words are 'O fuck', which the Crakers assume to be a vocative greeting: so Toby invents a God called 'fuck' to explain his invocation. The reading-effect of this naming is by making us laugh, to step back from the narrative content and draw attention to the ideas and spaces as satiric exaggerations. The very title *MaddAddam* riffs on parental responsibility and origin stories (ma/dda/addam), as well as suggesting a collective human folly in patriarchal origin stories (madd/addam), and more subtly gender politics and the intersection of male and female (ma/ddad/dam) or a world in which paternity is surrounded by femaleness (ma/(d)dad/dam). None of these connotations dominates: all are possible.

Just as More named his space 'no-place', and reimagined the use of gold as chamber pots and children's toys, so Atwood's punning and inversion enable the reader to laugh and stand aside from the plot. As Zeb jokes to Toby, 'Funny old thing the human race wasn't it? (228), a wry externalised perspective shared by any utopian writer. I want to discuss one extended joke, the elucidation of which enables us to see how Atwood implicitly nods at utopian debates. The Crakers are a genetically engineered species who turn blue when they are ready to mate, and who approach human women with a sexual openness which appears and feels alarming. It is ironic that the sexual contact is all from Craker men to human women, although the Crakers do listen and learn from human codes of behaviour. During the rescue of Ren from the painballers and the recovery of Snowman, a number of the Crakers have sex with Ren and Amanda, and as the MaddAddams continue to live with the Crakers, more sexual relationships develop and evolve, with the inevitable result of cross-species pregnancies and births (which the women choose actively to continue). The Crakers blue-print humans to help create a new hybrid species. By literalising blue-printing as a sexual and sexual-selection joke, Atwood suggests that any blue-print models (of utopia for example) are follies, and will produce difference and diversity not uniformity. This comic turn places conception and birth as central to an evolving relationship between human, non-human, earth and hybrid beings ('O, Fuck'). In this novel, women's voices and women's bodies literally figure forth a potential resolution to the perceived problems of the world and of the human in the first two books. Puns and bathos enable a serio-comic interpretative position outside the text's immediately bleak referential frame: positing perspectives from beyond the narrative which assume an active reader's continual sense of the relationships between here/there/somewhere.

Atwood herself has wittily and punningly argued that her recent work is 'ustopic': using possible scenarios through fiction to enable *us* to conceive of political action about our world (topos):

> Ustopia is a world I made up by combining utopia and dystopia—the imagined perfect society and its opposite—because, in my view, each contains a latent version of the other. In addition to being, almost always, a mapped location, Ustopia is also a state of mind, as is every place in literature of whatever kind [...] In literature, every landscape is a state of mind, but every state of mind can also be portrayed by a landscape. (Atwood 2011: 4)

There is no guarantee that humans can avoid the possible disasters envisioned in these novels: but alternative places and times act as distorting mirrors held up to our own times, acting in dialogue with our present to open up a space for thinking and action. Utopia is heuristic. Piercy and Atwood conceive of and construct utopia as a dynamic space between page and reader: not a blue print but a blank page on which we can write our own future.

The utopian mode is an open radical genre, self-consciously intertextual and flexible in form and mode. More's multi-voiced and multi-moded and voiced Mennipean satire perfectly matches the twenty-first-century conundrum of hybrid and crisis politics. The motif of the newly arrived disruptive stranger in contemporary fiction is a central tenet of utopian (as well as fabular and folk-tale) writing. Recent Young Adult fiction, for example Marcus Sedgewick's *Floodland* (2000), or Suzanne Collins immensely successful *Hunger Games* (2012) trilogy and its filmic spin-off shows how the utopian is a vital contemporary genre and a mode of critical political debate. The recent work of Sarah Hall (*The Carhullan Army*, 2010), Jeanette Winterson (*The Stone Gods* 2008), Liz Jensen (*The Rapture* 2009) and Julie Myerson (*Then* 2012) all represent alternative futures through female voices, shifting between different time frames. This strong feminist revisioning of a narrative mode, which begins with Piercy's rereading of More, is part of a contemporary feminist aesthetic that resists a model of time as necessarily linear, of the past and future as wholly distinct, and of the end of times as really upon us. Jameson's argument that utopia is a form that is 'itself a representational meditation on radical difference, radical otherness' (Jameson 2005: xii). radically opens it to alternative visions and voices. So how should we teach utopia? I leave it to future readers.

Notes

1. For example, the e-one at the British Museum: http://www.bl.uk/learning/histcitizen/21cc/utopia/utopia.html
2. See Aris Mousoutzanis's excellent summary (2014).
3. See Love (2007); E. Freeman (2010), and R. Weigman (2000).
4. See, for example, Adams 1991; Huckle 2012. Even Josephine Glorie's more sophisticated reading of the text (1997) that uses Benhabib to advocate a reading using critical social theory, which amounts to a dual explanatory-diagnostic reading of present ills, with an anticipatory-utopian aspect that imagines an alternative world nevertheless still assumes utopia to be a static concept, space and place.
5. McBean (2014) locates the text's circling between past, present and future in a similar way.
6. Dunlap (2013); Uygur (2014); Lubodova (2013); Wisker (2012: 176); Scurr (2013).

References

Adams, Karen (1991) 'The Utopian Vision of Marge Piercy in *Woman on the Edge of Time*', in *Ways of Knowing: Essays on Marge Piercy* (ed.) Sue Walker and Eugenie Hammer (Mobile, Alabama: Negative Capability Press) 39–59.

Atwood, Margaret (2003) *Oryx and Crake* (London: Bloomsbury)

——— (2009) *The Year of the Flood* (London: Bloomsbury)

——— (2011) 'The Road to Ustopia', *The Guardian*, http://www.theguardian.com/books/2011/oct/14/margaret-atwood-road-to-ustopia <accessed 25 February 2016>

——— (2013) *MadAddam* (London: Bloomsbury)

Collins, Suzanne (2012) *The Hunger Games Trilogy* (London: Scholastic Fiction)

Dunlap, Alison (2013) 'Eco-Dystopia: Reproduction and Destruction in Margaret Atwood's *Oryx And Crake*', *Journal of EcoCriticism* 5, 1–15.

Eagleton, Terry (2015) 'Utopias Past and Present', *The Guardian* 16th October, http://www.theguardian.com/books/2015/oct/16/utopias-past-present-thomas-more-terry-eagleton <accessed 26th October 2015>

Freeman, Elizabeth (2010) *Time Binds: Queer Temporalities, Queer Histories* (Durham, N.C. Duke University Press)

Glorie, Josephine (1997) 'Feminist Utopian Fiction and the Possibility of Social Critique', in *Political Science Fiction* (ed.) David Hassler and Clyde Wilcox (Columbia SC, University of South Carolina Press) 148–59.

Hall, Sarah (2010) *The Carhullan Army* (London: Faber and Faber)

Huxley, Aldous (1934) *Brave New World* (London: Chatto and Windus)
Jameson, Fredric (2005) *Archeologies of the Future: The Desire Called Utopia and Other Science Fictions* (London and New York: Verso)
——— (2004) 'The Politics of Utopia', *New Left Review* 25: 35–54.
——— (1977) 'Of Islands and Trenches; Naturalisation and the Production of Utopian Discourse', *Diacritics* 7: 2–21.
Jensen, Liz (2009) *The Rapture* (London: Bloomsbury)
Kumar, Krishan (2010) 'The Ends of Utopia', *New Literary History* 41 : 549–69
Love, H (2007) *Feeling Backward: Loss and the Politics of Queer History* (Cambridge MA, Harvard University Press)
Lubodova, Katerina (2013) 'Paradise Redesigned: Post-Apocalyptic Visions of Rural and Urban Spaces in Margaret Atwood's *MaddAddam* Trilogy', *Eger Journal of English Studies* 13: 27–36.
McBean, Sam (2014) 'Feminism and Futurity: Revisiting Marge Piercy's *Woman on the Edge of Time*', *Feminist Review* 27: 37–56.
More, Thomas (1973) *Utopia* (ed.) Robert Adams (Norton Critical Editions, New York: W.W. Norton & Co)
Mousoutzanis Aris (2014) *Fin-de-Siecle Fictions, 1890s/1990s: Apocalypse, Technoscience, Empire* (London and New York: Palgrave Macmillan)
Myerson, Julie (2012) *Then* (London: Vintage)
Piercy, Marge (1979) *Woman on the Edge of Time* (London: The Women's Press)
Sedgewick, Marcus (2000) *Floodland* (London: Orion)
Scurr, Ruth (2013) 'Clear-Eyed Margaret Atwood', *The Times Literary Supplement*, http://www.the-tls.co.uk/tls/public/article1300066.ece <accessed 26 February 2016>
Uygur, Mahiner (2014) 'Utopia and Dystopia intertwined: The Problem of Ecology in Margaret Atwood's *Oryx and Crake, The Year of the Flood* and *MaddAddam*', *The Journal of International Social Research*, 7: 42–8.
Weigman, Robyn (2000) 'Feminism's Apocalyptic Futures', *New Literary History* 31: 805–25.
Winterson, Jeanette (2008) *The Stone Gods* (London: Penguin)
Wisker, Gina (2012) *Margaret Atwood: An Introduction to Critical Views of Her Fiction* (London and New York: Palgrave Macmillan)
Slavov Zizek, (2011) *Living in the End of Times* (London: Verso)

Other Mothers and Fathers: Teaching Contemporary Dystopian Fiction

Oliver Tearle

A key preoccupation found in numerous works of contemporary dystopian fiction written since 2000 can be summed up in one figure: the parent. This ranges from biological and surrogate parents to metaphorical parents: 'Mothers' includes Mother Earth and Mother Nature as well as biological and filial ideas of motherhood, and reflect a preoccupation in recent dystopian fiction with environmental disaster and climate change. Similarly, the role of the 'Father' refers to both patriarchal terms, as well as to the literal role of the male parent. Since the year 2000, there has been an anxiety in genre fiction regarding the concept of caring for the world at large, and for fellow human beings, as well as for future generations. Although a similar trend can arguably be noted in postmillennial cinematic dystopias, this chapter focuses on a number of high-profile fictions—many of which have subsequently been made into successful films—to suggest ways in which modules based on contemporary dystopian fiction might be constructed to enable students' engagements with wider and meaningful dialogues between different strands of 'the dystopian'. This chapter outlines ideas that will hopefully go on to inform futures modules, or courses, on postmillennial dystopian fiction.

O. Tearle (✉)
Loughborough University, Loughborough, UK

© The Author(s) 2016

K. Shaw (ed.), *Teaching 21st Century Genres*,
DOI 10.1057/978-1-137-55391-1_6

Perhaps the post-apocalyptic dystopian novel that has attracted the most critical acclaim since the millennium is Cormac McCarthy's *The Road* (McCarthy 2006; adapted for cinema in 2009), about an unnamed man and his son who are making their way across America in the wake of an unspecified catastrophe that has killed most of the population and left little in the way of food for the survivors. Margaret Atwood's fiction has often addressed issues of motherhood and maternity, most famously in *The Handmaid's Tale* (1985), but her 2003 novel *Oryx and Crake* returns to this issue, interrogating the idea of the 'mother' in a more wide-ranging and metaphorical sense, reflecting recent scientific debates. Kazuo Ishiguro's novel *Never Let Me Go* (Ishiguro 2005; adapted for cinema in 2010) is about children who are raised as clones in order to serve as organ donors for other human beings or 'normals'. Its emphasis is on ideas of 'caring' in a more general sense, rather than examining this issue within the narrow confines of the literal family. Nevertheless, Ishiguro draws direct links between this dystopian idea of 'care'—enforced organ donation resulting in the donor's own death—and the traditional concept of motherhood.

As well as this recent concern with tropes of parenting, dystopian fiction published since the millennium has become increasingly aware of its position as an established literary genre. The burden of the past lies heavily on contemporary dystopias. It may seem odd to discuss the past in relation to dystopian fiction—a genre primarily known for depicting nightmare visions of a future world—yet recent dystopian fiction is as much a literary response to the past as it is a socio-political prediction of the future. Critics including Oliver Lindner have read recent works of dystopian fiction written in English as symptomatic of a widespread fear that the West is in decline (Lindner 2013). For Lindner, the symbol of cannibalism in post-apocalyptic and dystopian novels such as Cormac McCarthy's *The Road*, Margaret Atwood's *The Year of the Flood* (2009), and the futuristic sections of David Mitchell's *Cloud Atlas* (2004) suggests an atavistic return to an earlier, primitive stage of humanity, one reminiscent of late Victorian concerns of devolution, degeneration, and ideas of decadence and decline. However, what critics of recent dystopian fiction often overlook is the extent to which recent works in the genre reflect the same concerns that were found in much earlier works. In nineteenth-century dystopian novels, fears surrounding the consequences and implications of empire, Darwinian natural selection, and economic inequality loom large in texts such as Edward Bulwer-Lytton's *The Coming Race* (1871),

Richard Jefferies' *After London* (1885), and H. G. Wells's *The Time Machine* (1895). In dystopian works since 2000, the same themes can be found, although empire has been replaced by globalisation. Recent dystopian fiction often draws upon the genre's history in order to project the future, and illuminate the present. The crisis of parenthood which concerns recent dystopian novels—from *Oryx and Crake* to *The Road* and *The Book of Dave*—is also, we might say, a crisis of 'parental' literary influence, the struggle to write one's way out of the shadow of earlier famous dystopias such as *Brave New World* (1932), *Nineteen Eighty-Four* (1949), and *A Clockwork Orange* (1962), to offer just three examples. This same crisis, albeit with a different inflection, is operative in recent young-adult dystopian fiction, a related though slightly different genre. In devising modules that teach post-2000 dystopian fiction, it becomes necessary to determine how much of this rich literary history needs to be addressed. Can one understand Suzanne Collins's *The Hunger Games* (2008) without first addressing William Golding's *Lord of the Flies* (1954) or, for that matter, *Nineteen Eighty-Four*?

There is a cultural and historical issue here as well as a literary one. Modules that address contemporary dystopian fiction but do not also involve students reading earlier defining works in the genre run the risk of suggesting that recent dystopian novels are somehow peculiar to their times; that dystopia has risen in popularity in the last few decades in an attempt to reflect changing social and political attitudes. But to take one example, surveillance and the notion of the 'spectacle' have been a firm feature of the genre since at least Samuel Butler's anti-utopian work *Erewhon* (1872); recent popular dystopias such as *The Hunger Games* reflect the recent popularity of reality television, but also tap into a far older trope within dystopian fiction. When teaching contemporary dystopian literature, one needs to include a detailed history of the genre, to avoid certain assumptions among the students: strong critiques of totalitarian political regimes can be found in *Nineteen Eighty-Four*. Many students are aware of Orwell's novel, but how many will necessarily know of Yevgeny Zamyatin's *We* (1923), which heavily influenced Orwell's novel, or Jack London's even earlier dystopian novel and socialist critique, *The Iron Heel* (1908)?

Dystopian fiction has always displayed an allusive and intertextual quality in the past, frequently engaging with what has been, until recently, a fairly small field. George Orwell noted numerous precursors to his *Nineteen Eighty-Four*. In turn, *A Clockwork Orange* author Anthony

Burgess offered a critical-creative response to Orwell's own novel, in his novel *1985* (1977). E. M. Forster stated that he wrote his dystopian short story 'The Machine Stops' (1909) as a response to one of H. G. Wells's utopian novels, but such borrowings and creative engagements with previous works in the field have become more self-conscious and pointed in fiction produced since the millennium. Dystopian fiction is now more playful in its interaction with previous fiction belonging to the genre—and to other works of literature from outside the dystopian tradition. As Peter Brooks has noted in the context of late Victorian narratives, the 'sons are not free of the fathers but bound to the retracing of their traces. But yet again, the impossibility of original story, the need to retell, places the primary emphasis of the tale on the plane of narration itself, calls attention to the attempt to repeat, reconstruct, retell' (Brooks 1984: 262). Such borrowings, echoes and crossovers within the dystopian genre obviously make it easier to construct university modules and school syllabuses exploring numerous works from the genre since many dystopian novels already seem to be having a dialogue with each other. Recent contributions to this burgeoning genre are often acutely aware that they are part of a tradition which involves not only *Brave New World* and *Nineteen Eighty-Four* but a whole range of literary texts, both directly and indirectly 'dystopian', such as Absurdist theatre and early works of science fiction such as Mary Shelley's *Frankenstein* (1818). This issue might also be related to the question of style, a feature of dystopian fiction that is often overlooked in favour of political and thematic discussions. Several notable dystopian novels written since 2000 employ distinctive prose styles which raise additional questions relating to dystopian fiction's connections with, and borrowings from, very different traditions and modes, such as modernist and postmodernist fiction.

The primary focus of dystopia is disaster, nightmare made real—whether in the form of natural catastrophes, totalitarian political regimes or war. The millennium and the long period of anticipation which preceded it led to fears over what the year 2000 would bring in its wake. 'As the marker of a new year, decade, and millennium grew closer', Kirsten Moana Thompson writes, 'long-standing apocalyptic anxieties about the overdetermined year 2000 became evident in American popular culture, public policy, and journalism' (Thompson 2007: 1). This continued post-2000, but with a change from the disasters themselves, to their aftermaths and how, in the wake of environmental disaster and war, humanity might survive in an altered landscape.

Cormac McCarthy's *The Road* is at once a typical example of this and an atypical one. It is subtly allusive, but its strongest allusions are to previous texts not known for their dystopian qualities, and its multiple points of reference need to be addressed when it is being studied in the classroom, for the novel's power lies partly in what McCarthy does with these sources and precursor-texts. McCarthy's novel is about America in the wake of a terrible but unspecified catastrophe, whether global warming, an asteroid impact, or some other cataclysmic disaster (the novel is famously ambiguous and cryptic about what has caused the disaster). One of the most notable aspects of the novel is the absence of the mother figure from the narrative: it is as if there is no room for the maternal presence in the world of atavistic barbarity, Darwinian competition, and rampant cannibalism that McCarthy evokes. His title, too, evokes Jack Kerouac's classic American Beat novel, *On the Road* (1957)—but here, the absenting of women from the narrative is not a product of a male declaration of independence (leaving the family at home to discover oneself) but a device to underscore the difficulty of maintaining traditionally feminine or nurturing qualities in this post-apocalyptic hell. Pointedly, the mother to the young boy did not perish in the unnamed holocaust but committed suicide, choosing to desert her family rather than struggle on as one of the survivors. But the father is dying, too: a potent symbol of impotent fatherhood. The man can only do so much to protect his son from the harsh realities of the world they inhabit. Many of the objects that McCarthy draws attention to in the decaying world of *The Road* are relics of capitalist consumerism: the shopping trolley the man and boy use to transport their possessions, the cans of Coca Cola they find. Although the terrible disaster that has destroyed much of the population and altered the landscape may be a global one, the novel remains tightly focused on the United States. This is America stripped of its status as global superpower, reflecting—among other things—anxieties over the decline of the United States as the world power.

Everything about *The Road* is minimalist: the small cast of characters, the lack of character names, the lack of quotation marks indicating dialogue, even the omission of apostrophes in words like 'hadnt' and 'wont' develop a sparse style of language that McCarthy cultivated in a previous novel, *No Country for Old Men* (2005). The events and action are downplayed, curiously lacking in drama. Even the precise setting of the novel is not specified, although the 2009 film adaptation features a slightly more specific landscape identifiable as somewhere in the east coast of America. It is a world in which the 'names of things [are] slowly following those things into oblivion' (McCarthy 2006: 93), including the names of people. The only named character in *The Road* is a man named Ely, though the precise significance of this name is never explained. This minimalism reflects the scarcity of everything—food, survivors, hope—but also arguably reflects the lack of a guiding female presence in the waste land of *The Road*. The quintessentially American style of the novel's prose is in the tradition of Ernest Hemingway: taut, masculine, unadorned. Like T. S. Eliot's *The Waste Land* (1922) the dried landscape of dust and ashes reflects the lack of life-giving properties, the death and sterility that permeate this fallen world. It is a resolutely male text, which focuses almost exclusively on the father-son relationship of the two main characters. Yet McCarthy's father-protagonist is a far cry from the manly patriarch we might expect from such a spare and functional prose style. The very first image of the novel is that of the father 'reach[ing] out to touch the sleeping child beside him' (McCarthy 2006: 1), a tender act as much traditionally maternal as paternal.

The Road is dedicated to McCarthy's own son and, as Mark Busby has noted, the relationship between the father and son is the 'heart of the novel' (Busby 2009: 45). In his review of the novel, James Wood drew attention to the importance of children in the post-apocalyptic genre as it has developed since 9/11. For Wood, this is a result of the shift from fear of nuclear annihilation that dominated post-apocalyptic fiction from the Cold War era (when death was instantaneous or at least immediately present all around the survivors) to the altered focus in recent post-apocalyptic fiction, where fear of climate change looms large. 'The temporal reprieve', Wood writes, 'the deferral of the worst to later generations, may not be any consolation at all. It may, strangely enough, increase the fear: are you more agonisingly afraid of something that will happen to yourself or of something that will happen to your children?' (Wood 2013: 50). But 'father' and 'son' here can be interpreted in religious terms: Allen Josephs has drawn attention to the ways in which McCarthy's early drafts for the *The Road* more explicitly foreground the idea of God as one of the novel's themes, as a potential symbol of salvation and hope (Josephs 2013: 134). This preoccupation with God as an absent presence helps to explain one of the more surprising phantasmal intertexts for *The Road*: Samuel Beckett's play, *Waiting for Godot* (1953). Euan Gallivan has drawn attention to the fact that early reviewers of *The Road* pointed up the novel's 'Beckettian' qualities (Gallivan 2012: 145). But it is Beckett's drama rather than his fiction which McCarthy's novel most persistently evokes. *The Road* and *Waiting for Godot* both share an almost microscopic focus on two male characters. There is a curious lack of action in both texts, a minimalism. There is even a character referred to simply as 'the boy' in both Beckett and McCarthy, and both texts explore the notion of being on the 'look-out' (McCarthy 2006: 160–1) and it is notable that Beckett's play, as the stage directions reveal, also takes place on a country road. A road has become *The Road*, the one that all remaining humanity must trudge down without any real sense of long-term hope. The post-apocalyptic landscape of *The Road* must be seen partly through the lens of Beckett's play: 'Barren, silent, godless' (McCarthy 2006: 2) as McCarthy describes it in the novel's opening pages. Both texts also share a sense of waiting, though for what is at once crystal clear and shrouded in mystery. Both texts share an existentialist sense that hope may be empty and pointless but it is the only thing that keeps the characters in existence. But if the novel evokes Beckett's sterile landscapes from *Waiting for Godot* (and, to a lesser extent, the post-apocalyptic setting of *Endgame*), it ends with a slightly more positive suggestion of hope for the boy's future. The father's duty of care towards his son has led to the discovery of a new home for the boy. This message of optimism supports religious readings of the novel. As Erik Hage has observed: 'there are even suggestions that the son of the man is actually a Son of Man and that this road has all the gravity and importance of the biblical roads to Damascus and Emmaus' (Hage 2010: 143), a journey that again returns us to the final part of *The Waste Land*. As the father gazes at his son, he reflects: 'If he is not the word of God God never spoke' (McCarthy 2006: 3). The suggestion here of a wordless God and the 'Word of God', Jesus Christ, must sit uneasily alongside the novel's later nightmare vision of a 'charred human infant headless and gutted and blackening on the spit' (McCarthy 2006: 212), 'infant' literally meaning 'wordless' or 'unable to speak'. The infant Christ is presented in the potentially redemptive form of the son (who shares the kindness and compassion of Christ) but also in the horrific image of the child gutted and cooked for a cannibalistic feast in a Darwinian landscape of competitiveness and violence.

A quasi-Christian religious discourse can be glimpsed in what might be called the novel's 'neomedieval' atmosphere. Neomedievalism has been defined by Michael Spiegel as a term used to describe a world, real or fictional, that 'resembles that of Western Christendom during the Middle Ages, when the universalism of the Catholic Church coexisted with the fragmentation of kingdoms into fiefdoms' (Spiegel 2010: 120). The term reflects a 'simultaneous globalization and fragmentation where the nation-state persists, though weakened' (Spiegel 2010: 120). A discussion of neomedievalism when teaching post-2000 dystopian fiction seems essential, since it is a feature not only of McCarthy's novel but also of works by other recent 'dystopianists' such as Will Self, Margaret Atwood and Jim Crace. Although no real social infrastructure remains in *The Road*, not even one of post-national 'fiefdoms', the novel might be said to reflect the postmillennial turn to neomedievalism in fiction in its very use of Spiegel's word, 'christendom' (the lower-case letter being a clue to the term's dwindling power). At one point, as it begins to snow, the father catches a snowflake in his hand, and watches it 'expire there like the last host in christendom' (McCarthy 2006: 15). The fact that the word is summoned but only in a simile (and a weak one involving something as delicate and evanescent as a snowflake) is a stark reminder that this world is different from other recent post-apocalyptic novels and their more stratified neomedieval worlds, such as Will Self's British dystopia *The Book of Dave* (2006).

The Book of Dave has received less critical attention than *The Road*, but it was published in the same year and also centres on father-son relationships as the crucial human element. One productive point of comparison for McCarthy's American vision of a post-apocalyptic future would be *The Book of Dave* with its peculiarly British dystopian vision, which is inspired by satirical writers like Jonathan Swift and Aldous Huxley as much as dystopianists like Orwell or Burgess. Those wishing to construct a module or syllabus that addressed the differences between recent British and American dystopias could create a fruitful dialogue between McCarthy's and Self's novels.

The Book of Dave reflects current anxieties surrounding the role of the father in a postmillennial world, issues pertaining to divorce and child custody, and the clash between altruism and self-interest. Religion, too, is a central theme, as it is in McCarthy's novel. But where *The Road* places the father-son relationship in an extreme post-apocalyptic environment, *The Book of Dave* projects the present-day fear and anger of the titular father-protagonist, Dave Rudman, into a future vision of London in which Dave's 'Book'—written for the purpose of providing moral instruction for his son—has been taken up as a sacred text by Londoners dwelling in a neomedieval postdiluvian world five centuries hence. Parenthood in this future dystopia has undergone a sharp split—enforced by the religious mandate of the 'Book of Dave'—in which mothers and fathers divide up the care of their children equally between them, with fathers having custody for one half of the week and mothers for the other half, the twice-weekly 'Changeover' having become hardened into religious ceremony. Parenthood thus becomes a systematised case of what might be called dual single-parenthood, in which parents both raise their children, but separately from one another. Like *The Road*, the novel depicts a single-parent family unit. In both *The Road* and *The Book of Dave* we see similar themes explored in very different ways, although both McCarthy and Self use the device of apocalypse to provide an extreme backdrop to their novels' depictions of fatherhood. In both, parenthood has become a core part of a person's identity: just as the adult protagonist in McCarthy's novel is frequently referred to as 'the father', and Self's future London is populated by 'dads' and 'mummies' and gender has become defined in terms of parenthood.

The essential premise of *The Book of Dave* takes us back to Richard Jefferies' novel *After London* (1885), an early work of post-apocalyptic fiction which shows the industrial city transfigured by a catastrophic event into a rural, quasi-medieval, pre-industrial landscape. It is neomedievalist before the term was coined. This is also what has happened in the future world of Self's novel, where London has become Nú Lundun, a reversion to what Daniel Lukes has called a 'bucolic' world 'in which the country has replaced the city' (Lukes 2015: 288). The language used by Nú Lunduners, Mokni, is heavily influenced by the religion that has grown up around the titular Book of Dave, a book inscribed on metal plates by its disgruntled and mentally ill author, a London taxi driver, Nadsat for the Satnav generation. Indeed, parts of the Knowledge—the test that London cabbies have to undergo in order to drive taxis in the city—make their way into the Book of Dave, which later adherents interpret as sacred hymns. The Tree of Knowledge thus gives way to 'the Knowledge', an intimate mental familiarity with the geography of London, neatly encapsulating the neomedieval idea of the village—not so much Marshall McLuhan's 'global village' as merely one of many neomedieval villages within a globalised world.

The essential difference between *The Road* and *The Book of Dave* in their treatment of religion can be neatly observed in a very similar line which appears in the two novels. In *The Road*, it is the man Ely who declares to the man and boy that there 'is no God and we are his prophets' (McCarthy 2006: 181), echoing a line from the 1880 novel *Niels*

Lyhne by Danish writer Jens Peter Jacobsen: 'There is no God, and man is his prophet' (Jacobsen 1947: 160). Religious belief may be difficult to maintain in such a barren wasteland world, and the survivors' worldview is, if not entirely faithless, then full of doubt and questioning. Although Ely's statement is cryptic, he appears to be saying that godless worlds must also have their prophets—those who act as spiritual leaders for the new nightmare world and its survivors. Conversely, the title character and father-figure of *The Book of Dave* hears a voice saying, '*There is no god but you, Dave, It whispered, and you can be your own prophet* ...' (Self 2006: 345). It is after hearing such voices that Dave resolves to compose his own holy text, which eventually inspires a new patriarchal religion—a religion which, like the faith that is almost powerless to be (re)born in McCarthy's ash-choked world, emerges from a post-apocalyptic scene of devastation—and with true patriarchal resonance, in Self's novel it's a Noah-like flood). The faith that, whilst not thriving, cannot die altogether in McCarthy's novel ends up flourishing in Self's neomedieval world. In both novels religion is aligned with father-son relationships: Dave becomes his 'own prophet' in an attempt to reach his estranged son, inscribing his moral instruction on metal tablets which are buried in his wife and son's garden. Faith in McCarthy's novel is a less certain or dogmatic thing, but the father in *The Road* views his son as a potential saviour, like a new Christ who has come to earth after the apocalypse. Both novels stress the paternal as much as the patriarchal side of religion, the idea of 'God the Father', something which is rendered literally true in the spawning of Dave's religion in Nú Lundun.

It is important when teaching recent dystopian fiction to be aware of the rich layers of intertextuality present in many novels produced in the genre since 2000. There are several important influences and intertexts for *The Book of Dave*, ranging from Russell Hoban's 1980 novel *Riddley Walker* to Jefferies' *After London*, Burgess' *A Clockwork Orange*, and even works of comic satire like *Monty Python's Life of Brian* (1979). Unlike *The Road*, Self's novel is as much Swiftian satire as it is admonitory dystopia. Its subtitle, 'A Revelation of the Recent Past and the Distant Future', directs us to read the two narratives—presented alongside each other in alternate chapters—as interrelated in more complex ways than a simple cause-and-effect relationship might suggest. The revelation is as much to be found in the (almost) present-day narrative as it is in the future dystopian London Self depicts. The future world is not simply a product of the world of the novel's 'recent past' chapters, which take place between 1987 and 2003: the London of both time-settings is presented as an unpalatable nightmare world, with the present-day narrative exploring Dave's discontent and frustration as a modern-day father, and the 'distant future' half of the novel offering, in one sense, the opposite to this, a world in which patriarchy has been reinforced tenfold, at the cost of women's freedoms and dignity.

It is worth contrasting both *The Book of Dave* and *The Road* with a relatively little-known novel in the post-apocalyptic genre, Jim Crace's *The Pesthouse* (2007), about an America in decline. On a module devised to convey the sheer range of responses to the post-millennial world, Crace's novel could be placed into a productive dialogue with *The Road* in particular, given that it also offers a vision of a future post-apocalyptic America, yet treats the basic idea in a different way. The neomedievalism of the future world envisioned in *The Book of Dave*, and *The Road*'s anxieties over humanity's future, meet in Crace's novel, which appeared a year after the other two novels. America was a land built by "fathers": the Pilgrim Fathers, the Founding Fathers, the patriarchal Christianity that Atwood's *The Handmaid's Tale* had depicted as a forceful oppressor of women's rights. Yet the world of *The Pesthouse* is an emasculated and unmanned world: unmanned by plague and by environmental catastrophe. Technology has entirely disappeared from the world: this is extreme neomedievalism. Unlike *The Road*, *The Pesthouse* is populated by named characters; names are still deemed important in this future world, whereas they were not in McCarthy's future vision. Tellingly, Crace gives his male protagonist the name Franklin, an ironic reminder of that founding father, Benjamin Franklin; whereas one Franklin had helped to make the United States, this neo-Franklin will witness that country's disappearance from the world stage. This is not so much the American Dream as American nightmare. Suggestively, in the novel America had been in decline even before the virulent plague that threatens the remaining population came along. The figure of the child or infant in both *The Road* and *The Pesthouse* is a symbol of the new generation struggling to make its way in an inhospitable nightmare world in which America's future—and, in different ways, the world's at large—remains uncertain. The image in *The Road* of the charred human infant on the spit bleakly casts doubt over the long-term future of the human race. In *The Pesthouse*, the baby that Margaret acquires sounds a note of hope for the future, but it is a fragile one. Like *The Road*, Crace's novel ends with the makeshift family unit—Franklin,

Margaret, and the baby—reaching the coast and a more hopeful note being sounded.

Self's *The Book of Dave* would make a worthy addition to any syllabus outlining recent dystopian fiction not least because it can be used to spark discussions about other novels in the genre. As well as the points of comparison with the post-apocalyptic worlds of *The Road* and *The Pesthouse*, Self's novel might, perhaps more surprisingly, also be productively compared with the patriarchal hell depicted in Margaret Atwood's influential 1980s dystopia, *The Handmaid's Tale*. This would be particularly suited to a module that was designed to address the depictions of men and women in dystopian fiction, as well as other gender-related issues such as the recent crisis in masculinity and the role of women in what was, until *The Handmaid's Tale*, an overwhelmingly male-dominated genre in fiction.

As in Atwood's novel, Self presents a dystopian future in which patriarchal (literally 'father-ruling') society oppresses women, using the mandate of religion in both instances to support misogyny and control of women's bodies. *The Book of Dave* might also be viewed as a curious counterpart to Atwood's novel in that its recent past narrative offers, not a woman who is oppressed by legal and social conventions and regulations, but a father who is frustrated by, and feels a victim of, issues surrounding paternity and fatherhood. Both Offred and Dave are figured as parents whose role is to bring forth children whom they are then separated from (although, in a twist, we later learn that Dave isn't the biological father of his estranged son, Carl). Although a less extreme form of oppression from that witnessed in Atwood's Gilead, the legal and bureaucratic constrictions which deny Dave Rudman access to his son offer a bizarre form of present-day dystopia in which the pastoral role of the parent is displaced by an exclusive focus on biological models of parenthood. As Daniel Lukes has observed, paternity in *The Book of Dave* is reduced to a 'biological narrative' of insemination rather than a more complex nurturing role (Lukes 2015: 284), and when Dave Rudman discovers he is not the biological father of his son, an already fragile bond is all but severed.

Both novels present the reader with their protagonists' accounts in different ways, but both employ the device of the found text, the reception of which, in a future world several centuries hence, is designed to influence our ultimate response to the novel's events. Whereas Atwood reveals only at the end of her novel that Offred's account is being analysed at an academic conference two centuries in the future, Self's novel uses alternate chapters to move between the present-day world of London and the London of five centuries in the future, in which Dave's Book has been taken up as a holy text. This highlights that Dave's present-day world is as much a dystopia for him as the future world his Book creates: the novel's dual narrative invites us to ask whose dystopia it is anyway, and what we mean when we use such terms to discuss contemporary culture.

The Handmaid's Tale obviously belongs to the twentieth, rather than the twenty-first century; yet it is a vital source for many (especially female) writers of more recent dystopian fiction. Indeed, Atwood herself has continued to revisit the dystopian landscape she mapped out in *The Handmaid's Tale* with her more recent dystopias, such as *Oryx and Crake* (2003). The neomedievalism of *The Book of Dave* and *The Pesthouse* is also found in this novel. As Michael Spiegel has observed, '*Oryx and Crake* finds in neomedievalism the social structure necessary to understand how Atwood's portrayals of Oryx and Crake work to subvert the realist novel and challenge its claim to fully represent an increasingly post-national world' (Spiegel 2010: 121). Alongside the novel's neomedieval qualities we need to consider its attitude to the metaphor of the parent or God as creator of life. Mark A. McCutcheon has argued that *Oryx and Crake* is 'a specifically Frankensteinian science fiction' (McCutcheon 2010: 216). Suggestively, the biological parents of the novel's protagonist both end up rejecting the pseudo-parenthood that the novel's genetic engineering represents. Jimmy's mother leaves his father for what goes on at the HelthWyzer Compound, saying: 'It's wrong [...] it's a moral cesspool' (Atwood 2003: 57). Eventually, Jimmy's father decides to blow the whistle on the organisation (Atwood 2003: 212). The perverse form of mothering evoked by such genetic splicing and experimenting ends up eroding the literal parenthood of the novel's characters. Coral Ann Howells has pointed up the shift that has taken place in Atwood's treatment of dystopian fiction over the last few decades:

> *The Handmaid's Tale*, centered on human rights abuses and particularly the oppression of women under a fundamentalist regime, is entirely social and political in its agenda, whereas *Oryx and Crake* projects a world defamiliarized not through military or state power but through the abuse of scientific knowledge, where genetic engineering has created transgenic monsters and humanoid creatures in a post-apocalyptic scenario much closer to conventional science fiction. (Howells 2006: 163)

As Howells also points out, dystopian fiction is 'traditionally masculine' (Howells 2006: 163), but recent dystopias have questioned this gendering, with McCarthy's novel depicting a more sensitive and nurturing image of the father and Atwood's offering a horrific perversion of the 'mother' role into a scientific creator and modeller of new life. Even *The Book of Dave*, with its alternating chapters of emasculation and female oppression, attempts something more 'androgynous' than was the preserve in many defining dystopias of the mid-twentieth century. *Oryx and Crake* revisits the theme of 'mothering' that is central to *The Handmaid's Tale*, but has also been read as a response to a much older work of what might be called 'science fiction' that centres on the theme of unnatural mothers: Mary Shelley's *Frankenstein* (1818).

Kazuo Ishiguro's 2005 novel *Never Let Me Go* can be read as another contemporary updating of *Frankenstein*, picking up on several of the key themes from Shelley's novel and refashioning them for a modern scientifically advanced world of cloning, organ donation, and genetic engineering. As with Shelley's novel we have the theme of man playing God, and the idea of creating something—in a godlike or parent-like role—only to overlook the broader moral and psychological damage which such creation causes. It is also a novel in which the alternative dystopian world it depicts—in which children have been cloned for the purpose of later becoming compulsory organ donors for other human beings—contrasts the cloned characters explicitly with other humans who are able to have children and live full lives, so-called 'normals'. The central characters of *Never Let Me Go*—the trio of Kathy, the novel's narrator, and her friends Ruth and Tommy—cannot conceive children. They will never be parents, never have fulfilling jobs, never live out their three-score years and ten. When they leave Hailsham, the private school in which they are brought up, they will go on to be carers and, ultimately, donors, giving away their vital organs in a series of operations until, by the fourth operation, they 'complete' (the novel's sinister euphemism for 'die'), perishing in their prime of life. The song which provides Ishiguro's novel with its title is a love song, but Kathy interprets the lyrics ('Baby, baby, never let me go') as a *cri de coeur* for thwarted parenthood, with the word 'baby' being misconstrued and taken literally. She imagines a scenario in which 'a woman who'd been told she couldn't have babies, who'd really, really wanted them all her life' miraculously has a baby and 'holds this baby very close to her' (Ishiguro 2005: 70) for fear that something terrible will happen to it. Kathy quickly realises her interpretation of the song's meaning 'didn't fit with the rest of the lyrics' but 'that wasn't an issue with me' (Ishiguro 2005: 70). The word 'issue', mockingly suggesting the children or offspring Kathy will never have, is one of many subtly devastating touches to Ishiguro's prose.

What is *Never Let Me Go* saying about parenthood and the notion of care and welfare? And how might Ishiguro's novel be useful in classroom discussions, especially when compared with other recent novels about notions of parental responsibility and notions of care, such as *Oryx and Crake*? Assuming the novel should be read allegorically—that is, this alternative science-fiction world is a mirror of our own—Ishiguro can be read as suggesting a tension between the personal and the social, the idea of care on a private familial level and care as a politically sanctioned system. In order to provide care or donations for the world at large, the citizens of Hailsham must forgo the right to have children. Margaret Atwood, who reviewed Ishiguro's novel for *Slate*, drew attention to the similarity between 'Hailsham' and 'Havisham', that Dickensian false mother and 'exploiter of uncomprehending children' (Atwood 2005) who lurks behind Ishiguro's novel. The notion of breeding children for the purpose of their organs is morally repugnant, but Ishiguro presents Kathy's narration as that of a young woman who has already accepted her lot. Out-and-out rebellion from within the novel is resisted—unlike in *Oryx and Crake* and many twentieth-century dystopias which focus on rebellious dissenters—and is instead replaced by tacit and unquestioning compliance. There is an insidiousness to Ishiguro's nightmare alternative world that is supported by the blandness of Kathy's narration, and this makes the novel's set-up all the more unnerving. On a point of style, this raises questions about the moral role of the narrator in recent dystopian fiction, especially when Kathy's style of narration is compared with the omniscient third-person narration of *Oryx and Crake*.

Young-adult fiction tends to rely more on the established trope of the rebel figure, although even here it is often attenuated or downplayed. Recent popular dystopias aimed specifically at the young adult market, such as James Dashner's *The Maze Runner* series (2009–), Veronica Roth's *Divergent* trilogy (2011–13), and—most popular of all—Suzanne Collins' *The Hunger Games* trilogy (2008–10), invite similar readings to the ones already discussed, although their target audience is obviously more clearly defined. All three novels have been adapted for screen to various degrees of success, helping them to reach an even bigger audience. How to introduce and teach these novels alongside mainstream literary dystopias?

This is, in one sense, surprisingly easy: as has already been seen, much contemporary dystopian fiction discussed so far in this chapter centres in part on children, teenagers, and young adults. There is much common ground shared between literary dystopia and the burgeoning young-adult dystopian genre. Issues surrounding parents and guardians are present in these novels, sometimes through the removal or marginalisation of adult characters for the main section of the narrative (as in *The Hunger Games*), which enables the younger characters to foreground their qualities of care or control: while nursing Peeta, her fellow Tribute from the same district, Katniss tells him 'I'm no good at this. I'm not my mother' (Collins 2009: 312). Yet this moment of self-deprecation also draws attention to the maternal quality in Katniss's nature and the fact that her instinct to protect and survive is, at bottom, a motherly one. She rejects the Darwinian impulse of the Games, which are themselves reminiscent of *Lord of the Flies*, choosing to survive and help others survive rather than seeking to eliminate her rivals or vie for the role of 'alpha'—typically an aspiration among males and one which, as with Atwood's dystopian novels, raises interesting questions about gender in recent works in the genre. Katniss only kills when she has to, as an act of immediate self-preservation. The novel highlights that the maternal instincts of nurture and survival can win out over the rival impulses of death and destruction. Near the close of the first novel, rather than trying to kill each other, Katniss and Peeta resolve to poison themselves, sending out a strong message to the viewers of the Games that death and self-interest need not triumph. Friendship and love can conquer death and competitiveness. In this context, we are back to the tender father of *The Road*, stroking his son's sleeping face at the beginning of the novel, keeping himself alive long enough for his child to find a new life with the 'good guys'. Like a mother living long enough to wean her children, the heart of contemporary dystopia tends to lie not so much with rebels who transgress in a treasonous political way—as figures like Winston Smith and Ray Bradbury's Guy Montag do in twentieth-century dystopias like *Nineteen Eighty-Four* and *Fahrenheit 451* (1953)—as with figures whose compassion and kindness overrule the uncaring ideologies of the world at large. The 'motherly' instinct of nurture and care must resist the 'fatherly' instinct of rule and control.

Recent young-adult dystopian fiction does tend to emphasise notions of state control more than the novels previously discussed in this chapter.

This is understandable, given the fact that younger readers are more aware of systems of authority and feel more powerless to resist authority, even when it is clearly unjust or exercised too forcefully. Yet in terms of overarching themes, how much difference exists between *Never Let Me Go* and a novel like Scott Westerfeld's *Uglies* (2005), a young-adult dystopian novel published in the same year, is open to question. Both are about young people who are scientifically controlled and altered without their permission (Westerfeld's novel centres on a future world in which plastic surgery is compulsory at age 16, in order to render everyone 'pretty'). Therefore the discussion of Ishiguro alongside Westerfeld, or Atwood's hybrid creatures from *Oryx and Crake* alongside the 'muttation' hybrids from Collins' *The Hunger Games*, presents few problems for the designer of a course or module in contemporary dystopia. Writers in both aspects of the genre tackle the same themes, and often even focus primarily on characters from the same age group. Similarly, some critics, such as Amy S. Kaufman, have read Collins' trilogy as a young-adult example of neomedievalism, something that is 'implicit in the relationship between the Capitol and the districts' (Kaufman 2013: 15).

The Hunger Games might be viewed as a miscellany of numerous popular tropes of dystopian fiction, what we might call a 'superdystopia', an allusive medley of different dystopic traditions. The novel cleverly blends the strict totalitarian control of Orwellian and other dystopias, the idea of children and adolescents fighting each other in a contained space that is also the focus of *Lord of the Flies*, and the emphasis on surveillance which is found in *Nineteen Eighty-Four*. It also contains echoes of the culture of killing as a television spectacle envisioned in Richard Bachman's cinematic adaptation of the Stephen King novel *The Running Man* (1982 [1987]) and Koushun Takami's novel *Battle Royale* (1999), also later adapted for cinema. This may suggest that young-adult dystopian fiction and literary dystopian fiction have merged to some extent. Is the future of mainstream dystopian fiction the superdystopia, where numerous established tropes of the genre are merged and recycled, like so much cultural detritus? Perhaps, for this reason, young-adult fiction provides the ideal point at which to conclude a survey of contemporary dystopian fiction, not because it suggests a culmination, but because it raises the most stimulating questions about the genre's future, and the future is where the dystopian always points.

References

Atwood, Margaret (2003) *Oryx and Crake* (London: Virago Press)

——— (2005.) 'Brave New World', *Slate*, April 1, http://www.slate.com/articles/arts/books/2005/04/brave_new_world.html <accessed 31 October 2015>

Brooks, Peter (1984) *Reading for the Plot: Design and Intention in Narrative* (London: Harvard University Press)

Busby, Mark (2009) 'Review of *The Road*', *Cormac McCarthy Journal*, 7:45–46.

Collins, Suzanne (2009) *The Hunger Games* (London: Scholastic)

Crace, Jim (2007) *The Pesthouse* (London: Picador)

Dashner, James (2013) *The Maze Runner* (Frome: The Chicken House)

Gallivan, Euan (2012) 'Cold Dimensions, Little Worlds: Self, Death, and Motion in *Suttree* and Beckett's *Murphy*', in *Intertextual and Interdisciplinary Approaches to Cormac McCarthy: Borders and Crossings*, (ed.) Nicholas Monk (Abingdon: Routledge) 145–54.

Hage, Erik (2010) *Cormac McCarthy: A Literary Companion* (London: McFarland & Company)

Howells, Coral Ann (2006) 'Margaret Atwood's Dystopian Visions: *The Handmaid's Tale* and *Oryx and Crake*', in *The Cambridge Companion to Margaret Atwood*, (ed.) Coral Ann Howells (Cambridge: Cambridge University Press) 161–75.

Ishiguro, Kazuo (2005) *Never Let Me Go* (London: Faber and Faber)

Jacobsen, J. P. (1947) *Niels Lyhne* (trans.) Hannah Astrup Larsen (London: Oxford University Press)

Josephs, Allen (2013) 'The Quest for God in *The Road*', in *The Cambridge Companion to Cormac McCarthy* (ed.) Steven Frye (Cambridge: Cambridge University Press) 133–146.

Kaufman, Amy S (2013) 'Our Future is Our Past: Corporate Medievalism in Dystopian Fiction', *Studies in Medievalism* 22:11–20.

Lindner, Oliver (2013) 'The End of the West in Contemporary Anglophone Fiction', in *From Popular Goethe to Global Pop: The Idea of the West Between Memory and (Dis)Empowerment* (eds.) Ines Detmers and Birte Heidemann (New York: Rodopi) 71–90.

Lukes, Daniel (2015) 'Surrogate Dads: Interrogating Fatherhood in Will Self's *The Book of Dave*', in *Configuring Masculinity in Theory and Literary Practice* (ed.) Stefan Horlacher (Boston: Brill Rodopi) 271–300.

McCarthy, Cormac (2006) *The Road* (London: Picador)

McCutcheon, Mark A (2010) 'The Medium is…the Monster? Global Aftermathematics in Canadian Articulations of *Frankenstein*', in *Local Natures, Global Responsibilities: Ecocritical Perspectives on the New English Literatures* (ed.) Laurenz Volkmann, Nancy Grimm, Ines Detmers, and Katrin Thomson (New York: Rodopi) 205–222.

Self, Will (2006) *The Book of Dave* (London: Penguin Books)
Spiegel, Michael (2010) 'Character in a Post-national World: Neomedievalism in Atwood's *Oryx and Crake*', *Mosaic*, 43:119–134.
Thompson, Kirsten Moana (2007) *Apocalyptic Dread: American Film at the Turn of the Millennium* (New York: State University of New York Press)
Westerfeld, Scott (2010) *Uglies* (London: Simon & Schuster)
Wood, James (2013) *The Fun Stuff and Other* Essays (London: Jonathan Cape)

Pathways to Terror: Teaching 9/11 Fiction

Mark Eaton

This chapter focuses on the growing subset of genre fiction that we might call '9/11 fiction'. The coordinated terrorist attacks that took place on 11 September 2001 resulted in almost 3000 deaths, the largest death toll of any terrorist attack in history. Writers have been trying to assess the impact and implications of the attacks ever since. 'Though a glut of material has appeared on the subject of September 11', the writer Joyce Carol Oates observed in 2006, 'very few writers of fiction have taken up the challenge and still fewer have dared to venture close to the actual event' (Oates 2006: 33). This assessment now seems premature at best. At least one short story about the events of 9/11 appeared as early as 2002—John Updike's 'The Varieties of Religious Experience' (2002)—but around the same time that Oates complained about a dearth of fiction on the subject, novels and short stories about 9/11 started appearing regularly, marking a new literary genre.

Even a partial listing gives us a sense of the sheer number and range of 9/11 fictions: Jonathan Safran Foer, *Extremely Loud and Incredibly Close* (2005); Ian McEwan, *Saturday* (2005); Ken Kalfus, *A Disorder Peculiar to the Country* (2006); Claire Messud, *The Emperor's Children* (2006); John Updike, *Terrorist* (2006); Jess Walter, *The Zero* (2006); Don

---

M. Eaton (✉)
Azusa Pacific University, Los Angeles, USA

© The Author(s) 2016

K. Shaw (ed.), *Teaching 21st Century Genres*,
DOI 10.1057/978-1-137-55391-1_7

DeLillo, *Falling Man* (2007); Andre Dubus III, *The Garden of Last Days* (2007); Moshin Hamid, *The Reluctant Fundamentalist* (2007); Joseph O'Neill, *Netherland* (2008); Zoe Heller, *The Believers* (2009); and Amy Waldman, *The Submission* (2011). All of these novels represent the terrorist attacks of 9/11 in some way, whether through characters who were directly involved as victims, perpetrators, survivors, rescue workers assigned to dig through the rubble at Ground Zero, or through characters who witnessed them from afar but have been impacted nonetheless. In much 9/11 fiction the attacks themselves function as a subtext for events that may be only tangentially related. Such indirect approaches to writing about 9/11 are increasingly evident in a number of recent novels, including Colum McCann's *Let the Great World Spin* (2009), about Philippe Petit's extraordinary stunt in 1974 when he walked on a wire suspended between the twin towers; Tom Perotta's *The Leftovers* (2011), about the aftermath of a Rapture-like event called the Sudden Departure; Colson Whitehead's *Zone One* (2011), a post-apocalyptic novel about the resettlement of lower Manhattan after a devastating pandemic; and Donna Tartt's *The Goldfinch* (2013), about a precocious teenager who survives a similar terrorist attack on the Metropolitan Museum of Art in which his mother is killed. Whether direct or indirect, explicit or implicit, 9/11 fictions arguably constitute an important twenty-first century literary genre.

In my own teaching, I have explored what this new literary genre can offer students who are struggling to understand the changing landscape of global terrorism today. Among other things, many 9/11 novels and short stories provide a rather compelling glimpse into various pathways to radicalisation taken by would-be terrorist characters, or 'pathways to terror'. By probing into some of the reasons why characters become enamored with political and religious ideologies associated with radical jihad, 9/11 fiction can offer students an 'insider', almost ethnographic account of terrorist organisations and their members. Through techniques of interiority such as free indirect discourse, writers can explore some of the reasons why terrorism might appeal to those who find a Manichean view of the world persuasive, and for whom jihad is an entirely justified struggle against perceived and real Western incursions into their homelands. While in no way justifying terrorist atrocities committed in the name of jihad, fiction about 9/11 and its aftermath prompts students to think deeply about what terrorists want and why they believe violence is justified.[1]

Students stand to gain a great deal, for instance, from the way fiction about 9/11 parses the toxic mixture of religion and politics that is promulgated by so many terrorist organisations. In *Terror in the Mind of God: The Global Rise of Religious Violence* (2003), sociologist Mark Juergensmeyer has argued that terrorism must be understood as a form of religious violence, a phenomena 'for which religion has provided the motivation, the justification, the organization, and the world view'. Juergensmeyer tries to dig a little deeper into the terrorist mindset to see if he can figure out why and how exactly religion can motivate, for instance, suicide bombings:

> I have tried to get inside the mindset of those who perpetrated and supported such acts. My goal is to understand why these acts were often associated with religious causes and why they have occurred with such frequency at this juncture in history. Although it is not my purpose to be sympathetic to people who have done terrible things, I do want to understand them and their world views well enough to know how they and their supporters can morally justify what they have done. (Juergensmeyer 2003: 7)

What he discovers is that terrorist leaders often invoke the notion of a cosmic war between forces of good and evil as an explanation for this-worldly social struggles, and that this reframing of social and political struggles into what is essentially a religious war has powerful effects. When followers begin to see their personal struggles within a framework of spiritual warfare and become part of an exclusive in-group devoted to a sacred cause, the potential for religious violence is vastly increased: 'That happens only with the coalescence of a peculiar set of circumstances—political, social, and ideological—when religion becomes fused with violent expressions of social aspirations, personal pride, and movements for political change' (Juergensmeyer 2003: 10). For Juergensmeyer, then, religion alone is necessary but not sufficient to explain suicide bombings.

Fiction confers a certain amount of freedom on writers to tease out the coalescence of religious and political motives that combine to create the conditions necessary for violence. In fiction, writers can represent the inner lives of would-be terrorists with remarkable psychological depth, even as they reconstruct the social determinants of terror in almost ethnographic detail. Scott Atran has found that 'what inspires the most lethal terrorists in the world today is not so much the Koran or religious teachings as a thrilling cause and call to action that promises glory and esteem in the eyes of friends' (Atran 2010). Atran replaces the hypothetical 'rational actor' of most political theories with what he calls a 'devoted actor' model:

an individual who becomes 'willing to protect morally important or sacred values through costly sacrifice and extreme actions, even being willing to kill and die, particularly when such values are embedded in or fused with group identity' (2010). Elsewhere, Atran and his colleague Jeremy Ginges elaborate on the features that distinguish devoted actors from rational actors: first, their devotion to an 'imagined kin' of 'brotherhoods, motherlands, fatherlands, homelands, and the like' takes precedence over any obligation or responsibility to their actual families; second, they tend to follow a 'rule-bound logic' and subscribe to a Manichean view of good and evil that overrides the usual calculus of costs and consequences; and third, they may exhibit a 'backfire effect' when 'outsiders' try to extricate them from their in-group (Atran and Ginges 2015: 70–1). When Hasib Hussain, Mohammad Sidique Khanand, and two other suicide bombers led a series of coordinated attacks in central London on 7 July 2005, for example, they were fulfilling what they considered a 'sacred commitment' to undertake terror in Europe (Lynch 2012: 2). As Khanand explained in a video recorded before his death: 'I and thousands like me are forsaking everything for what we believe. Our driving motivation doesn't come from tangible commodities that this world has to offer. Our religion is Islam, obedience to the one true God, Allah and to follow in the footsteps of the final prophet and messenger Muhammad. This is how our ethical stances are dictated' (quoted in Lynch 2012: 2).

Fictions about 9/11 and terrorism corroborate many aspects of this field research. By showing how characters drawn to extremist ideologies may eventually become devoted actors, subordinating their own interests to some larger cause and potentially sacrificing their lives for that cause, 9/11 fiction arguably fleshes out field research in ways that researchers often cannot. Researchers can only infer motivations from what their subjects tell them, whereas fiction writers can freely enter into their characters' heads and create their dreams, fears, and hatreds. According to Joseph M. Conte 'the novelist has the capacity to reveal that which cannot be represented in predominantly visual media or by nonfiction journalism' and by imaginatively entering into the minds of terrorists themselves, the novelist in effect supplies 'an interrogation of motives' (Conte 2011: 567–8). Because realist fiction depends on characterisation, and because characterisation in turn depends on the plausible motivation of characters' actions, novels and short stories about terrorism open a window on the shadowy world in which radical extremists operate. In short, teaching 9/11 fictions can serve to provide students a valuable perspective on pathways to terror.

In a few years, most students entering colleges and universities will not have been born before 2001. Yet they will have grown up at a time when the war on terror dominated headlines, even as scores of terrorist attacks were carried out in places like Bali, Madrid, London, Mumbai, Paris, San Bernardino, and so on. Students cannot help but be familiar with the barbarous acts of the Islamic State. No sooner did they learn of Osama Bin Laden's demise than ISIS had emerged Phoenix-like from the ashes of protracted wars in Afghanistan and Iraq, attracting young people to training camps in Syria and elsewhere from all over the world. Indeed, among the thousands of young people who have travelled to Syria to join the Islamic State, at least some are students themselves. Regardless of whether our students remember 9/11, or were even alive at the time, they have lived through what several prominent historians have described as the Age of Terror.[2]

Many scholars working on global terrorism—an elusive, shadowy subject—concur about the need to understand the pathways to and away from radicalisation, so that governments and law enforcement agencies can more effectively prevent terrorist attacks. As scholars and teachers in literary studies, we might suppose there is little we can contribute to such efforts. I contend that a sub-category of genre fiction offers compelling evidence of the pathways to radicalisation. Hence, 9/11 fictions offer a resource to generate discussion and critical thinking about one of the most alarming problems of our times. By studying 9/11 fictions in the classroom, students may feel they have a better grasp of how radicalisation occurs, if not necessarily how to prevent it. In his book *After the Fall: American Literature Since 9/11*, Richard Gray points out that among the ever-increasing number of works comprising this new genre 'only some are concerned with the crisis of terrorism and counter-terrorism since September 11' and the 'fictions that get it right, as I see it [...] [are] rooted in the conviction that the hybrid is the only space in which the location of cultures and the bearing witness to trauma can really occur [...] These fictions resist [...] the oppositional language of mainstream commentary—us and them, West and East, Christian and Muslim' (Gray 2011: 17). Teaching 9/11 fictions that specifically focus on the pathways to terror works best in my experience when it provokes neither outrage nor empathy but rather careful, nuanced critical thinking about radicalisation, religion, pluralism, and so on.

If nothing else, reading 9/11 fictions requires students to consider religious others. Each section of DeLillo's novel *Falling Man* closes with a short vignette of a young jihadist who goes by the name of Hammad. Since none of the 19 hijackers on 9/11 were named Hammad, 'we're entitled to imagine his character as DeLillo's representation of the mindset of the young jihadist' (Conte 2011: 565). In the first of these vignettes, titled 'On Marienstrausse', Hammad is part of a terrorist cell operating out of an apartment in Hamburg, Germany, just as the 9/11 conspirators had. 'The talk was fire and light, the emotion contagious', the narrator tells us. 'They were in this country to pursue technical educations but in these rooms they spoke about the struggle' (DeLillo 2007: 79). Hammad is increasingly influenced by the teachings of a radical Islamist leader named Amir, who turns out to be Mohamed Atta, the suspected mastermind behind 9/11. Amir is said to be 'very genius' and leads their discussions when he is not in a back room 'doing blueprints', telling them things like the following: 'The world changes first in the mind of the man who wants to change it. The time is coming, our truth, our shame, and each man becomes the other, and the other still another, and then there is no separation' (DeLillo 2007: 79–80). Alongside more practical forms of training, such as studying architecture and engineering, they are steadily being indoctrinated as part of a closed, tight knit group of terrorists: 'There was a feeling of lost history. They were too long in isolation. This is what they talked about, being crowded out by other cultures, other futures, the all-enfolding will of capital markets and foreign policies' (DeLillo 2007: 80).

The passage speaks to the terrorists' growing sense of alienation. Unlike his roommates on Marienstrasse, Hammad has a girlfriend, Leyla, but Amir admonishes him for conforming to Western norms: 'What is the difference between you and all the others, outside our space?' (DeLillo 2007: 83). Their fraternity has no room for girlfriends or wives, as Hammad knows. After Amir's dressing down, Hammad vows to resist temptation: 'He had to fight against the need to be normal. He had to struggle against himself, first, and then against the injustice that haunted their lives' (DeLillo 2007: 83). As he becomes all the more invested in ideology, and the group becomes ever more insular, or cut off from outside influences, he gives up his relationship with Leyla: 'He was becoming one of them now, learning to look like them and think like them. This was inseparable from jihad. He prayed with them to be with them. They were becoming total brothers' (DeLillo 2007: 83). In passages like these, *Falling Man* is nothing less than an astute fictional account of pathways to radicalisation, which sociologists tell us involve separation from friends and family for the sake of the in-group.

The second vignette in *Falling Man* is titled 'In Nokomis'. We pick up the trail of the Hamburg terrorist cell, which has now relocated to Florida's Gulf Coast, where they are renting a pink stucco house: 'They sat around a table on day one and pledged to accept their duty, which was for each of them, in blood trust, to kill Americans' (DeLillo 2007: 171). The terrorists shave their beards: The idea is to go unseen' (DeLillo 2007: 172). At the supermarket, Hammad observes: 'He was invisible to these people and they were becoming invisible to him' (DeLillo 2007: 171). Amir opens a bank account in his name, 'first and last, Mohamed Atta, because he was basically nobody from nowhere' (DeLillo 2007: 172).

DeLillo's fictional representation of the planning phase in the 9/11 attacks highlights the surreptitious machinations of the plotters, the near misses that might have exposed them, and the virulent anti-capitalist ideology that motivates them, which pits them in a 'cosmic war' against a demonised enemy. 'There was no feeling like this ever in his life', Hammad tells us in a passage of free indirect discourse, 'He wore a bomb vest and he knew he was a man now, finally, ready to close the distance to God' (DeLillo 2007: 172). We learn, too, of time spent in Afghanistan, where they trained as soldiers and were further indoctrinated into a militant, and highly Manichean, version of jihad: 'They received instruction in the highest jihad, which is to make blood flow, their blood and that of others' (DeLillo 2007: 173). Again, DeLillo emphasises brotherhood:

> Here they were in the midst of unbelief, in the bloodstream of the *kufr*. They felt things together, he and his brothers. They felt the claim of danger and isolation. They felt the magnetic effect of plot. Plot drew them together more tightly than ever. Plot closed the world to the slenderest line of sight, where everything converges to a point (DeLillo 2007: 174).

The plot soon converges to a suicide attack: 'They were soon to perform another kind of duty, unwritten, all of them, martyrs, together' (DeLillo 2007: 175). Mohamed Atta insists: 'There is no sacred law against what we are going to do. This is not suicide in any meaning or interpretation of the word. It is only something long written. We are finding the way already chosen for us' (DeLillo 2007: 175). In his study *The Looming Tower: Al-Qaeda and the Road to 9/11*, Lawrence Wright has argued that Mohamed Atta and the 9/11 attackers believed they were called by God, and as such they were able to override the Koran's injunction against suicide: 'They believed that they were answering God's call. If they were truly blessed, God would reward them with a martyr's death' (Wright 2006: 108). They were not committing suicide so much as becoming heroic martyrs. In *Falling Man*, Hammad is sceptical about this explanation and he asks Amir about the innocent victims: 'What about the others, those who will die?' (DeLillo 2007: 176). Annoyed, Amir explains that he had covered this objection already in Hamburg, but he answers anyway: 'Those who will die have no claim to their lives outside the useful fact of their dying' (DeLillo 2007: 176). Hammad is reassured by this answer, which sounds to him like 'philosophy' (DeLillo 2007: 177). DeLillo's character sums up the appeal of martyrdom as follows: 'We are willing to die, they are not. This is our strength, to love death, to feel the claim of armed martyrdom', a shared 'vision of heaven and hell, revenge and devastation' (DeLillo 2007: 178).[3]

The final vignette 'In the Hudson Corridor' is the shortest, but it is also the most intense. In this section, DeLillo ventures so close to the actual event as to put readers directly inside the airplane as it approaches the North tower. The author opens the section *in medias res*, as it were, after American Airlines Flight 11 has already been 'secured', with Mohamed Atta presumably at the controls while readers are with Hammad outside the cockpit, sitting in the jump seat where flight attendants normally sit for takeoff and landing. There is no sign of any flight attendants, or passengers, but we know that hijacking the plane has not been easy because the 'air was thick with the Mace he'd sprayed and there was somebody's blood, his blood, draining through the cuff of his long-sleeved shirt' (DeLillo 2007: 237). Hammad has apparently been cut 'by one of his brothers, how else, accidentally, in the struggle', but he 'doesn't know where the box cutter was' and the pain 'was becoming hard to bear' (DeLillo 2007: 237–8). We know that the 9/11 hijackers used box cutters to overtake the planes, of course, yet DeLillo is less interested in how they pulled it off than in why they undertook it in the first place. To get at the reasons why, he allows readers privileged access to the mind of a suicide bomber in the moments before death:

> Forget the world. Be unmindful of the thing called the world.
> All of life's lost time is over now.
> This is your long wish, to die with your brothers. …
> Recite the sacred words.
> Pull your clothes tightly about you.
> Carry your soul in your hand. …

> The pious ancestors had pulled their clothes tightly about them before battle. They were the ones who named the way. How could any death be better?
> Every sin of your life is forgiven in the seconds to come.
> There is nothing between you and eternal life in the seconds to come.
> You are wishing for death and now it is here in the seconds to come.
> (DeLillo 2007: 238–9)

Inspired by previous martyrs, or pious ancestors, Hammad looks for his sins to be forgiven in heaven. There is no mention of virgins, only the ironic detail: 'He fastened his seatbelt' (DeLillo 2007: 239). The passage then abruptly shifts in mid-sentence to the novel's protagonist, Keith Neudecker, sitting at his desk inside the North Tower when all of a sudden 'the aircraft struck the tower, heat, then fuel, then fire, and a blast wave passed through the structure that sent Keith Neudecker out of his char and into a wall' (DeLillo 2007: 239). With stunning economy, DeLillo shifts from the forward galley of the airplane to an office inside the towers, several floors above where it sliced into the building with tremendous force: 'The movement was beneath him and then all around him, massive, something undreamed. It was the tower lurching' (DeLillo 2007: 240). DeLillo could not resist the temptation of narrative as a means of trying to revisit, if not fully understand, the events of 9/11. 'These are the days after', one character states. 'Everything now is measured by after' (DeLillo 2007: 138).

John Updike's short story 'Varieties of Religious Experience', published in *The Atlantic Monthly* in 2002, also delves into the minds of two fictional terrorists in order to consider the nature of their attraction to martyrdom. Although their 'instructions were to blend in' so as to go undetected as they plan the last-minute details of a most spectacular suicide mission, with 'its many finely interlocked and synchronized parts', Mohamed and Nawaf find themselves in a Florida bar, seething in their rage against an 'unclean society disfigured by an appalling laxity' of morals, a 'godless democracy' that would suffer perdition under '*a blazing Fire*' when the signal came for them to carry out their mission on that 'fateful morning (Updike 2002: 96–7). At one point, the whole mission appears to be in jeopardy, 'but the All-Merciful had extended His protecting hand', and Mohamed and Nawaf continue their preparations 'for the great deed that had been laid out like a precision drawing in an engineering class' (Updike 2002: 98). Drawing upon the details of Mohammed Atta's handwritten letter to his fellow hijackers, Updike takes us behind-the-scenes as these 'masterminds of evil' plan to commit an audacious form of 'self-sacrifice', no mere suicide bombing but a mission that calls for hijacking commercial planes and flying them into the World Trade Center towers (Updike 2002: 103). The narrator gives us access to their thoughts:

> The greatness of the deed held him pressed upward like a species of nausea, straining his throat with a desire to cry out, to proclaim, as did the prophet whose name he bore, the magnificence, beyond all virtues and qualities imaginable on earth, of God and His justice. *For the unbelievers We have prepared fetters of chains, and a blazing Fire. Flames of fire shall be lashed at you, and melted brass.* (Updike 2002: 98)

Like DeLillo, Updike penetrates into the minds of men who feel threatened by Western culture, revealing the Manichean mindset that drives them to commit terror against presumed enemies. 'Determined men who have inwardly transposed their own lives to a martyr's afterlife can still inflict an amount of destruction that defies belief', he wrote in an essay in *The New Yorker*. 'Can we afford the openness that lets future kamikaze pilots, say, enroll in Florida flight schools?' (Updike 2007: 118).

Updike's subsequent novel *Terrorist* (2006) takes up this question by providing an all too plausible account of the radicalisation of a young Muslim convert named Ahmad Ashmawy Mulloy, who comes under the influence of a radical imam named Shaikh Rashid at a New Jersey mosque, Shaikh Rashid. In light of recent examples of young men and women leaving the US and attempting to join terrorist organisations abroad, the novel seems prescient.[4] By focusing on the pathways to terror for a young convert, *Terrorist* offers a compelling psychological profile of radicalisation. Consider this passage just after Ahmad has agreed to commit a suicide bombing:

> A certain simplicity does lay hold of Ahmad in the troughs between surges of terror and then of exaltation, collapsing back into an impatience to be done with it. To have it behind him, whatever 'him' will then be. He exists as a close neighbor to the unimaginable. The world in its sunstruck details, the minute scintillations of its interlocked workings, yawns all about him, a glistening bowl of busy emptiness, while within him a sodden black certainty weighs. He cannot forget the transformation awaiting him, behind, as it were, the snapped camera's shutter, even as his senses still receive their familiar bombardment of sights and sounds, scents and tastes. The luster of

> Paradise leads backward into his daily life. [...] Ahmad's every minute has taken on the intimate doubleness of prayer, the self-release of turning aside and addressing a self not his own but that of Another, a Being as close as the vein in his neck. (Updike 2006: 251–2)

For a writer who once declared 'my only duty was to describe reality as it had come to me—and to give the mundane its beautiful due', this passage is doing something rather different (Updike 2003: xvii). Far from giving the mundane its beautiful due, this passage registers a sort of 'enraptured' focus on an ineffable, transcendent realm that infuses the character's mundane world with meaning. Updike burrows into the mind of a potential suicide bomber and forces his readers into a sort of complicity with an enchanted, if also perverted, worldview that might compel submission, or what the narrator calls the 'slaglike dark weight nagging within him [that] skews his view of the world' (Updike 2003: 252). Granted, this is a fictional account of radicalisation, not an account derived from fieldwork. Nonetheless, it alerts us to the fact that whatever motivates terrorism typically does not conform to rational standards of political discourse. As Atran and Ginges persuasively argue, the most egregious acts of terror 'defy the logic of *realpolitik* (Atran and Ginges 2015: 82).

In the words of Shaikh Rashid, Ahmad's 'glorious act' of self-sacrifice will be performed in service of 'the cause of the true God, and God never deserts those who wage war on His behalf. *Allahu akbar!*' (Updike 2006: 269; 271). Ahmad draws on his faith to sustain him while performing his mission: 'we must each meet death with what faith we have created within, and stored up against the Event' (Updike 2006: 272). There is an apocalyptic aspect to his mission: 'Yes. Ahmad will be God's servant. Tomorrow' (Updike 2006: 274). No wonder he refers to Mohammed Atta and his co-conspirators as 'inspired martyrs' (Updike 2006: 275). Ahmad wakes up the next day ready to join them in Paradise, and like them, he is almost preternaturally alert and focused on the task at hand:

> He moves swiftly, without running. He must not attract attention, he must slip through the city unseen. Later would come the headlines, the CNN reports filling the Middle East with jubilation, making the tyrants in their opulent Washington offices tremble. For now the tremble, the mission are still his, his secret, his task [...] because what he does now occurs within the palm of God's hand, His vast encompassing will. (Updike 2006: 281–282)

Ahmad's mission is to drive a truck full of explosives into the Lincoln Tunnel and detonate it, killing everyone inside, including himself. Mindful of his special role as 'the final piece' of the terrorist plot, Ahmad proceeds to his intended target, the Lincoln Tunnel: 'He is not thinking normally, in this exalted yet thin atmosphere of last things. He must keep his head level by conceiving of himself as God's instrument, cool and hard and definite and thoughtless, as an instrument must be' (Updike 2006: 284–5). The novel offers a terrifying glimpse into the mind of terror.

Compare these fictional treatments of radicalisation with Martin Amis' short story 'The Last Days of Muhammad Atta' in *The Second Plane September 11: Terror and Boredom* (2008). Like DeLillo and Updike, Amis approaches the problem of terrorism from the inside, as it were, by trying to understand what motivated the mastermind behind the 9/11 attacks. 'Muhammad Atta was not religious; he was not even especially political', the narrator tells us. 'He had allied himself with the militants because jihad was, by any magnitudes, the most charismatic idea of his generation. To unite ferocity and rectitude in a single word: nothing could compete with that' (Amis 2008: 99). Similarly, Amis' short story delves into the group dynamics of the terrorist cell: 'A peer group piously competitive about suicide [...] was a very powerful thing, and the West had no equivalent to it. A peer group for whom death was not death—and life was not life, either' (Amis 2008: 113). And when he probes further into the mind of Mohammad Atta, Amis begins to demonstrate what fiction can do to disclose the ideological contortions of terror: 'Strapped in, Muhammad Atta managed the following series of thoughts: You *needed* the belief system, the ideology, the ardor' (Amis 2008: 116). As in *Falling Man*, Amis' narrator then ventures inside the character's mind at the moment of impact:

> American 11 struck at 8:46:40. Muhammad Atta's body was beyond all healing by 8:46:41; but his mind, his presence, needed time to shut itself down. The physical torment—a panic attack in every nerve, a riot of the atoms—merely italicized the last shinings of his brain. They weren't thoughts; they were more like a series of unignorable conclusions, imposed from without. Here was the hereafter, after all; and here was the reckoning. His mind groaned and fumbled with an irreconcilability, a defeat, a self-cancellation. Could he assemble the argument? It follows—by definition—if and only if...
>
> And then the argument assembled all by itself. The joy of killing was proportional to the value of what was destroyed. (Amis 2008: 120)

What distinguishes this fictional account of Muhammad Atta's worldview from the one represented by DeLillo, however, is that it seems 'more like a series of unignorable conclusions, imposed from without'. Arguably, Amis cannot resist being a bit too pedantic in this short story. 'Here was the primordial secret', he tells us. 'No longer closely guarded—no longer well kept. Killing was divine delight. And your suicide was just part of the contribution you made—the massive contribution to death' (Amis 2008: 119).

Two additional novels about 9/11, Mohsin Hamid's *The Reluctant Fundamentalist* (2007) and Zoe Heller's *The Believers* (2009), represent somewhat similar attempts to account for the apparent appeal of extremism as a sort of crusade against Western domination. Far from being shocked while watching the events of 9/11 unfold, the reluctant fundamentalist recognises instead 'that I had always resented the manner in which America conducted itself in the world; your country's constant interference in the affairs of others was insufferable' (Hamid 2007: 156). The character even goes so far as to say that 'no country inflicts death so readily upon the inhabitants of other countries [...] as America' (Hamid 2007: 182). On the verge of losing his job with Samson Underwood anyway, he feels like a pawn in someone else's game and decides he can no longer work for the company. 'I had become', he says, 'a servant of the American empire at a time when it was invading a country with a kinship to mine and as perhaps even colluding to ensure that my own country faced the threat of war' (Hamid 2007: 152). So he quits his job and converts to Islam, refusing 'to participate any longer in facilitating this project of domination' (Hamid 2007: 156). The narrator's motivations are notably less religious than political in nature, for according to the reluctant fundamentalist: 'finance was a primary means by which the American empire exercised its power' (Hamid 2007: 156). Later, he lectures his interlocutor throughout the novel, Jim, on the hubris of American exceptionalism:

> As a society, you were unwilling to reflect upon the shared pain that united you with those who attacked you. You retreated into myths of your own difference, assumptions of your own superiority. And you acted out these beliefs on the stage of the world, so that the entire planet was rocked by the repercussions of your tantrums [...] Such an America had to be stopped in the interests not only of the rest of humanity, but also in your own. (Hamid 2007: 168)

Jim turns out to be an undercover CIA agent sent to assassinate the reluctant fundamentalist, a Marlow to the narrator's Kurtz, as evidenced by the 'glint of metal' that flashes when the agent pulls some object out from inside his jacket in the final pages of the novel (Hamid 2007: 184). Hamid's *The Reluctant Fundamentalist* follows its protagonist down the path of radicalisation, even though the novel's ambiguous ending suggests that whatever terrorist plot he had in mind was averted.

Zoe Heller's novel *The Believers* covers similar terrain, but from a different point of view. In this novel, the lawyer Joel Litvinoff is defending a man accused of plotting terrorism, Mohammed Hassani, who is allegedly one of the fictional Schenectady Six, 'a group of Arab Americans from upstate New York who had visited an al-Qaeda training camp in Afghanistan' (Heller 2008: 22). While Joel defends his client on religious grounds, arguing before the court that Hassani had 'traveled to Afghanistan on the understanding that he was to take part in a spiritual retreat', not realising that it was in fact a terrorist training camp, since the Imam at his local mosque 'had deliberately misrepresented the camp as a religious center' (Heller 2008: 22). Joel's wife Audrey disagrees with this tactic; she believes her husband should defend Hassina 'on grounds of legitimate Arab rage', or in other words, as 'a perfectly rational anger against the American hegemon' (Heller 2008: 23; 36). 'People bang on about fundamentalist Islam and religious fanatics', Audrey declares, 'but it's obvious no one is inspired by bin Laden for *religious* reasons' (Heller 2008: 35). In a brilliant twist, however, Heller subtly reveals that Audrey's radical views are themselves a form of fundamentalism not unlike that of the religious fundamentalists whom she abhors. For all her antipathy to religion, she clearly has 'a gift for conviction' (Heller 2008: 37). Indeed, 'Audrey's attachment to her dogma' was such that not 'even the cataclysmic events of the previous September had put her off stride for more than a couple of hours. By lunchtime on the day that the towers fell, when the rest of New York was still stumbling about in a daze, Audrey had already been celebrating the end of the myth of American exceptionalism and comparing the event to the American bombing of a Sudanese factory in 1998' (Heller 2008: 37). A lifelong friend, Jean, finds Audrey's response to 9/11 chilling. Heller intriguingly suggests that Audrey too is among the believers indicated by the novel's title. *The Believers*, then, dares to explore possible continuities between different forms of radicalism, prompting us to question whether there really is greater polarisation along political and religious lines, as many pundits have alleged. A sophisticated fictional account of ideological blind spots that afflict the left and right alike, *The Believers* is surely among the more nuanced 9/11 fictions.

'In the last decade', John Duvall writes, 'American fiction has articulated important political, aesthetic, and psychological contexts for understanding the wounds of September 11' (Duvall 2012: 181). Critical accounts of literature about 9/11 have tended to focus on the problem of representation, asking what literature can possibly say in the wake of such a traumatic event?[5] Instead, this chapter focuses on the problem of radicalisation, asking what literature can potentially tell us about the pathways to terror that have led to atrocities committed in the name of God. Drawing on the work of sociologists who contend that suicide bombings and the like are committed by 'devoted' rather than rational actors, this chapter has tried to understand the roots of terrorism. With its highly developed techniques for representing interiority, such as free indirect discourse, literary fiction affords a supple means to explore conflicted and often contradictory motivations of these devoted actors—by entering into the minds of actual terrorists themselves, for instance, or by representing the paths taken by those who seem drawn, for whatever reasons, to extremism. By dramatising these internal and ideological conflicts as lived experience, fiction writers have disclosed the complex processes by which individuals may come to understand their world through a distorting, Manichean lens that pits believers against apostates, while understanding their martyrdom as a calling by God to sacrifice themselves for the sake of a supposedly sacred mission. Novels of terror are by no means reassuring—indeed, they are downright dystopian—yet they are nonetheless instructive. We could do worse than to learn what we can from them. Teaching 9/11 fictions will not likely do much to ameliorate the current crisis of global terrorism, but perhaps it will give students tools for thinking about how we might divert pathways to terror.

Notes

1. In *What Terrorists Want: Understanding the Enemy, Containing the Threat*, Louise Richardson rejects the view that trying to understand what motivates terrorists is tantamount to sympathising with their cause. She insists, on the contrary, 'that the best way to contain terrorism is to understand its appeal and to use this understanding to forge effective counterterrorist policies' (2006: xx).

2. Strobe Talbot and Nyan Chanda, *The Age of Terror: America and the World After September 11* (New York: Basic Books, 2002).
3. In his remarkable essay 'In the Ruins of the Future' (2001), DeLillo ascribes the same tactical advantage to terrorists but inverts the point of view from which he describes it: 'We are rich, privileged, and strong, but they are willing to die. This is the edge they have, the fire of aggrieved belief' (DeLillo 2001: 34).
4. A number of US citizens have attempted to join terrorist organizations in recent years, from the adolescent in Texas who journeyed to Afghanistan to be trained in terrorist camps to the Pennsylvania housewife who became well known by her Internet moniker, Jihad Jane. See Elliott (2010).
5. Gray begins his study of American literature since 9/11 by citing Toni Morrison's elegiac tribute: 'I have nothing to say—no words stronger than the steel that pressed you into itself; no scripture older or more elegant than the ancient atoms you have become' (Gray 2011: 1).

References

Amis, Martin (2008) *The Second Plane September 11: Terror and Boredom* (New York: Knopf)

Atran, Scott (2010) 'Pathways to and from Violent Extremism: The Case for Science-Based Field Research', in *Statement Before the Senate Armed Services Subcommittee on Emerging Threats & Capabilities*, https://edge.org/conversation/pathways-to-and-from-violent-extremism-the-case-for-science-based-field-research <accessed 7 December 2015>

Atran, Scott, and Jeremy Ginges (2015) 'Devoted Actors and the Moral Foundations of Intractable Intergroup Conflict' in *The Moral Brain: A Multidisciplinary Perspective* (eds.) Jean Decety and Thalia Wheatley (Cambridge, MA: The MIT Press) 69–86.

Conte, Joseph M (2011) 'Don DeLillo's *Falling Man* and the Age of Terror', *Modern Fiction Studies* 57.3, 559–83.

DeLillo, Don (2007) *Falling Man* (New York: Scribner's)

DeLillo, Don (2001) 'In the Ruins of the Future: Reflections on Terror and Loss in the Shadow of September', *Harpers*, 33–40.

Duvall, John N. (2012) 'Fiction and 9/11', in *The Cambridge Companion to Post-1945 American Fiction*, (ed.) John N. Duvall (Cambridge: Cambridge University Press) 1–14.

Elliott, Andrea (2010) 'The Jihadist Next Door', *The New York Times Magazine* 27 January, http://www.nytimes.com/2010/01/31/magazine/31Jihadist-t.html?pagewanted=all&_r=0 <accessed 14 July 2010>

Gray, Richard (2011) *After the Fall: American Literature Since 9/11* (Oxford: Wiley-Blackwell)

Hamid, Moshin (2007) *The Reluctant Fundamentalist* (New York: Harcourt, 2007)

Heller, Zoe (2008) *The Believers* (New York: Knopf)

Juergensmeyer, Mark (2003) *Terror in the Mind of God: The Global Rise of Religious Violence* (Berkeley: University of California Press)

Lynch, Gordon (2012) *The Sacred in the Modern World: A Cultural Sociological Approach* (New York: Oxford University Press)

Oates, Joyce Carol (2006) 'Dimming the Lights', *New York Review of Books* 6 April, 33-36.

Richardson, Louise (2006) *What Terrorists Want: Understanding the Enemy, Containing the Threat* (New York: Random House)

Updike, John (2007) *Due Considerations: Essays and Criticism* (New York: Knopf)

Updike, John (2006) *Terrorist* (New York: Knopf)

——— (2003) *The Early Stories: 1953-1975* (New York: Random House)

——— (2002) 'Varieties of Religious Experience', *The Atlantic Monthly* November, 93–104.

Wright, Lawrence (2006) *The Looming Tower: Al-Qaeda and the Road to 9/11* (New York: Knopf)

PART FOUR

World Literature

Teaching Translit: An Unsettled and Unsettling Genre

Bianca Leggett

Translit is a new genre of literature characterised by a fragmented narrative structure which shifts, not only between different periods and places, but also between different genres. The term was first coined by author Douglas Coupland in his book review for *The New York Times* on 8 March 2012. In the weeks that followed, 'translit' appeared in a number of literary blogs which debated the validity of the term and the likelihood of its 'slipping into the lexicon' (Coupland 2012).[1] Following this, translit largely disappeared from view until, in 2015, the term was referenced by a small number of academic essays and books in both the USA and UK.[2] Translit has proved to be of interest chiefly to postcolonial scholars and theorists of contemporary literature more broadly, although it is also referenced briefly in the writings of the eminent geographer David Lowenthal (2015: 68).

The link between the fields of literary studies, geography and translit is offered by transnationalism. Coupland argues that the emergent genre of translit, in which an over-arching plot is pieced together from fragments of narrative scattered across history and throughout the world, is 'an embodiment of our new world of flattened time and space' (2012). Central to Coupland's definition is, however, the insistence that

B. Leggett (✉)
Birkbeck, University of London, London, UK

© The Author(s) 2016

K. Shaw (ed.), *Teaching 21st Century Genres*,
DOI 10.1057/978-1-137-55391-1_8

translit is 'genre shifting', and that science fiction forms a distinct part of the eclectic blend which it represents. The translit novel is, he argues, one in which time-travel and UFOs might sit alongside commentary on twenty-first-century economics or a historical passage about the conquest of the New World. It is perhaps surprising, then, that there is no evidence of translit being adopted as a term of interest to scholars of genre, or of science fiction. Nevertheless, translit, a hybrid form of genre fiction which remains relatively obscure, is a fascinating and valuable topic on which to focus as part of a module which looks at genre fiction more broadly.

By outlining the genesis of the term translit, my intent has been to underline the extent to which translit remains an unsettled term. It is this unsettled quality which makes translit such an interesting, and indeed unsettling, topic to teach. While genre fiction modules often aim to introduce students to what is considered to be most central and salient in the developing field of genre literature studies, translit is by contrast a peripheral, perhaps an ephemeral, term. In this chapter I will suggest reasons for teaching translit, outlining a series of practical exercises which dwell on the term itself as well as on the literary text for which the term was first coined, Hari Kunzru's *Gods Without Men* (2014). The module I explore here is designed to prompt students to think critically about the terminology they use, raising questions about how a critical discourse is created and sustained as well as how it effects the way that they approach a literary text.

I draw here on my own experience of teaching translit as a session within a wider ranging module of twenty-first-century fiction, which I co-designed and co-taught in 2013–14.[3] What follows, however, are suggestions for a more sustained treatment of translit over a period of four classes which might make up part of a larger module concerned with genre fiction. This intense focus on translit is also designed to touch on broader concerns as regards the purpose and functioning of cultural criticism in the academy and beyond. Translit is best taught to students who have some familiarity with genre fiction already so that, on encountering a hybrid translit text, they can recognise that different fragments of the story manifest characteristics of distinctly different genres. For such students, translit's tendency to move outside of the boundaries of the genres in which it locates itself—to set up expectations of certain rules only to break with them—should prove an intriguing object of study.

Introducing Translit ('for Lack of a Better Word')

A module which teaches translit must begin by spending significant time answering the seemingly simply question—what is it? Your students should be told to prepare for their first class by reading Coupland's article 'Convergences' (2012), which offers a book review of Hari Kunzru's *Gods Without Men* which posits a theory that this novel belongs to a larger emergent genre, namely translit.

Translit texts, as Coupland describes them, are defined by shared features which relate to structure, hybrid genre and thematic concerns as well as a shared general outlook on the zeitgeist, or rather—as Coupland has it—an age in which 'we have a lot of *zeit* but not much *geist*'. Translit texts are network narratives in which multiple plot strands—often taking place in a diverse range of global locations and/or at different points in the past, present or future—intersect only loosely. Coupland lists translit's precursors as 'say, *Winesburg, Ohio* and *Orlando*' while 'the genre's 21st-century tent poles are Michael Cunningham's novel *The Hours* and David Mitchell's *Cloud Atlas*'. Coupland writes that, a 'long-form solidity emerges, even though the links between substories can be as ethereal as a snatch of music'. The fragmentation of the narrative has implications for the way such novels are read, calling for the reader to take a pronouncedly active part in assimilating the plot since the 'author assumes the reader has the wits to connect the dots'. Coupland speculates that the ability to move between and manipulate genre conventions may be becoming a prerequisite of 'being a writer in 2012', with translit—which practises 'genre shifting'—displaying the tendency at its most marked. He moves from this idea to the rather grander claim that such 'genre shifting' is, in fact, a 'statement of fact about the 21st-century condition'. This 'condition' is one which Coupland suggests is mutable and 'extreme', yet also affectless, flat and 'psychically sparse'. This, he argues, accounts for translit's tendency to move hectically between different temporalities, since ours is an age in which time and space have collapsed in upon themselves so that 'all eras coexist at once [...] a state of possibly permanent atemporality given to us courtesy of the Internet'.

You may wish to spend some time in class reading the article or otherwise ascertaining whether your students have understood the article by asking them to summarise its main points back to you. Ideally these should be gathered together on a board or screen where they can be returned to later in class, helping students to organise their responses to the article as they move from summarising its contents to beginning, tentatively at first, to evaluate them.

With this definition of translit complete, you are free to throw open a wider discussion about genre itself, namely: what is a genre, and what purpose does it serve? Students may be drawn to answers which reflect on how genre is used in teaching and learning within the academy, so it may be useful to direct them to think more broadly by asking them what reasons a cultural critic might have for inventing a new term to describe a genre. The point here is to prompt students to move on from simply understanding and assimilating a critical position and instead to think about the mechanisms of criticism itself, setting the tone for the rest of the module. Discussions might touch upon the relative authority of critic and author in defining genre, perhaps bringing in the question of the role of booksellers and readers too. This should go some way to helping students to understand that genre classifications are artificial constructs which, though they can usefully guide the way we respond to a text, are nevertheless always open to question.

Having established that a genre can be critiqued, ask your students to consider how we can go about critiquing the claims which Coupland makes. Here your summarised points of the different claims made within the article will prove useful. Some of the claims which Coupland makes are merely descriptive of the novel he reviews so can be easily evaluated: either the novels he mentions conform to certain thematic or formal characteristics he describes or they do not. Others are clearly more subjective, particularly the claims which Coupland makes for what he calls our 'extreme present', that is, the quality of contemporary life. The testing of these ideas will make up the central focus of subsequent classes, to which I will return.

In this first class, however, attention should be focused on Coupland's claim that translit is 'what must undeniably be called a new genre'. Ask your students how we can test such a claim. They may suggest that the authority of the article depends on where it appears, here *The New York Times*. They may also suggest that the author's reputation is important to our conclusions and for this it may be useful to supply students with a brief biography and bibliography of Douglas Coupland. Coupland's reputation for popularising terms such as 'McJob' and 'Generation X' merits discussion, although whether this history reveals Coupland to have talent for describing the zeitgeist or simply for perpetuating soundbites is, of course, open to dispute.

The discussion should be turned to the more challenging matter, how can we know if Coupland is right about the newness of translit? To move this discussion forward, give your students a second article to read: Bruce Sterling's 1989 article 'Catscan 5: Slipstream', which appeared in *SF Eye*. Translit's tendency towards 'genre shifting', as Coupland calls it, is certainly similar to Sterling's slipstream, that is, that genre of novels which deploys the tropes of science fiction and/or magical realism in the service of a text which is largely received as realist. By placing these articles side by side, we can ask the question: has Coupland simply cluttered the debate with a term of his own when an older and more established one might have served better?

Since there are valid arguments to be made on each side, this has the potential to be a lively debate whose final implications can be left open. It could be argued that Coupland's failure to mention slipstream is suspicious, suggesting either that he is falsely exaggerating the novelty of the phenomenon he describes, or perhaps that he is unfamiliar with the term. The article gives the impression that Coupland is a somewhat reluctant reader of science fiction: he congratulates the author of the novel he reviews for keeping 'the extraterrestrial hokum to a minimum'. It seems possible that slipstream novels and the discourse which surrounds them have passed him by, giving a skewed impression of just how new a phenomenon so-called translit novels really are. This might also account for the lack of interest in translit displayed, to date, by scholars of science fiction.

On the other hand, the term translit, though it bears similarities to slipstream, exceeds the definition. It also carries suggestion of a particular structure, that is, one which is fragmented, moving between different times and places. The fact that the term arises 25 years later may also be significant, particularly given Coupland's insistence that translit responds to particular aspects of its twenty-first-century context, particularly the more globalised nature of the world and the impact of digital technologies. More subtly, it might be remarked that the term 'slipstream' carries with it the suggestion of a bygone era when it was taken for granted that genre fiction and the mainstream were mutually exclusive, perhaps even that the common reader would only encounter science fiction if it were 'slipped' to them. It could be argued that slipstream is an important precursor of translit, but that Coupland's term reveals that the process first remarked upon by Sterling—the mingling of science fiction tropes with realist texts—has become part of the mainstream itself rather than a mere tributary. Conducting this discussion as a debate, allocating students a position for which they must find evidence, might help to prompt them to take a decisive position as well as providing a link to the next class in which students will see how other cultural critics have responded to Coupland's article, beginning with literary bloggers.

Geeks and Academics

In the last session, your students will have gained some understanding of what translit is and how we can approach the task of evaluating its validity as a piece of critical terminology. This next session looks more at questions of how translit has been received, requiring students to think about how critical terminology acquires authority once it has been proposed. Such investigations carry students into thinking about the function of the academy and of forums for criticism outside it, particularly those in the digital sphere. Each class should ideally begin with a question that students can wrangle over, trying to solve through the process of the class. In this case, the question moves from 'What is translit?' and 'Is translit really a new genre?' to, 'How has translit been received?' and, more challengingly, 'Do some opinions matter more than others?'

The central reading for this class is an article by Robert Eaglestone 'Contemporary fiction in the academy: a manifesto', in which he asks, 'When reading contemporary fiction, what differentiates a geek or journalist or member of a reading group from an academic?' (2013: 1089). The answer, it transpires, is not very much: experts who operate outside of the academy have their own 'specialist publications', 'forms of writing', 'prizes' and are comprised of people who 'like we academics, can read carefully and closely' (2013: 1090). Eaglestone fears that the boundaries which demarcate the discipline are becoming 'all too permeable', diluting the academy's claims of 'mastery' over its subject matter. In response, he sets out a manifesto which looks to delineate those boundaries more clearly by defining the nature of what the academic's 'mastery' should ideally be. Academics are different primarily in that they are part of a discipline who can agree on their shared field of study and, more importantly, on what questions are asked within that field: 'You have come close to understanding a discipline when you know what questions its practitioners ask and how they are answered' (2013: 1092). That field reaches 'maturity' in its ability to question its own founding principles, to move forwards through a series of crises.

The debate as to what this 'mastery' means in contemporary literary studies is one in which students and teachers are heavily invested. It matters to students because the question of how to evaluate sources is a pressing one in literary studies, but particularly in regards to responding to a contemporary text, which often provokes an abundance of accessible online responses from journalists and bloggers well before academic criticism is readily available. It also matters to students in the grander sense because they have invested considerable time, effort and funds in securing a qualification whose value rests on a claim to the expertise to which Eaglestone alludes. The evaluation of the term 'translit', which originates in literary journalism but has migrated to the periphery of academic discourse, allows for these matters to be discussed in a seminar setting. This is potentially disquieting: in an age in which universities speak nervously about enrolment numbers and retention rates, academics might be forgiven for avoiding a conversation which encourages students to question the value of their university education. Yet, the question of hierarchies of cultural value is one which is already a necessary discussion in the teaching of genre fiction. It has been my experience that students not only emerge from such conversations with their faith in liberal education intact, but satisfied that they are better able to articulate a robust defence of its values.

Alongside reading Eaglestone's article, students should be given a task to complete: find one online source which considers translit and assess how useful it is as an academic source. For example, a student might chance upon James McGirk's article 'Translit is neither new nor subversive' (2012). In assessing McGirk's credentials as critic, it should be noted that a link is provided to a biographical paragraph which makes mention of his qualifications and teaching experience within the academy alongside his publishing record as a literary journalist. The article appeared in *3quarksdaily*, an online magazine that describes itself as a place to present 'interesting items from around the web each day in the areas of science, design, literature, current affairs, art, and anything else we deem inherently fascinating'. This, taken from the site's 'About Us' section, is accompanied by a number of testimonials of esteem, mostly from academics. One reads:

> I have placed *3 Quarks Daily* at the head of my list of web bookmarks.
> (Richard Dawkins, previously Charles Simonyi Professor of the Public Understanding of Science at Oxford University, 2012)

On one level, this testimonial suggests a spirit of deference by online journalism towards the academy, yet the use of Dawkins—whose cultural capital rests largely on his role as a public intellectual—hints again at the uncertain standards by which 'mastery' is judged. The evidence suggests that online content claims a relationship to academic authority to boost its own prestige, but leaves open the question of how we evaluate whether it represents a parallel or subordinate form of commentary.

This question can be answered in part by drawing attention to the use McGirk's 2012 article makes of academic thinkers. McGirk makes a comparison between Coupland's article and those of Francis Fukuyama: 'Fukuyama's End of History perished in the flames of the World Trade Center,' he concludes, 'No need to revisit it in our fiction.' The implication is that Coupland's article, and Fukuyama's ideas, are inherently conservative; that the idea that the weight of history can be dispensed with lightly betrays a deep complacency that the neoliberal world order cannot be challenged. This reference to Francis Fukuyama evidences that online journalism can draw on academic discourse, a reminder once again of the permeability of the membrane which separates one from the other. Yet it also provides a reminder of the kind of long form thinking which takes place in the academy; short think-pieces such as these can draw on this discourse, but cannot reciprocate with more than an impressionistic response. An example such as this can help students to understand why such journalism can justifiably be viewed as secondary, a place in which ideas are responded to or digested, but rarely generated.

Students could also be encouraged to note the differences between online magazines and academic journals along formal lines. They may note obvious differences relating to the length of the article or the lack of footnotes, or perhaps differences in style or tone. To these, the tutor of the class might raise questions of who edits the article or explain the value attached to peer-review in academic circles. By comparing this to the Eaglestone article, a discussion might be staged which not only helps students to recognise what sets an academic article apart, but allows for some discussion as to what the academy is for. Ultimately the exercise may serve to heighten critical awareness of how academic 'mastery' manifests itself in the sources we read, even while it admits that the permeability of the boundary between academic writing and other modes of discourse is quite fragile. Although it invites students to make use of sources like *3quarksdaily*, the exercise also instils the importance of evaluating such sources within the context of a larger conversation, which tends to find fullest, most original and most rigorous expression in academic sources. Students should now have gained a fuller sense of how translit has been received and begun to appreciate why academic discourse carries the weight that it does without closing down the question of whose opinion matters too definitively. Having completed this task, students will be ready to move from evaluating literary criticism to practising it for themselves.

'Genre Shifting'

Having spent two sessions thinking about the term translit itself, its initial definition and its reception, the third session moves on to a literary text, that is, the novel which is, according to Coupland, translit's exemplar, Hari Kunzru's *Gods Without Men* (2012). Since the novel, at 400 pages, is quite long, students should be warned to begin reading in plenty of time. The novel's hybrid approach to genre can be disorienting, making it hard for the reader to form expectations of the plot or a stable sense of the conventions at work. In this it is clearly an example of 'genre shifting', as Coupland calls it, but is it—as he claims—more than just a 'postmodern party trick' (2012)? This question should form the focus of the subsequent session.

This question requires some analysis before proceeding, since students may not readily recognise why the charge of 'postmodern party trick' is undesirable, or indeed feel confident that they can recognise characteristics associated with postmodernism. If this presents problems, the question might be simplified to 'Are there artistic reasons which justify the author's use of multiple genres, or is it just a gimmick?' You might begin by asking students how the use of multiple genres affected their enjoyment of the novel but, having allowed some time for the sharing of these kinds of responses, they should be gently guided towards more technical questions. Ask students what genres they can identify and where the shifts occurred then move on to asking what purpose they think these shifts in genre serve.

Students are likely to find this second question much more difficult to answer. Here a focus on the text can help build a more complex response to the novel which allows students to come back round to the question in hand after greater reflection. An initial exercise might look closely at the epigraphs with which Kunzru's novel begins. They read as follows:

> Dans le désert, voyez-vous, il y a tout, et il n'y a rien… c'est Dieu sans les hommes.
> (Balzac, 'Une passion dans le désert', 1830)
> De Indio y Negra, nace Lobo, de Indio y Mestiza, nace Coyote…
> (Andrés de Islas, *Las Castas*, 1774)
> My God! It's full of stars!
> (Arthur C. Clarke, *2001: A Space Odyssey*, 1968)

True to translit's tendency to shift between time, place and genre, these extracts point to Kunzru's intention to look to a range of influences that originate from three different centuries, are expressed in three different languages and, key to this discussion, represent three different genres. The juxtaposition of Balzac and Arthur C. Clarke is particularly important for hinting at the slipstream qualities that are central to translit, in which the influence of a nineteenth-century realist and of a twentieth-century science fiction writer can sit side by side. The de Islas quote suggests two other genres which are woven into the novel's fabric. Certain sections of *Gods Without Men* are set in 1798, made up of the letters of a Spanish missionary who reports back on the progress made by his Mission amongst a group of Native Americans in the Mojave Desert, an element of a historical novel in an otherwise twentieth- and twenty-first-century narrative. Secondly, the reference to 'coyote' introduces a trope, taken from Native American mythology, that will recur throughout the novel, a means by which a kind of magical realism enters the text. In this epigraph, however, 'coyote' refers to an archaic racial term used by the Spanish in the eighteenth century as part of an elaborate taxonomy of the peoples they encountered in the New World. The quote from de Islas is, in fact, a series of captions to his paintings that depict taxonomies of race. 'Coyote' is the term used to describe a person whose origins are part Native American, part mixed race.[4]

With this information, the conversation can be moved on from considering what the epigraphs can tell us about the way Kunzru intends to use genre and temporality, to how it sets up thematic concerns. By asking students to find these connections, they begin to 'connect the dots', as Coupland (2012) has it, to bring attention to elements of correspondence throughout the novel which they may have missed on the first reading. The de Islas quote, for example, might suggest that Kunzru is interested in the wider implications of European cultural imperialism for the way identity is understood, particularly in the rendering of certain groups as other or inferior. While this theme plays out most obviously in the 1798 sections, it might also be traced to the twenty-first-century stories, most suggestively to a plot thread which offers an oblique angle on the war in Iraq and its aftermath. The thread is focalised through an Iraqi-American girl who has reluctantly agreed to play the role of an insurgent in a surreal military training exercise, which requires her to live in a simulated version of an Iraqi village. The village is constructed in the Mojave Desert, which is to say, on the same site as the eighteenth-century Spanish Mission. Like the missionaries before them, the soldiers' apparently benevolent motives towards the 'villagers' prove to be severely compromised by elements of self-interest and the skewed power-structure which underpins their interactions.

By bringing together these two apparently unrelated stories which take place centuries apart, Kunzru draws a telling parallel between two different stories of cultural imperialism.

While, arguably, *Gods Without Men* has no core plot, it has certain fables which are discernible in several different plot threads which acquire resonance through repetition. There is a strong argument to be made that interconnectivity is both a formal principle at work in the novel and, as Coupland claims, its 'ultimate theme'. If students can recognise this, they will be able to access a level of the novel which may not have been apparent to them on first reading; they will move from an impression of the novel as a collection of impressionistic stories to being able to 'connect the dots'. In this way, an understanding of the term translit can heighten our awareness of certain features of the novel. As such, this exercise demonstrates one of the ways in which the term translit could be useful to us as readers.

What emerges from this exercise are ideas which potentially refute the possibility that Kunzru's structure is more than a 'postmodern party trick', or rather, make a strong argument that the fragmented novel is integral to the novel's thematic concerns. According to Coupland the 'ultimate theme' of the novel is itself 'connectivity', an idea which can be linked back to his suggestion that the novel echoes something about the world itself in 2012. This last point offers a useful bridge to the last class in which students will look more closely at what ideas Coupland expresses about the properties, qualities and major concerns of life in 2012 and, more challengingly, consider how we go about evaluating whether there is any substance in what he says.

'Our Extreme Present'

Students should now be accustomed to a structure in which the class begins with a question, which in turn forms part of an evaluation of the term translit, which draws on a context beyond the article itself including the ideas of earlier critics, contemporaries and literary texts. In the final class, focus turns to Coupland's description of translit's capacity to reflect what he calls 'our extreme present', which is described variously as a 'spiritually sparse age' with 'zeit' but not 'geist', and as an era of 'flattened time and space' in which technology 'connects us to our cores' and yet also 'fails'. This final question has two parts. First, does Coupland's review represent an insightful reading of *Gods Without Men* and second, more challengingly, how accurate is his description of the world in 2012?

Begin by breaking down aspects of Coupland's commentary that may require word definitions or further explanation, leading into a discussion in which students' personal responses are invited. Do we live in an unspiritual age? Does technology alienate us from each other and from ourselves, or can it connect us to each other at our 'core'? Students often become opinionated and lively in conversations that allow them to give insights taken from their personal experiences. The risk here, of course, is that students come to believe that an instinctive response is all that is required. Students need reminding that one of the ways in which we reach the multiple possibilities of meaning within a literary text is by uncovering the ways it connects to other thinkers, writers and literary texts as to its social and political context. To access this level of meaning requires the reader to work harder, drawing on a larger frame of reference than personal experience.

Return then to the text in order to find evidence that supports just one of Coupland's insights about the novel's reflection of the 'extreme present', for example, the complicated relationship he suggests between technology and spirituality. A useful starting point here would be to familiarise students with 'Clarke's Third Law', that is Arthur C. Clarke's edict, that 'Any sufficiently advanced technology is indistinguishable from magic' (1974: 39). Students may readily suggest that technology has a negative effect on our capacity for introspection and represents a barrier to intimacy with others. The idea that technology—or perhaps the promise of technology—can simultaneously represent a kind of re-enchantment, the means by which a sense of the numinous or magical enters day-to-day life, may be less readily apparent. Challenge your students to find something in the novel in which science and technology are linked to the promise of a magical, spiritual or otherwise other-worldly realm. *Gods Without Men* is a rich and fascinating novel and with luck your students will find multiple examples: a story which concerns a cult whose followers believe in a divine species of aliens, for example, or a reference to the techno-fable *2001: A Space Odyssey* in the novel's epigraph.

One of the most intriguing examples is perhaps a plot thread which concerns a quantitative analyst named Jaz Matheru. At a key point in the novel, Jaz contemplates the strange and seemingly autonomous functioning of 'Walter', a mathematical formula which he is using to predict activity in the financial market. Like *2001*'s HAL, Walter is a formulation so complex that its functioning becomes unfathomable to its creator, a quality which becomes increasingly disturbing as it slips beyond its makers control. Jaz notes with alarm that it is as if the formula is acquiring a kind of consciousness:

> The math, Jaz thought, was some of the most beautiful that he'd ever encountered. The problem that would come to tug at him like an importunate child was something else. Something about Walter's responsiveness its voracious thirst for data. It was more like an organism than a computer program. It felt *alive*. (134)

This 'organism', Jaz begins to suspect, is not only anticipating the market but also influencing it:

> A thought occurred to him, which he tried his best to suppress. What if Walter had precipitated the crash–or, if not precipitated, then nudged it along, influenced it in some way? He dismissed the idea. The problems in the mortgage market were vast, systemic. (338)

Ask students to pick out words or phrases which encourage us to think of Walter as sentient, blurring the line between monster and monstrous analogy. Build on this by asking students to compare the language used in the extracts of the novel considered here to snippets of journalism reporting on economic matters that use imagery of myth, magic and science fiction. An apt example is an article entitled 'The mathematical equation that caused the banks to crash', which appeared in *The Guardian* in 2012, the same year as *Gods Without Men* was published. It discusses the role played by the Black-Scholes equation in contributing to the economic crisis: the author speaks of a 'Midas Formula' that was used 'as a kind of talisman, a bit of mathematical magic', which 'has its roots in mathematical physics, where quantities are infinitely divisible'. The article concludes, however, 'It may be rocket science, but magic it's not' (Stewart 2012). Reading this article will not only help your students to grasp why journalists and novelists alike saw analogies comparing high finance to the supernatural as an apt comparison in the context of the 2008 economic crisis, but also suggests the subtle distinction between the way the journalist uses such analogies (finally insisting 'magic it's not') and the way that a novelist can extend such an analogy into the realm of science fiction. The exercise triangulates Coupland's review, Kunzru's novel and contemporary journalism, using the three together to make a case which goes some way to vindicating Coupland's notion that translit echoes an 'extreme' quality which can be linked to a more broadly accepted perspective on global events leading up to 2012.

The challenge now is to use a different triangulation of sources to carry out a similar exercise, this time using a critical theorist in the place of the newsaper article. Ask your students if they can find a correlation between the ideas that Coupland describes in relation to the quality of contemporary life in the work of a critical theorist. This task can be adapted to suit the abilities of your students. More advanced students, given time to carry out the exercise, may be able to find a correspondence in a critical thinker they have already encountered in their studies. For others, it may work better to provide an article in which such a connection exists, asking students to find and explicate it. For example, the comment that translit is 'an embodiment of our new world of flattened time and space' might be connected to a number of thinkers on globalisation, for example David Harvey on 'space-time compression' (1999) or postmodernity, perhaps Zygmunt Bauman's notion of 'liquid modernity' (2013).[5] Since students will have encountered a reference to Fukuyama before, a useful comparison might be made between his ideas and those of a contrasting thinker. In *The End of History and the Last Man* Fukuyama claims that

> Technology makes possible the limitless accumulation of wealth, and thus the satisfaction of an ever-expanding set of human desires. This process guarantees an increasing homogenization of all human societies, regardless of their historical origins or cultural inheritances. All countries undergoing economic modernization must increasingly resemble one another (1992: xiv).

This might be placed alongside the contrasting ideas of a more contemporary critic, Arjun Appadurai:

> The various flows we see—of objects, persons, images, and discourses—are not coeval, convergent, isomorphic, or spatially consistent. They are in what I have elsewhere called relations of disjuncture. By this I mean that the paths or vectors taken by these kinds of things have different speeds, axes, points of origin and termination, and varied relationships to institutional structures in different regions, nations, or societies. Further, these disjunctures themselves precipitate various kinds of problems and frictions in different local situations. Indeed, it is the disjunctures between the various vectors characterising this world-in-motion that produce fundamental problems of livelihood, equity, suffering, justice, and governance. (2000: 5)

Though certain kinds of boundary are easily transcended in the contemporary world, it remains the case that difference and inequality remain, or are even accentuated, in the globalised world of the twenty-first century. Students will now have encountered ways in which we can test the validity of the claims that Coupland makes for what the world was like in 2012, first by comparing his comments to the novel itself, then to a journalistic text and finally to the writing of a cultural theorist. The session should be ended by asking students what conclusions they have reached and by discussing how they can use these opinions in an assessment, of which I will say more in my concluding remarks.

Towards Teaching Translit

The purpose of this chapter has been not only to make the case that there is value in teaching translit, but to suggest practical ways in which such a subject might be taught with attention to teasing out larger questions relating to the study of contemporary fiction in general. Coupland's article has been used as a source of ideas which have been drawn out to bring students into contact with a wider frame of reference and more academically rigorous explorations of concepts which they have encountered there in nuggatory form. The classes I have proposed are structured around four questions which take different approaches towards the larger concern of evaluating Coupland's translit, first defining the term, second considering its reception, third using it as a guiding principle for reading a literary text and finally evaluating its commentary on the 'extreme present'. Assessment should ideally draw on all four of these questions by asking students to write an essay that responds to Coupland's article, with the stipulation that they must refer to other literary critics (digital or otherwise), critical theorists, aspects of the article's social and historical context and the novel *Gods Without Men*. You might also ask them to comment on whether they see a future for the term translit, which is to say, do they think it can become (as Sterling proposed of slipstream) an 'acknowledged genre and a workable category' (1989). In the best tradition of the liberal arts, the study of translit can help to encourage your students, not only to engage in a larger critical debate, but to become cultural critics in their own right.

Notes

1. For other examples, see James McGirk, 'Translit is neither new nor subversive', *3QuarksDaily*, 19 March 2012, http://www.3quarksdaily.com/3quarksdaily/2012/03/translit-is-neither-new-nor-subversive.html <accessed 15 December 2015>; Margaret Jean Langstaff, '"Translit" Lit', *Good Reads*, 11 March 2015, https://www.goodreads.com/author/show/4135782.Margaret_Jean_Langstaff/blog/tag/douglas-coupland <accessed 15 December 2015>.
2. See Catherine McKinnon,'Translit as thought-events: Cloud Atlas and Storyland' in G. Pittaway, A. Lodge and L. Smithies (eds.) *Minding The Gap: Writing Across Thresholds And Fault Lines Papers – The Refereed Proceedings Of The 19th Conference Of The Australasian Association Of Writing Programs*, http://ro.uow.edu.au/lhapapers/1994/ <accessed 15 December 2015>.
3. I owe thanks to my colleagues Zara Dinnen and Tony Venezia, with whom the course was designed, and to the Department of English and Humanities at Birkbeck, University of London, for its support.
4. For discussion of these images see Ilona Katzew, *Casta Painting: Images of Race in Eighteenth-century Mexico* (New Haven and London: Yale University Press, 2005).
5. See David Harvey, 'Time-Space Compression and the Postmodern Condition' in Malcolm Waters (ed.), *Modernity: After Modernity* (London: Routledge, 1999) and Zygmunt Bauman, *Liquid Modernity* (Cambridge: Polity Press, 2013).

References

Appadurai, Arjun (2000) 'Grassroots Globalization and the Research Imagination', *Public Culture,* 12.1, 1–19

Clarke, Arthur C. (1974) 'Hazards of Prophecy: The Failure of Imagination', in *Profiles of the Future: An Inquiry into the Limits of the Possible* (London: Victor Gollancz)

Coupland, Douglas. 'Convergences', *The New York Times,* 8 March 2012, http://www.nytimes.com/2012/03/11/books/review/gods-without-men-by-hari-kunzru.html?_r=0 <accessed 10 October 2015>

Eaglestone, Robert (2013) 'Contemporary fiction in the academy: a manifesto', *Textual Practice,* 27.7, 1089–1101.

Fukuyama, Francis (1992) *The End of History and the Last Man* (New York: Macmillan)

Kunzru, Hari (2012) *Gods Without Men* (London: Penguin)

Lowenthal, David (2015) *The Past is a Foreign Country—Revisited* (Cambridge: Cambridge University Press)

McGirk, James (2012) 'Translit is neither new nor subversive', *3 Quarks Daily,* 19 March 2012, http://www.3quarksdaily.com/3quarksdaily/2012/03/translit-is-neither-new-norsubversive.html <accessed 4 October 2015>

Sterling, Bruce (1989) 'Catscan 5: Slipstream', *SF Eye,* 5, https://w2.eff.org/Misc/Publications/Bruce_Sterling/Catscan_columns/catscan.05 <accessed 12 October 2015>

Stewart, Ian (2012) 'The mathematical equation that caused the banks to crash', *The Guardian,* 12 February, http://www.theguardian.com/science/2012/feb/12/blackscholes-equation-credit-crunch <accessed 15 December 2015>

Teaching Contemporary Cosmopolitanism

Kristian Shaw

Over the last 20 years there has been an undeniable acceleration in transnational mobility, globalising processes and the use of digital communicative technology, generating an unprecedented interconnection between people and places. These catalysts have led to a global resurgence in Humanities and Social Sciences scholarship regarding the development of a new contemporary manifestation of cosmopolitanism. The socio-cultural, economic, and anthropological strands of cosmopolitan theory are very well established and will be discussed in this chapter alongside the key theorists in cosmopolitan thought. What now needs to be addressed is how such socio-cultural changes can be applied pedagogically to literary studies. Literature, like other academic disciplines, must move beyond established paradigms and frameworks to find answers for the post-millennial state. The aim of this chapter is to provide an explanation of cosmopolitanism and how its values can be applied to academic provision, offering new perspectives on the teaching of English in the twenty-first century. Although there is much written on the subject of cosmopolitanism, there is little work on cosmopolitan pedagogy. The chapter will begin by outlining the basic tenets and principles of the concept, before going on to demonstrate its usefulness in pedagogical practice. Drawing

K. Shaw (✉)
University of Lincoln, Lincoln, UK

© The Author(s) 2016

K. Shaw (ed.), *Teaching 21st Century Genres*,
DOI 10.1057/978-1-137-55391-1_9

on a case study of a taught module focused on cosmopolitanism, it will conclude by offering a potential rubric for pedagogical approaches to the concept and a conceptual framework by which literature may embrace new forms of cultural theory.

Cosmopolitanism has a long history of application, stretching from the Greek writing of Diogenes to the Enlightenment philosophy of Immanuel Kant, promoting the optimistic ideology of an interconnected global community where diverse cultures can come together to engage in dialogue and progress. Classical Stoic cosmopolitanism introduced the idea that individuals may exist as citizens of the world, mediating between new and existing loyalties, and balancing local allegiances with an abstract commitment to global others. Kant, on the other hand, tried to combine the philosophical concept with democratic forms of governance. These earlier conceptions of cosmopolitanism possessed a purely normative edge, resulting in the term evoking connotations of utopianism. Contemporary use of the term needs to acknowledge the complexity of twenty-first century life, emphasising that the ethical ideals of shared belonging, cooperation and cohabitation must function in order to confront cosmopolitical threats and address global inequalities. One of the key concerns in clarifying the usage of cosmopolitanism is identifying the ethical ideals associated with the concept. Although the term is interpreted in various ways, Steven Vertovec and Robin Cohen attempt to both pin down its meaning and acknowledge its multiplicity, defining it as: 'a socio-cultural condition' arising as a result of contemporary globalising processes; 'a kind of philosophy or world-view' that acknowledges the common values existing between all humans regardless of race or affiliation; a project aimed towards 'building transnational institutions' that override the potency of the nation-state; a 'political project for recognizing multiple identities' and the multiple allegiances a citizen feels with regards to local, national and global concerns; 'an attitudinal or dispositional orientation' that demonstrates an openness to cultural experience and otherness; or simply 'a mode of practice' that acknowledges and embraces the internal effects of globalisation on cultures and communities (2002: 9). By progressing away from an impractical 'us vs. them' mentality—which both homogenises and marginalises non-Western perspectives on the one hand, and assumes an uncritical stance towards cultural or ethnic difference on the other—cosmopolitanism offers new approaches to the teaching of belonging and identity. In the search for a term that simultaneously reflects both the diversity and cultural interdependence of the globalised world, cosmopolitanism seems to be an exceptionally fecund appellation.

Literary Cosmopolitanism

> Narratives, especially novels [...] speak to the reader as a human being, not simply as a member of some local culture; and works of literature frequently cross cultural boundaries far more easily than works of religion and philosophy (Nussbaum 1990: 391).

Teaching faces new ethical and cultural challenges to confront the critical changes of the twenty-first century, including unprecedented levels of transnational engagement and heightened awareness of global others. Ulrich Beck argues that the globalising conditions of millennial society necessitate 'a new historical reality [...] a cosmopolitan outlook in which people view themselves simultaneously as part of a threatened world and as part of their local situations and histories' leading individuals to reorient their lives accordingly and pay attention to the cultural asymmetries that govern global relations (2006: 48). Such diversity poses immediate problems in academia, as lecturers begin to recognise the need for an incorporation of the realities of cultural difference in academic provision. In the last two decades, higher education has employed the abstract ideal of 'the global' as the means of achieving an outward-facing promotion of institutions' practices and programmes. Engagement with global concerns is increasingly perceived as a measurement of a university's ability to cater to multicultural changes in society. Yet little has been written on how global perspectives may hold a pragmatic purpose with regards to learning goals or pedagogical approaches to teaching, often because the notion of 'the global' remains a vague signifier for cultural engagement. This is not to say that the inclusion of wider cultural concerns is not a productive means of engaging and educating students; indeed, it often fosters deeper engagement with cultural theory and leads to greater self-reflection and critical examination of textual material. In an age of unprecedented globalisation and cultural interconnectedness, the need for empathy and tolerance is greater than ever before. Curricula should reflect the diversity of backgrounds and experiences, educating students on not only their own culture but that of global others.

Literature is a late arrival to the critical study of cosmopolitanism, and yet the term is uniquely suited to literary analysis. Kwame Anthony Appiah perceives the novel in particular 'as a testing ground for [...] cosmopolitanism, with its emphasis on dialogue among differences'; the novel itself being 'a message in a bottle from some other position' and narrative empathy is thus an integral component of reader response (2001: 207; 223). Appiah argues that by becoming exposed to 'the extraordinary diversity of human responses to our world and the myriad points of intersection of those various responses', we will witness the development of 'cosmopolitan reading practices' (2001: 203; 2005: 258). By offering diverse insights available from limitless subjectivities, fictional representation and construction can encapsulate cosmopolitanism's fundamental focus on heterogeneity and the value of difference. Pheng Cheah concurs, contending that by reflecting socio-cultural connections, literature forges 'cosmopolitan bonds' and generates a form of 'universal communication' (2008: 27). Due to its universal connotations, cosmopolitanism has become a portmanteau for various planetary processes defining our contemporary present, including mounting human rights issues, global security threats, the radical inequalities of transnational mobility, the spread of globalisation, and the socio-political effects of digital communicative technologies. In essence, the values of cosmopolitanism indicate how to preserve individual cultural identities while acknowledging the presence and respecting the validity of disparate cultures in the new millennium.

The question is whether these socio-cultural changes and ethno-political changes provoke a reappraisal and revision of existing pedagogical approaches to better understand the globalised conditions of the emerging twenty-first century. Globalised society has forced a rethinking of issues such as identity, allegiances and citizenship, and students increasingly possess cross-cultural belongings which complicate existing cultural paradigms and heighten the need for cosmopolitan educational strategies. Universities undoubtedly play a key role in cultural transmission, exposing students to the shifting ethno-political realities of the contemporary moment. From an educational perspective, cosmopolitanism, as an interdisciplinary theory, holds much weight in its practical application. After all, teaching for cross-cultural communication and the application of cosmopolitan ideals simply extends upon the acknowledgement of diverse cultural values, beliefs and prejudices. The United Kingdom, as a polyethnic nation-state which encourages diversity and tolerance, allows for the retention of ethnic bonds while exposing individuals to the values of other belief systems. By forcing students to rethink and critically examine the fluid cultural flows and ethnic groupings of the post-millennium, as well as exposing students to both the diversity of their own culture and literature beyond their culture, literature acts as a transmitter for recognisable socio-cultural change. A pedagogical approach to cosmopolitanism offers a form of creative autonomy in the act of reading and creates the educational conditions for a re-evaluation of literature and culture in the twenty-first century. In implementing and analysing texts that reflect shifting negotiations regarding belonging and identity, it is possible to remove the burden of accommodation from pedagogical literary practices. By assuming a descriptive, rather than prescriptive, stance to cultural changes and globalised concerns, it is suited to open-ended English assessments, requiring critical reflection and evaluation.

The argument that educational bodies need to reflect cultural change is not a new one. In recent years there have been several attempts to introduce multicultural accommodations into curricula at all ages. Since the early 1960s, English began to incorporate terms such as 'cultural pluralism' into the curriculum. These terms were often linked to a vague paradigm of multiculturalism that marginalised and corralled non-Western cultures into a homogenous group of otherness. Yet cultural pluralism and diversity in the classroom has always been tightly linked to the notion of critical pedagogy. The model of cosmopolitanism proposed in this chapter assumes a critical stance to tenets first advanced under 'multicultural education' paradigms, questioning how both students and academic provision can acknowledge and appreciate socio-cultural and ethnic difference without marginalising such difference in the process. However, it is important to highlight the ways in which the term marks a break from late-twentieth century multicultural educational strategies. The main difference is that cosmopolitanism focuses on the identity of an individual, rather than that of a group (ethnic or otherwise). While multiculturalism implies a form of homogeneity at the group level, cosmopolitanism explores heterogeneous forms of belonging both individually and culturally. In this sense, the term is distinct from multiculturalism in that it rejects allegiance to group dynamics and resists the temptation to attach individuals to ethnic ties entirely. Individuals are therefore able to choose which ideals and practices with which they identify, as opposed to ones traditionally associated with their background. Further, a valid criticism of multicultural educational strategy, as Farideh Salili and Rumjahn Hoosain point out, is that it assumes an '[u]ncritical reliance' on multiple cultural perspectives and accepts 'them all as equally valid no matter how outrageous they are', leading to the 'uncritical glorification of the culture of nondominant groups'

(2001: 8). Pedagogical approaches to multiculturalism often result in assimilationist policies that gloss over any discussion of racism or ethnic difference, and assume a simplistic stance towards diverse perspectives on contemporary concerns. Such assimilation fostered the misconception that Western values are universal, rather than fluid constructions.

What is required is a broader pedagogical approach to identity and belonging that acknowledges the heterogeneous nature of post-millennial cultural relations. By requiring a re-evaluation of assumed signifiers, cosmopolitanism interrogates the identifying agents by which we determine attachments or allegiances. As Rob Reich notes, '[i]nsofar as mutual learning between cultures is valued, so too should a conception of autonomy that permits choice among cultures be valuable' (2003: 317). Nor should we 'conceive of intercultural choice as binary'; instead, Reich argues for 'the freedom to be a cosmopolitan hybrid, appropriating the values of other cultures for oneself, renegotiating the value of the culture(s) one is born into, asserting shifting allegiances and affiliation, and, in the end, constructing for oneself a context of choice that extends beyond the culture of one's birth' (2003: 317). Exposure to diversity, both in pedagogical practice and literary texts, removes the barriers that sustain multicultural grouping and introduces the freedom of negotiating one's own identity politics into the creative process of reading. In allowing for such freedom of association, a natural consequence of transnational movement and more ethnically diverse societies, the concept also rejects established paradigms of identity politics, making it possible for individuals (and readers) to assume their own responses to literature and culture free of group dynamics. Cosmopolitanism, then, offers new forms of identification aside from merely communal or ethnic allegiances, and becomes a process of becoming that is sensitive to multiple forms of affiliation.

Cosmopolitan Pedagogy

> Through cosmopolitan education, we learn more about ourselves [...] By looking at ourselves through the lens of the other, we come to see what in our practices is local and nonessential, what is broadly or deeply shared. (Nussbaum 1996: 11)

In recent years, interest in cosmopolitanism has re-emerged through the philosophical and sociological work of Martha Nussbaum, among others. Nussbaum was one of the first theorists to recognise the natural links between cosmopolitanism and pedagogy. In her 1996 essay, 'Patriotism and Cosmopolitanism', she introduced a strong ethical intent to educational practice, arguing that by studying and recognising the similarities and differences between rights of other world citizens, the theory would enable students to learn more about their own position in the world (a position now reconfigured due to a new awareness of the lives of others). Such an approach pays greater attention to wider cultural allegiances than national and parochial concerns:

> We should regard all human beings as our fellow citizens and neighbours [...] We should not allow differences of nationality or class or ethnic membership or even gender to erect barriers between us and our fellow human beings, we should recognize humanity wherever it occurs and give its fundamental ingredients, reason and moral capacity, our first allegiance and respect. (Nussbaum 1996: 7)

She reiterated this stance in her 1997 text *Cultivating Humanity*, which posited that contemporary pedagogical approaches need to focus on the students' capacity to perceive themselves as outward-facing citizens who can identify and emphasise with global others. At its core, Nussbaum's approach suggests that the cultural interdependencies of the post-millennial environment necessitates a need for students to appreciate 'the ways in which common needs and aims are differently realized in different circumstances' (1997: 10). This would engender a movement away from predominately Western paradigms. Nussbaum also calls attention to the potential of cosmopolitan theory to literature specifically, identifying that the 'narrative imagination' involves an understanding of 'what it might be like to be in the shoes of a person different from oneself, to be an intelligent reader of that person's story, and to understand the emotions and wishes and desires that someone so placed might have' (1997: 11). The notion of the narrative imagination is crucial for literary studies where self-reflection and empathetic identification with otherness is central to understanding characters and thematics.

However, her universalist claim that 'we should give our first allegiance to the moral community made up by the humanity of all human beings' demonstrates a turn away from localised forms of belonging and membership, neglecting the more realisable and everyday forms of cultural engagement (1996: 7). Due to the progressive interdependence of the contemporary world, one cannot simply rely on a polarised binary between the spheres of locality and globality. Her statements also remain rather vague on the issue of how cosmopolitan thought may be pragmatically applied to pedagogical practice, relying on the liberal, universal values of morality and global empathy. Nussbaum tends towards the belief that cosmopolitan thought holds a pedagogical purpose simply by allowing students to recognise sameness in the other or at least to respond to such otherness in a positive and progressive sense. It is perhaps more accurate to call for a less normative approach to cosmopolitanism with regards to pedagogical practice, paying attention to conflict and discord, as much as openness and harmony: a critical cosmopolitan stance to the post-millennial environment. Also, the liberal values Nussbaum identifies are more dominant in Western societies and fail to acknowledge the conflicting values of non-Western nations. Nussbaum, by privileging the universal over the parochial, neglects that the global and the local must be thought about relationally and need not operate in opposition to one another, but rather function dialogically. D. Hansen recognises how cosmopolitanism differs from cultural pluralism and multiculturalism, while at the same time identifying the flaws in Nussbaum's global/local dynamics: 'the cosmopolitan does not privilege already formed communities. It seeks to defend emerging spaces for new cultural and social configurations reflective of the intensifying intermingling of people, ideas, and activities the world over. However, cosmopolitanism does not automatically privilege the latter' (2008: 294). Indeed, Nussbaum's dichotomy of patriotism and cosmopolitanism ignores that an individual may possess multiple forms of citizenship and these shape their identity in mutually progressive ways (this is predominantly the case in multicultural societies).

Opponents of Nussbaum consequently claim that what this abstract form of cosmopolitan thought:

> obscures, even denies, are the givens of life: parents, ancestors, family, race, religion, heritage, history, culture, tradition, community—and nationality. These are not 'accidental' attributes of the individual. They are essential attributes [...] To pledge one's fundamental allegiance to cosmopolitanism is to try to transcend not only nationality but all the actualities, particularities, and realities of life that constitute one's natural identity. (Himmelfarb 1996: 77)

Jeremy Waldron, however, refutes the position that a citizen of the world is an abstract entity simply because there is no such thing as world citizenship.

He counters that individuals in a globalized, interdependent society 'do not pretend they have no responsibility for the world simply because there is no world state to enforce that as a matter of obligation' (2003: 44). Rather, citizens will recognise that awareness and consciousness of global others and wider concerns necessitates a willingness to shoulder responsibility, no matter how informal that role may be. Younger generations now recognise their identities to be both fluid and transient—cultural loyalties and acts of citizenship often overlap and can be reconstituted at any time. Digital communicative technology alone brings into play new ties or virtual communities which allow for greater forms of social participation or cross-cultural interaction on an unprecedented scale, and are equally as valid as corporeal engagement. A cosmopolitan pedagogical stance must acknowledge that a student may experience several social, cultural or ethnic commitments and avoids a confrontation between local and global forms of belonging. Nussbaum's arguments, though not without their inherent weaknesses and contradictions, can contribute to current thinking on the application of cosmopolitan thought in modern classrooms. She recognises that the interconnection and interdependence of the globalised world necessitates a change in educational reform and pedagogical practice to reflect engagement with differing traditions and ways of life. The approaches she outlines remain a valid means of implementing empathy, cultural tolerance and respect into the curricula.

We do, however, need to move beyond Nussbaum's frameworks to account for a critical understanding of cosmopolitan educational frameworks in the new millennium. According to Miriam Sobre-Denton and Nilanjana Bardhan, cosmopolitan pedagogy should not simply reflect the need for intercultural communication, but involve 'an ethical orientation towards and recognition of difference'; they suggest this to be a pedagogical process of 'cosmopolitan peoplehood' through which the student engages with 'notions of the stranger, the imagination, empathy and implicature' enabling students to become 'more Other- and world-oriented' (2013: 151, 160). In this way, cosmopolitan pedagogy becomes 'much more about lifelong learning processes of critical self-transformation rather than about the specific "outcome" of global citizenship', and prepares 'students to engage in transformative research and social action at the local and global levels of teaching, learning, being and becoming' (2013: 151, 166). With regards to pedagogical practice, we can adapt this framework to suggest that cosmopolitanism:

- Encourages students to assume a critical stance towards cultural and political concerns;
- Contributes to an active process of relating to others;
- Enhances the pedagogical importance of inclusivity;
- Leads to greater levels of self-reflection and self-identification in the act of reading as a creative process;
- Prevents the homogenising effects of globalisation, and dominant Western attitudes, taking hold in the classroom;
- Fosters a civic responsibility to both global and local frames of reference and concerns;
- Develops an intellectual openness to diversity;
- Challenges students to reassess their preconceived beliefs on cross-cultural interaction and cultivates new forms of global knowledge;
- Promotes more empathetic identification with forms of cultural otherness, fostering mutual understanding in the classroom;
- Inspires deeper engagement with the contemporary global condition.

Course Content

> The study of literature in the last two decades has increasingly invoked "cosmopolitanism" as a label for literature's [...] claim to continued relevance in a globalized world. (Vermeulen 2015: 83)

While many pedagogical texts have outlined what cosmopolitanism involves, few have interrogated how such beliefs should be pragmatically applied in the classroom, other than as a vague acknowledgement of the need for cultural difference. I recently designed an undergraduate module, 'Contemporary Cosmopolitanism', which discusses the ways by which disparate fictions interrogate and re-evaluate approaches to race and belonging in the twenty-first century, alongside a critical stance towards cultural or technological developments. Global processes are particularly important to any discussion of British and American fiction. As Jonathan Xaxier Inda and Renato Rosaldo argue, 'the nation-states of the West have become homes to a host of diverse and sometimes incommensurable cultures [...] They have developed into sites of extraordinary cultural heterogeneity', justifying the module's concentration on British and American fiction (2008: 23). The module proposes that the concept of cosmopolitanism provides a direct response to ways of living in relation to others and answers urgent fears surrounding global convergence.

As the introduction theorised, through literature, readers can begin to develop broader perspectives on socio-cultural issues, and feel empathy for the lives of others—tenets of cosmopolitan idealism. Students, as readers, draw circles of identification around themselves, demarcating identities and widening the stance between self and other. Fiction enables readers to identify with those different to themselves, appreciate commonality, and acknowledge shared concerns that threaten wider communities. In so doing, narrative concerns become universal. By forcing students to perceive themselves through the eyes of others, cosmopolitanism allows for a re-evaluation of personal identity, as well as increased empathy for the plight of others. As N. Hansen-Krennig, D. T. Mizokawa and Z. Wu emphasise, '[i]nitial encounters with other ways of seeing the world evolve into the understanding and acceptance of social responsibility, which calls for each human being to see beyond a moral or civic obligation to one's own home, community, province or state, and country to a global, world-encompassing responsibility'; however, they recognise that developing cultural empathy does not simply emerge from the creative process of reading, but rather 'through a guided response to literature' that requires students to reassess their cultural attitudes, values and beliefs (2001: 212, 214). In this sense, this chapter follows their reasoning that literature can play an integral role in the recognition of ethical values and development of social and ethnic identities.

The novelists chosen for the module demonstrate an awareness of emerging cultural interdependencies, and their works seem especially adept in disseminating cosmopolitan values and perspectives. Although the selected fictions are what we might term 'Western', the global perspectives and environments they imagine exceed national space, exemplifying the diverse manifestations of cosmopolitanism within contemporary fiction. They give voice to the need for ethical responsibility and global awareness to combat the interdependent risks of the twenty-first century and there are tentative signs of a movement towards a decentring of the Western perspective. In discussing these works, the module attempts to identify a trend in fiction to engage with the notion of global ethics, as well as placing societal interaction at the heart of pedagogical practice. The various forms of cosmopolitanism explored in the chosen fictions reveal the multidimensionality of the concept, sensitive to geographical and cultural idiosyncrasies. Despite this, the set texts do not exist in isolation, but interrelate with one another, fostering a unity in diversity and allowing a clear commonality to run throughout the module. Notably, their diverse subject matter reflects the intrinsic heterogeneity of contemporary British and American fiction, tackling issues as wide-ranging as deterritorialisation, racial solidarity, digital migrant labour, trans-species empathy, and post-human futures. Particular attention is paid to the role of ethical agency in activating global discourses and facilitating cross-cultural dialogue. Rather than responding to a classical conception of universal cosmopolitanism, the texts demonstrate a sense of urgency in reacting to emerging cosmopolitical threats, and foreground the interplay between local and global contexts as the basis for a critical cultural commentary. The module consequently follows Bruce Robbins in perceiving cosmopolitanism to involve an inscription of '(re)attachment, multiple attachment, or attachment at a distance' (1998: 3). Students must both work through the connotations of Western elitism associated with the term, and interrogate assumptions regarding ethnic heritage or racial grouping. This cosmopolitan pedagogical approach not only reconfigures the term to respond to modern processes, but makes important steps towards reflecting non-Western and non-dominant modes of cultural understanding in twenty-first-century teaching.

The works examined on the module are twenty-first-century novels in order to suggest a future-oriented approach to cosmopolitan thought. The first two weeks of the module examine the global fictions of David Mitchell. Both *Ghostwritten: A Novel in Nine Parts* (2000) and *Cloud Atlas* (2004) combine differing literary styles and genres to reflect the complex globality of the new millennium. His narratives involve a concentration on humanity's capacity for ethical engagement, particularly with regards to transnational mobility as a catalyst for the creation of cosmopolitan dispositions. Through a deconstruction of the shared fates of the narratives, students engage with the notion of cosmopolitical interconnectedness and must determine how Mitchell's structural and aesthetic choices reflect recent transformations in global society—not least the notion of convergence culture. By examining how individuals' lives may be bound up with those from other cultural or ethnic backgrounds, students are asked to understand the conflicting nature of narrative events and diverse perspectives, as well as recognising the roles of active collaboration and individual agency in aiding humanity's progression.

The following two sessions concentrate on how cosmopolitanism specifically relates to local communities and landscapes, beginning with the urban suburbs of London in Zadie Smith's *NW* (2012). The module encourages students to consider how Smith's limited geographical focus in the narrative works against Nussbaum's claim that universal and abstract attachments are more vital than more local forms of belonging in developing meaningful relations. As Sobre-Denton and Bardhan note, cosmopolitan pedagogy should concern 'the interconnectedness of the local with the global, and the use of the labor of the imagination to create links between the two' (2013: 166). The module therefore considers the ways in which Smith and Cole create 'glocal' spaces—local landscapes affected by wider globalising forces—which complicate established forms of belonging and identity. *NW* specifically examines the nature of cultural belonging in an area of intense ethnic and racial diversity and interrogates how disparate individuals strive to create a cohesive society. The students are asked to consider how social and cultural values are constantly in a state of flux, and appreciate an individual's agential multiplicity in negotiating a range of ties and belongings.

Teju Cole's *Open City* (2011) provides a transatlantic comparison to Smith's fiction by exploring the urban cityscapes of New York following the catastrophe of 9/11. By paying attention to the non-elite mobilities of African migrants, Cole's text reveals a critical cosmopolitanism that allows students to question the very nature and limitations of cultural empathy. More than any other text in the module, *Open City* problematises the ideals of cosmopolitanism in a post-9/11 context, suggesting that human rights inequalities and the persistence of racial exclusion are setbacks (or at least regressive tendencies) to the implementation of active ethical agency. The inclusion of Smith and Cole allows the module to contradict the assumption that transnationalism is a natural precursor to cosmopolitan dispositions. Indeed, as Owen B. Sichone points out, the positioning of transnationalism as a catalyst of cosmopolitanism neglects 'the immobile 97 per cent of the global population that never leaves home' (2008: 313). Developing this thinking, students consider who exactly may be termed a 'cosmopolitan', as cosmopolitanisation of territory enables global forces to impinge upon an individual's life without the need for mobility. The module thereby confronts how cultural concerns operate at the micro-level and examines the actually existing strategies of racially diverse citizens to bridge social divides.

The following two weeks expand upon racial tension in through a sustained analysis of the fiction of British author Sunjeev Sahota. Sahota's debut novel, *Ours Are the Streets* (2011), inhabits the mind of a potential suicide bomber as he negotiates the political landscape of millennial Britain. His recent follow-up, *The Year of the Runaways* (2015), revolves around the lives of Indian migrants workers in Sheffield, questioning the choices and identities they assume. The module utilises the novel to confront the Kantian cosmopolitan notion of universal hospitality and questions whether all global citizens are entitled to exist in a moral community. Students must determine whether global interconnectedness has fostered the development of solidarity across established borders and examine the role of the 'stranger' in British life. In so doing, the module develops an engagement with the geopolitics and power relations surrounding migration, revealing who belongs and who is excluded from Western life.

The focus of the module then shifts to address the role of digital communicative technologies in facilitating cross-cultural dialogue. The Internet in particular has become a cosmopolitan construct, facilitating and effecting cultural change, while simultaneously raising global awareness of the lives of others. Virtual communities are beginning to override geographical divides and students need to understand how these developments reshape identity and belonging. However, cultures have also become marginalised by the advent of the digital age and the rise in communicative technologies. The module therefore considers two texts that offer very different perspectives on digital engagement: Dave Eggers's *The Circle* (2013) and Hari Kunzru's *Transmission* (2005). *The Circle* identifies the hegemonic corporate forces who control digital connectivity and invites the suggestion that the digital is merely a new manifestation of cultural imperialism, responsible for the exacerbation, rather than amelioration, of global inequality. Students must critically engage with new transformations in society and evaluate their role in establishing more ethical forms of integration. *Transmission*, by comparison, offers a non-Western perspective on digital connectivity, charting the dislocation of migrant labourers as they try to engage with the power-structures of transnational corporations. The narrative complements the previous week's focus on *The Circle* by questioning the extent to which digital companies are insensitive or ignorant of the plight of non-Western others. The texts also illustrate that social movements are increasingly formed, as well as identities and communities negotiated, through digital networks. In order to understand the wider cosmopolitical ramifications of the digital real, students must consider the recent application of social media in social movements—the Arab Spring, London student riots, Occupy Wall Street—movements organised and developed using the internet. A cosmopolitan approach to the digital not only raises awareness of the shift towards new forms of societal integration and collaboration, but reveals how digital connectivity simultaneously disrupts established communal bonds.

The final two weeks explore how cosmopolitanism can be adapted to the study of science-fiction or fantasy literature in order to confront radical forms of otherness. The module considers how Philip Pullman's *His Dark Materials* (2001) serves as an allegory for post-millennial concerns, including ecological degradation, the spread of globalisation, and the fluidity of national borders. Although cosmopolitanism is often criticised in the social sciences for remaining too abstract and having no practical application, literary studies is not restricted by such concerns. As Cheah argues, because one cannot literally '*see* the universe, the world, or humanity, the cosmopolitan optic is not one of perceptual experience but of the imagination', transforming literature into a 'world-making activity' (2008: 26, 29). The ethical ideals of cosmopolitan thought can be explored across imaginative space, being a unique medium through which to envision societal reconfigurations not yet possible in the new millennium.

The module is sensitive to the question of whether current assessment styles adequately address the changing nature of society. Assessments that hold real-world applicability can create graduates who will thrive in an increasingly competitive and diverse global marketplace. The module uses critical journals or seminar sheets rather than essay-based forms of assessment that allow students to hide behind cultural or literary theories of academics without real engagement. The critical journals necessitate an engagement with the issues of each session and require personal reflection on post-millennial themes. Classes would begin with an informal lecture that provided background information on a cultural theory or contemporary process; effort was made to connect the issues raised to the lives of the students. A group discussion subsequently followed, allowing for evaluation and exploration of different perspectives. Through this process, the module reveals literature to be a key driving force in the appreciation of diverse cultural perspectives and ethical values. The discussion and practical application of such values fosters an inclusive learning environment built upon tolerance and openness to difference and raises awareness of socio-cultural and ethno-political concerns unique to the post-millennium.

Towards a Cosmopolitan Classroom

> Literature educates not only the head, but the heart as well. It promotes empathy and invites readers to adopt new perspectives. It offers opportunities [...] to learn to recognize our similarities, value our differences, and respect our common humanity. (Bishop 1994: xiv)

This chapter has attempted to adapt the framework of cosmopolitanism to reflect the need for cultural awareness in pedagogical practice, and suggest ways by which the concept may be taught within literary studies. The global interconnectedness of the contemporary moment means cosmopolitan dispositions become all the more relevant and vital in addressing the cultural asymmetries, racial divides, terrorist threats and environmental challenges at the forefront of post-millennial life. A subsequent pedagogical engagement with (or resistance to) emerging global flows is consequently necessary for twenty-first-century teaching. Despite the argument that individual agency becomes the domain of cosmopolitan ethics, it is undeniable that governments and educational institutions are primarily responsible for the implementation of ethical ideals and reforms that allow a more egalitarian global community to emerge. And yet, cultural theorists remain sceptical regarding the emergence of cosmopolitan ethics at an institutional level. Cosmopolitanisation requires constant implementation at both educational and institutional levels, necessitating a transformation of existing social relations within networks that pay attention to the consolidation and maintenance of community at the micro, meso and macro scale. Fiction itself plays a vital role in this process; after all, fiction offers the cosmopolitan imagination a means of envisioning alternative configurations by which we may modify our relations with one another, thereby possessing a progressive socio-cultural function.

There are, of course, limitations to cosmopolitan educational frameworks, especially with regards to literary studies. Firstly, as Sobre-Denton recognises, '[i]n an era where schools are cutting funding across curricula from elementary schools to universities, teaching cosmopolitanism in a nuanced manner that represents non-Western, non-elitist, vernacular viewpoints may not be given the time nor the attention needed' (2012: 110). The task remains for the Humanities to embrace an outward-looking approach to pedagogical practice. Further, the ideals and tenets of cosmopolitanism are difficult to assess, relying on value judgements and creating abstract learning outcomes. The formation of cosmopolitan dispositions involve lifelong learning processes that can only be developed over time and are not perfectly suited to a classroom environment. There is a danger that the development of such frameworks can result in a simplistic approach to intercultural communication or identity politics. Striving for openness and cultural empathy in the classroom creates problems of its own, and leaves unanswered questions regarding the point at which radical views should be rejected to pacify inclusivity for inclusivity's sake.

However, teachers in general have a moral obligation to confront cultural, political or ethical issues that define the contemporary moment, and which emerge in the classroom. After all, the cultural and racial heterogeneity of the twenty-first-century classroom serves as a microcosm for contemporary globalised society—a place where differing cultures come into close and unavoidable contact with one another. A cosmopolitan pedagogical approach simply allows students to find common values across the established divides of race, class or cultural identity. And yet, that is not to say that we are now dealing with global students who are free-floating cosmopolitans. As Pippa Norris (drawing on empirical data from the World Values Survey) points out, whilst 47% of respondents considered themselves 'as belonging primarily to their locality', only 15% felt a predominant relation to 'the world as a whole' (Norris 2000: 161). National identity is still upheld as the true signifier of geographical belonging.

While this chapter has suggested that no singular model of cosmopolitanism exists, it has resisted the contention that the term exists as a floating cultural signifier—there must remain some coherence and specificity in the term's values for the concept to possess a pragmatic purpose. The various situated cosmopolitanisms evident in the works studied on the module indicate that the term should not be attached to vague universalising or progressive ideals with no tangible expression, but instead demonstrate how cosmopolitanism at large can be routinely negotiated and rooted in place in order for its ideals to possess any pedagogical relevance or demonstrate any practical application. Practically applied in this way, the term establishes itself as a positive analytical framework for interpreting social issues and a pragmatic heuristic tool for enabling students to reach and clarify their own understanding of cultural interactions and conflicting belief systems. Such a dynamic framework encourages students to express differing views and leads to more productive debates on sensitive issues. As a result, cosmopolitanism does not simply emerge as an abstract ideal, but a pedagogical practice and an ethical disposition that can be implemented individually, communally and institutionally. Moreover, cosmopolitanism proves itself to be a reactive genre, reflective of modern conditions and adaptable to cultural change, encapsulating states of belonging and shifts in cultural identities in the new millennium. There must be active engagement with societal changes of the twenty-first century to prevent literature modules becoming esoteric and delimited in their scope, having no interdisciplinary application or indeed application outside of the module itself. Contemporary cosmopolitanism therefore need not merely be an academic tool by which to provide socio-cultural analysis in literary studies, but a new genre that informs and re-evaluates existing pedagogical frameworks already taught in academia.

References

Appiah, Kwame Anthony (2001) 'Cosmopolitan Reading' in *Cosmopolitan Geographies: New Locations in Literature and Culture* (ed.) Vinay Dharwadker (New York and London: Routledge) 197–227.

——— (2005) *The Ethics of Identity* (Princeton, NJ: Princeton University Press)

Beck, Ulrich (2006) *Cosmopolitan Vision* (trans.) C. Cronin (Cambridge: Polity)

Bishop, Rudine Sims (1994) *Kaleidoscope: A Multicultural Booklist for Grades K-8* (Urbana, IL: National Council of Teachers of English)

Cheah, Pheng (2008) 'What Is a World? On World Literature as World-Making Activity', *Daedalus* 137:3, 6–38.

Hansen, D (2008) 'Curriculum and the idea of a cosmopolitan inheritance', *J Curric Stud* 40: 3, 289–312.

Hansen-Krennig, Nancy, Donald T. Mizokawa, and Zhongming Wu (2001) 'Literature, A Driving Force in Ethnic Identity and Social Responsibility Development' in *Multicultural Education: Issues, Policies, and Practices* (ed.) Farideh Salili and Rumjahn Hoosain (Greenwich, CT: Information Age Publishing) 211–23.

Himmelfarb, Gertrude (1996) 'The Illusions of Cosmopolitanism' in *For Love of Country: Debating the Limits of Patriotism* (ed) Joshua Cohen (Boston: Beacon Press) 72–77.

Inda, Jonathan Xavier, and Renato Rosaldo (2008) 'Tracking Global Flows' in *The Anthropology of Globalization: A Reader* (ed.) Jonathan Xavier Inda and Renato Rosaldo (Oxford: Blackwell) 3–46.

Norris, Pippa (2000) 'Global Governance and Cosmopolitan Citizens' in *Governance in a Globalizing World* (ed.) Joseph S. Nye and John D. Donahue (Washington, DC: Brookings) 155–77.

Nussbaum, Martha C (1997) *Cultivating Humanity: A Classical Defence of Reform in Liberal Education* (Cambridge, MA: Harvard UP)

——— (1990) *Love's Knowledge: Essays on Philosophy and Literature* (Oxford and New York: Oxford UP)

——— (1996) 'Patriotism and Cosmopolitanism' in *For Love of Country: Debating the Limits of Patriotism* (ed.) Joshua Cohen (Boston: Beacon Press) 2–17.

Reich, Rob (2003) 'Multicultural Accommodations in Education' in *Citizenship and Education in Liberal-Democratic Societies: Teaching for Cosmopolitan Values and Collective Identities* (ed.) Kevin McDonough and Walter Feinberg (Oxford: Oxford University Press) 299–324.

Robbins, Bruce (1998) 'Introduction Part 1: Actually Existing Cosmopolitanism' in *Cosmopolitics: Thinking and Feeling beyond the Nation* (ed.) Pheng Cheah and Bruce Robbins (Minneapolis, MN: University of Minnesota Press) 1–19.

Salili, Farideh, and Rumjahn Hoosain (2001) 'Multicultural Education: History, Issues and Practices' in *Multicultural Education: Issues, Policies, and Practices* (ed.) Farideh Salili and Rumjahn Hoosain (Greenwich, CT: Information Age Publishing) 1–13.

Sichone, Owen B (2008) 'Xenophobia and Xenophilia in South Africa: African Migrants in Cape Town' in *Anthropology and the New Cosmopolitanism: Rooted, Feminist and Vernacular Perspectives* (ed.) Pnina Werbner (Oxford and New York: Berg) 309–24.

Sobre-Denton, Miriam (2012) 'Landscaping the Rootless: Negotiating Cosmopolitan Identity in a Globalizing World' in *Identity Research and Communication: Intercultural Reflections and Future Directions* (ed.) Nilanjana Bardhan and Mark P. Orbe (Lanham, MD: Lexington Books) 103–18.

Sobre-Denton, Miriam and Nilanjana Bardhan (2013) *Cultivating Cosmopolitanism for Intercultural Communication: Communicating as Global Citizens* (New York: Routledge)

Vermeulen, Pieter (2015) *Contemporary Literature and the End of the Novel: Creature, Affect, Form* (Basingstoke: Palgrave Macmillan)

Vertovec, Steven, and Robin Cohen (2002) 'Introduction: Conceiving Cosmopolitanism' in *Conceiving Cosmopolitanism: Theory, Context, and Practice* (ed.) Steven Vertovec and Robin Cohen (Oxford: Oxford University Press) 1–22.

Waldron, Jeremy (2003) 'Teaching Cosmopolitan Right' in *Citizenship and Education in Liberal-Democratic Societies: Teaching for Cosmopolitan Values and Collective Identities* (ed.) Kevin McDonough and Walter Feinberg (Oxford: Oxford University Press) 23–55.

Index

Note: Page numbers with "n" denote notes.

© The Author(s) 2016

K. Shaw (ed.), *Teaching 21st Century Genres*,
DOI 10.1057/978-1-137-55391-1